SPANISH NIGHTS

The Secret of Sedo Mare

By Michael R. Ellis
United States Navy Retired

Rigney Page Adventures:

For those unfamiliar with navy terminology, a Glossary of Navy Terms and a chart of the navy rank structure are located at the end of this story.

Chapter 1

October 1978
Southwest Coast of Spain

A damp and chilled gust of Atlantic Ocean wind blows over Sedo Mare Pueblo. Construction debris flutters and twirls along roads and empty lots of this growing, residential community. The gusty wind rattles shutters and penetrates even the tiniest cracks around windows and doors.

The construction of dwellings is designed to protect the indoors from the heat of long summer days, but that design does not aid in keeping homes warm during cold weather. None of the buildings have central heating or fireplaces, and the only defense against the typical cold weather at this time of year is warm clothing and portable gas-bottle heaters.

One-thousand families live in Sedo Mare Pueblo, but few walk the streets this evening. It's a weekday night, and the cafés and restaurants on the beach are sparsely occupied.

Inside one of those single-family homes, Lieutenant Malcom Coleridge, USN, sits on the couch in the living room. Lieutenant, junior grade, Harrison Willmont, USN, sits in an overstuffed chair on the other side of the coffee table and faces Coleridge. The setting is casual. Both men wear sweaters to shield themselves from the chill of the evening. They sip bourbon. Several feet away, fire from a portable gas-bottle heater casts a glow and warms the room.

Lieutenant Coleridge is assigned as the Communications Department Head aboard the USS *Antares*—a submarine tender home-ported in Rota, fifteen miles to the south of Sedo Mare Pueblo.

Lieutenant, junior grade, Willmont, USN, serves as the USS *Antares* Assistant Communications Department Head and Radio Division Officer.

The two naval officers have the house to themselves. Their wives and Coleridge's daughter are attending BINGO night at the Rota Naval Base Officers Club.

Lieutenant Coleridge tells his assistant, "I have discovered a Spanish criminal organization using extortion to obtain classified information from American sailors. This criminal organization is…"

The door slams open and two men wearing ski masks barge through the doorway. They fire suppressor-equipped, automatic pistols at the two naval officers.

Each officer is shot four times, including shots to the head. They die within seconds.

Chapter 2

December 1978
U.S. Naval Base Rota, Spain

The U.S. Navy Intelligence Center Rota, Spain is housed in a non-descript, single-story, gray-colored, stucco building that stands among a dozen similar type buildings. The only distinguishing markings on the exterior of the building are the building number and a sign on the main access door that reads, U.S. NAVY WEATHER SERVICE ROTA SPAIN. The sign satisfies queries about the antenna arrays on the roof. One small office inside the building issues one weather report each day. The report is actually a summary of weather reports received over the teletype weather broadcast.

Access to the windowless building is through a cipher-lock-protected steel door on the west side of the building. The only emergency exit is on the east side of the building and can be opened only from the inside. A copper-mesh screen inside the walls, ceiling, and floors protects the intelligence center from electronic surveillance probing from the outside. The copper-mesh screen, telephones, and radio communications devices have secure (red) electronic-grounding systems to prevent classified signals from riding out of the building on electromagnetic signal waves.

Mr. Arleigh Rouston, OIC Task Force 152 Detachment Rota, sits at his desk in his office adjacent to the Naval Intelligence Operations Center. He concentrates on next quarter's budget. He shakes his head while considering that he is assigned missions requiring unrestricted funding, but restrictive funding is all he gets.

He takes his eyes off the budget and focuses on a picture of

President Carter on the wall across the room. In his mind, the face of Jimmy Carter turns into a dartboard target.

Rouston's yeoman enters the room, hands Rouston some stapled sheets of paper, and advises, "That's the report you requested from the Spanish Liaison Office. The reason it took so long is I had to have it translated from Spanish to English. That took almost a month to get that done."

Rouston's staff has been without a Spanish Translator for three years. The Office of Naval Intelligence, ONI, had deleted the Rota Intelligence Center billet for a Spanish translator, citing federal budget cuts and shortages of translators with a security clearance. Each year Rouston requests the billet be reinstated and each year the request is denied.

"Okay, I'll study it now. Hold all my calls."

"No problem," the yeoman responds; then, he exits the office and shuts the door behind him.

The OIC moves to the overstuffed chair and reads the report:

The History of Sedo Mare

The first historic records regarding the Spanish seaside village of Sedo Mare date back to 62 B.C. Ancient Roman records tell of a Roman soldier hunting party that came upon the fishing village by accident, after losing their way during a storm. When the malnourished and dehydrated hunting party stumbled into the village, the villagers took in the soldiers and nursed them back to health.

Months later when the soldiers returned to their garrison in Cadiz, scribes recorded the unusual stories that the soldiers told. Those soldiers described a fishing village of 120 fair-skinned, light-colored-hair people who wore animal skins for clothes.

Most of the villagers lived communally in three large, rectangular, barracks style, structures made of stone walls and thatched roofs. The largest of the buildings housed children. Men lived in the second largest structure. Women lived in the third largest structure. There were a number of small stone huts that housed one man and one woman each but no children. The social standing of those couples who lived in the small huts was never made clear to the Roman soldiers.

The village was located in a valley that was bordered by a rocky shoreline on the west and high rocky hills on the north, east, and south. The soldiers estimated the valley to be about two square miles. The villagers' language was unrecognizable to the Roman soldiers. With a mixture of body gestures by the villagers, the soldiers interpreted the name of the area to be "calming water" or "calming sea." The soldiers, who spoke Latin, named the area "Sedo Mare."

The villagers were fishermen and hunter-gatherers. The village economy was communal with all contributing to the food, housing maintenance, and clothing supply. Each morning, half the males took the fishing boats to sea. The other males went to the other side of the hills on the north and east to hunt and to gather wild fruit and nuts.

Each Roman soldier described the inhabitants of Sedo Mare as a loose knit group with no tribal structure. There was no leader, although the older men lead the hunting and fishing parties and older women led the child rearing and organized the communal food preparation.

The inhabitants were kind, pleasant, and always good natured. Their diet was mostly fresh fish from the sea and wild berries, olives, and nuts from the forest to the east. Wild animals were killed for meat and the skins were distributed to those in most need. Fresh water came from a well located at the east end of the village.

The most unique object in the village was a human-sized carved marble statue that was erected over the water well. The statue was an image of a naked woman holding her arms out over the well. The villagers called the statue Nirta, and they worshiped the statue like a goddess.

Each evening, the villagers chanted and engaged in water-drinking rituals around the statue. The ritual included male and female villagers stripping naked and copulating on the grass in the view of everyone.

Participation and choice of sexual partners was voluntary. However, those couples who lived alone in the small huts did not participate in the open sexual activities. The villagers invited the Roman soldiers to participate, and the soldiers did so willingly. The soldiers assumed Nirta was a goddess of fertility.

The Roman soldiers viewed the life and culture of the villagers to be near utopia. Violent acts between villagers were nonexistent. Stress was nonexistent. Envy was nonexistent. Men and women shared their bodies willingly and openly. Children were the wards of the community; parental identity meant nothing. A selected group of women were responsible for collective child care. When children passed into adolescence, they participated in the nightly copulation rituals.

The Romans investigated the mechanics of the water well. The well shaft was lined with stones as far down as they could see. They measured the length of the water-bucket rope, made of woven leather strands, to be one-hundred-twenty feet. When the Romans measured the incline of the land from the shoreline, the water level at the bottom of the well was ten feet higher than the ocean. The Romans were curious as to how such an undeveloped people could locate the exact location of groundwater and build such a solid utility to the length of more than one-hundred feet.

Members of the Roman soldier hunting party speculated that the village had not been previously discovered because of its surrounding geography: A rocky shoreline with no harbor on the west side of the village and steep rocky hills on the north, east, and south. A salt marsh lays to the south of the southern hills, stretching miles inland from the seashore.

Each soldier commented in his individual report that during their time with the fair-skinned villagers the personality of each soldier changed from a disciplined, fierce, hardcore Roman soldier to a peaceful person who was concerned about the wellbeing of others. Then, after four days on the trip back to Cadiz, their Roman soldier demeanor returned. They had discussed their changes in behavior among themselves and agreed they were puzzled by it. When providing their verbal reports to the scribes, each Roman soldier spoke well of the villagers and hoped that the villagers would survive and prosper.

When departing Sedo Mare, the Roman soldiers knew that they would find Cadiz by progressing south along the coast. They mapped their trek back to Cadiz. Roman geographers at the Cadiz garrison estimated the location of Sedo Mare to be seventeen kilo passus (approximately fifteen miles) northwest of the small port town of Speculum Rotae, which was the name the Romans gave the town now known as Rota.

Historic records of later that year tell of desertions from the Roman Garrison at Cadiz. The officer that had led the hunting party that spent months at Sedo Mare had speculated to his superiors that the deserting soldiers could be found at Sedo Mare. The officer stated that the same soldiers who had deserted were also hesitant to depart Sedo Mare. The officer described the fair-skinned villagers' lifestyle as without stress and living in maximum freedom. And the mood of the people was enticing and sometimes euphoric. The deserted soldiers had established relationships with some of the village women.

One month later, the same Roman officer led a platoon of soldiers on a mission to Sedo Mare to arrest the deserters. However, when they arrived at Sedo Mare, the villagers and the deserted soldiers were nowhere to be found. All the structures were bare inside. The fishing boats were gone and the statue of the goddess Nirta was gone. The location of the well could not be found.

The platoon of soldiers camped for several weeks near the river located over the hills two miles to the east of the village, waiting for the villagers and the deserted soldiers to return. The villagers and deserted soldiers never appeared.

Twice during the next year, the Cadiz garrison sent a platoon to capture the deserted soldiers. Each time, the Sedo Mare village was found unoccupied. During the second mission, the Romans carved into the flat side of rock a five-foot-high declaration of Roman ownership of the Sedo Mare area. The rock and eroded engraving can still be seen today on the northern slope of the valley.

One hundred years passed before another entry regarding Sedo Mare *was recorded. A newly arrived Roman Commander of the Cadiz garrison toured the area under his command during the year 57 AD. The Roman Commander had read the documents that recorded the treks to Sedo Mare a century before. This time, the Romans found the village populated with over 170 people. Most of the villagers were fair-skinned and fair haired and spoke a language unintelligible to the Romans. However, a few villagers spoke several words of Latin and accurately welcomed the Roman soldiers in Latin.*

Village structures were the same as the one-hundred-year-old documents described. The statue of Nirta stood over the water well. The behavior of the villagers was the same as described in the old documents.

The new Roman commander levied taxes on the villagers to be paid monthly in volumes of smoke-dried fish, wild animals, and barrels of olives. The commander stationed a squad of soldiers to oversee the first two deliveries of villager taxes to the Cadiz Garrison.

Neither the villagers of Sedo Mare nor the soldiers who were tasked to oversee the villagers' delivered the specified tax. After the third month of non-delivery, the Cadiz Garrison Commander sent a battalion of soldiers on an investigative mission to Sedo Mare. The village had been abandoned. The squad of soldiers tasked to oversee the villagers was nowhere to be found.

The Roman records of the Cadiz garrison tell of several annual patrols throughout the province. Each patrol returned and reported the village of Sedo Mare to be deserted. As the years wore on, Sedo Mare was mentioned infrequently in the Roman records. Eventually memories of Sedo Mare faded into the mist of time.

During the next fourteen-hundred years, southwest Hispania was occupied by the Goths and later by the Moors. The few records that survived those brutal times made no mention of Sedo Mare or fair-skinned villagers on Hispania's southwest coast.

The next reference to Sedo Mare in the archives of the Spanish National Museum was for the year 1443. The Christian Inquisition Tribunal in Cadiz heard rumors of a fishing village to the north that had recently sprouted to life and was occupied by pagans who worshipped a stone statue.

During the summer of 1443, the Christian Inquisition Tribunal deployed several Inquisitors with a platoon sized security guard of soldiers. The deployed inquisitors camped on top of the hill to the east of the Sedo Mare village and observed the villagers for a week. The lead Inquisitor dispatched daily messages to the Tribunal describing the sacrilegious behavior of the villagers in the valley below.

The last message received by the Tribunal from the deployed Inquisitors was written the night before the planned invasion into the valley. The deployed Inquisitors and guard of soldiers never returned to Cadiz.

Months passed, and the Cadiz Tribunal had not received any dispatches from the deployed Inquisitors. The Tribunal deployed a military squad to search for the missing Inquisitors. Three weeks later, the military squad returned to Cadiz and reported that the fishing village was deserted and the Inquisitors could not be found. The military squad had discovered the rock with the engraving claiming Roman ownership of the valley. The military squad leader advised of their discovery of the engraved rock that referred to the valley as Sedo Mare. From that date forward, the name Sedo Mare stuck and was used to identify the valley in all future documents.

The next mention of Sedo Mare was from the year 1532 and is found in the records of the town of Rota that lay fifteen miles south of Sedo Mare. A report by the Rota town government described Sedo Mare's dwellings as constructed of stones and tree trunks and listed the village population at two-hundred. The village economy was communal and no trading took place outside the village. The report specified that the villagers were not Christians and practiced pagan rituals. Villagers were observed dancing in trance-like motions around a carved stone statue at the village well. At the end of each ritual, the villagers stripped off their clothes and fell to the ground. Some engaged in sexual activities and others just fell asleep. The report also mentioned the rock on the northern slope that declared the valley to be the property of the Roman Empire.

Several weeks later, the Rota government sent a contingent of soldiers, clergy, and government bureaucrats to convert the Sedo Mare villagers to

Christianity and to integrate the village into the economics of the province. After two months, nothing had been heard from the contingent. A team of town representatives was dispatched to investigate. The investigators returned to Rota and advised that the Sedo Mare villagers had disappeared and the contingent of soldiers, clergy, and bureaucrats could not be found.

Nothing significant was recorded regarding Sedo Mare for another 400 years. Then, during the 1950s, a land developer, Empire Construction, with headquarters in London sought to purchase the land known as Sedo Mare Valley. A title search was conducted for the current owner; but no title to the land was found in Spanish records. The only physical evidence regarding ownership was the claim by the Roman Empire engraved in the rock at Sedo Mare. Eventually, the Spanish courts awarded ownership to the Spanish government. Then, the Spanish government auctioned the land. There were only three bidders, and the Spanish subsidiary of Empire Construction, Imperio Construir, was the highest bidder.

During Phase One of the building project, Imperio Construir built condo buildings and single-family homes in the Sedo Mare Valley— totaling 500 living units. Imperio Construir named the community Sedo Mare Pueblo. A road was carved out of the hills on the southeast side of the valley and was connected to the road leading to Rota. The shoreline on the west of the valley was cleared of rocks and a sandy beach was constructed. Several cafés and a gift shop were established on the beach.

The land developer was speculating on the growing population of the area because of the new Spanish Naval Base at Rota that would also provide a section of the Spanish base for the U.S. Navy. The developer was also speculating on the growing number of United Kingdom citizens retiring to the Rota area.

Currently, more than one-thousand families live in the Sedo Mare Pueblo. The population is a mix of Spanish, American, and U.K. citizens.

Sedo Mare Geology

A topographic survey of the valley was performed at the time the

Spanish Courts awarded the valley to the Spanish government. The survey states that the valley known as Sedo Mare was formed by lava flows from an ancient, now defunct volcano that lay to the northeast. The valley measures one-mile north-to-south by one-and-a-half miles from the shoreline on the west to the hills on the east. The hills on the east are the rim the defunct volcano. The hills on the north and south of the valley were formed by prehistoric lava flows. No record of a geological survey exists in Spanish national records.

Rouston lays the report on his desk. His eyes move to the large whiteboard calendar on the wall next to his desk. He notes that Senior Chief Page arrives two days from now.

Chapter 3

The U.S. Naval Air Terminal at Rota, Spain is a single story, stucco building with a red tile roof. The interior is five-thousand square feet and decorated in military drab. Shades of green are the primary interior colors.

As he walks through the crowded Air Terminal, Senior Chief Petty Officer Rigney "Rig" Page does not expect anyone to greet him. He did not advise anyone in Rota of his arrival date. Nevertheless, he glances around the air terminal to see if he recognizes anyone. No one looks familiar.

As usual, his image draws many stares. The tall, lean, broad-shouldered, ruggedly handsome senior chief wearing service dress blue uniform with only three gold hash marks causes many to turn their heads toward him.

Senior Chief Page carries a bulky, navy-blue-colored canvas suitcase in each hand. One suitcase contains all his uniforms. The other suitcase includes selected civvies and personal records that will accommodate him until his personal-goods shipment arrives in Rota.

When he exits the air terminal and walks into the parking lot, Rig is met by the sunny, chilly, December morning air. As he walks across the parking lot toward awaiting buses, he considers that he made a mistake by not packing his pea coat in his suitcase. His military and civilian winter coats are stuffed into his personal-goods shipment that is located somewhere between Washington DC and Rota.

During the flight from Charleston, Rig arranged a seat on the bus with the Chief-of-the-Boat of the USS *John Hancock* Blue Crew. Navy buses wait in the parking lot to transport the *John Hancock* Blue Crew to the submarine tender, USS *Antares*. The *Antares* is home-ported at the Rota Naval Base.

Thirty minutes later, Rig steps off the bus at the head of the pier. He looks to the end of the pier and sees that the USS *Antares* is MED moored—the ship is positioned perpendicular to the pier with the stern tied to the pier.

As he walks along the pier toward the *Antares*, Rig notes all the usual sounds and activities of ships and submarines in port for maintenance and upkeep. A United States cruiser is moored to the left side of the pier. One fast attack submarine and one ballistic missile submarine are moored to the right side of the pier. Sailors in dungarees and in khakis move about the pier with tool bags in hand. Store supplies are being offloaded from trailer trucks. A crane is lifting large machinery off the deck of the cruiser. Sailors on one of the submarines paint the sail. The sound of pneumatic tools dominates the din.

After performing the prescribed ceremonial boarding procedures at the *Antares* quarterdeck, Senior Chief Page departs the quarterdeck and walks along the starboard side toward the Chiefs Mess.

After entering the Chiefs Mess, he drops his suitcases against a bulkhead. Then, he scans the mess. He observes several mess cooks setting up for the midday meal. Half the tables have white tablecloths and plates arranged. Three chiefs who wear short-sleeve working-khaki uniforms sit at a center table; they drink coffee and engage in conversation.

Rig walks to the table where the chiefs sit and asks, "Reporting aboard. Who do I see about checking into Chiefs Berthing?" His eyes jump from chief to chief while awaiting an answer.

The short and thin senior chief with jet-black hair and short-trimmed beard answers, "That would be Master Chief Tollerson. He'll be the one wearing the Command Senior Enlisted Advisor Badge. He'll assign you a rack appropriate to your rank and time in grade. He'll be here during lunch. You can place your bags on the deck in Chiefs Berthing. They'll be safe there."

"Where can I find Chiefs Berthing?"

The senior chief with the beard responds, "Through the forward door, past the scullery. Can't miss it."

Rig asks, "Mind if I join you for a cup of coffee?"

"Take a seat."

Rig goes to the coffee urn and draws a cup of coffee. He adds a dash of cream.

After sitting down at the table, the ceremony of introductions, shaking of hands, and "welcome aboard" takes place. Page notices that each chief wears wrinkled and soiled khakis.

One of the chiefs questions, "Rigney Page? How do you spell your first and last name?"

"R I G N E Y P A G E, but, please, call me Rig."

"Your name is familiar. Have we been stationed together somewhere?"

Rig knows that his name and picture appeared in the Navy Times several times during the past three years, and during the last year his name and photograph appeared repeatedly in the Washington Post and other major newspapers.

Rig responds, "I don't think so."

The chief stares curiously at Rig while attempting to remember.

"What was your last command?" asks the senior chief sonarman with a beard.

"Commander Naval Telecommunications Command, Washington D.C."

One of the chiefs comments, "That's unusual—coming off shore duty and not going to sea duty."

Rig exhibits surprise and questions, "Isn't the USS *Antares* sea duty?"

"No," the chief responds, "*Antares* rarely goes to sea. So, it's Type 4 duty—neutral duty."

Rig nods and expresses understanding. His duty station assignments are based on naval intelligence needs and not the standard sea-shore rotation for radiomen.

Rig listens to the conversation of the three chiefs. They have just come off a twelve-hour shift working on upgrading a sonar system and a navigation system aboard one of the two boomers moored alongside the tender. The boomer is in port for emergency repairs after a major electrical fire while submerged on patrol.

When the three chiefs finish their coffee, they rise from their chairs. The senior chief sonarman informs Rig, "We are off to our racks. Any questions before we leave?"

Rig asks, "Where's the Communications Office?"

"On the oh-four level."

After the three chiefs depart the Chiefs Mess, Rig remains seated and sips coffee. He looks toward the overhead and sees the typical shipboard array of cables, junction boxes, and valves.

Several minutes later, a door opens in the forward bulkhead. The noises of echoing clashing pots and pans fill the Chiefs Mess. A chief who wears short sleeve khakis and a mess cook wearing a steward's jacket walk through the doorway and enter the Chiefs Mess. The chief is twenty feet away and has his head turned away from Rig as he issues orders to the mess cook.

Rig recognizes the chief from the past. He spends a few moments recollecting. Then, he remembers Commissaryman Second Class Gordon Benedict from ten years ago at U.S. Naval Communications Station Nea Makri, Greece.

Rig stands up and calls out in a raised voice, "Hey, Gordon Benedict, remember me?"

Chief Benedict turns his head toward the voice. He spends

a few moments staring at Senior Chief Page. Then, his eyes go wide and he expresses surprise. He walks toward Page with his hand outstretched.

Rig moves toward Benedict with his right hand outstretched.

They meet in the center of the room. They shake hands.

With an enthusiastic tone and expression, Chief Benedict says, "Of course, I remember you, Rigney Page. How could I ever forget you? You're the most notorious sailor I know."

Rig responds, "And I remember you well. You are one of the most compassionate, dedicated, and caring sailors I ever met."

"I've read about you in the papers," Benedict states. "You've been busy."

"Don't believe everything you read in the papers." Rig expresses amusement.

Benedict nods. Then, he says, "I read about you being shot. Are you recovered now?"

"Yes."

Benedict cocks his head to one side, dons a quizzical expression, and asks, "Newspapers say you were accused of shooting some labor union people and blowing up their buildings. Did you?"

"All charges were dropped."

Benedict nods and expresses amusement at Rig for not answering the question. Then, he comments. "I read about you and Ralph Hilton killing terrorists at a navy base in Scotland. I read that in the Navy Times. Was the Navy Times wrong?"

Rig responds, "The Navy Times got it right. But other newspapers omitted the brave actions of other chiefs that night."

"I would've never thought Ralph Hilton was capable of fighting terrorists. I remember him from Nea Makri. He was such an asshole. Whatever happened to him?"

"He is retired now and working as a civilian in COMNAVTELCOM in Washington—same command I was stationed at before coming here."

"What is your assignment here?"

"Communications Department."

"You'll be onboard for a full tour, then?"

"Probably."

"Glad to hear it." Benedict pauses as he glances toward the sound of clanging pots and pans in the galley. "I must get the cooks started on preparing for lunch. I would like to talk some more, later. Okay?"

Rig responds, "Sure, we will meet at the chiefs club for a beer one afternoon, soon."

"Looking forward to it," Benedict states sincerely. Then, he turns and walks through the forward door.

Chapter 4

After Rig drops his suitcases in the Chiefs Berthing compartment, he proceeds to the 0-4 level in search of the communications office.

The Communications Office includes a small outer office where the department yeoman has a desk and a larger inner office where the Communications Officer works.

As Rig enters the communications department yeoman's office, he can see Lieutenant Christine Hawthorne through the doorway to her office. She sits at her desk. Her head is bent over a stack of papers.

Rig recalls the first time he saw Christine three years ago in Thurso. She was a boot ensign fresh out of Communications Officer School. He had quickly evaluated her physical features. She was wearing Working Blue uniform. Her short and wispy frame, dark-brown hair, narrow eyes, pointed nose, and austere manner reminded him of his high school librarian who was nicknamed *The Wicked Witch of the West*. Later, he discovered she was the opposite of that, especially when she dressed up in sexy civilian clothes, wore her hair long and teased, and different style make up. They became lovers within a few weeks but kept that secret from the public.

Rig says to the yeoman, "Senior Chief Page reporting for check in with the communications officer."

Christine hears Rig speak to the yeoman. She would recognize his deep, mellifluous, sexy voice anywhere. She lifts her head and casts a happy smile toward Rig.

Rig returns the smile and nods his head.

The yeoman says to Rig, "I need to schedule all your reporting aboard interviews."

Christine comes to her office doorway and tells the yeoman,

"Petty Officer Barnes, I will see Senior Chief Page now."

The yeoman's desk is only a few feet from the lieutenant's office door. After Senior Chief Page enters the lieutenant's office, Barnes observes the lieutenant close the door. He hears the click of the door lock. He becomes puzzled by the violation of regulations that male and female sailors are not allowed to gather behind closed doors.

Christine wraps her arms behind Rig's neck and pulls herself to standing on her toes. She feels her shirttail pull free from her trousers.

He moves his hands under her shirt and holds on to the middle of her back.

Their kiss is long, wet, and passionate. They become aroused quickly, as always happens when lovers have been separated for a long time.

Christine moves her cheek to his. She says in panting breaths into his ear, "I am so glad to see you. I became so worried when reading about you and your family in the newspapers. After you get settled, you must tell me the truth of it all."

Rig relaxes his embrace. He is flushed and panting also.

She is about to take a step backwards; then, changes her mind. She grabs his biceps, pulls herself up on her toes, and kisses him again on the mouth.

The second kiss lasts only moments and is less passionate than the first.

She takes a step back and says appraisingly, "You still have those muscles. How do you find the time?"

"I make time."

Christine tucks in her shirttail. Then, she takes a tissue from a box on her desk. She wets the tissue with her tongue; then, she rubs lipstick off Rig's mouth.

Rigney grins sheepishly.

She stares at the jagged, one-inch-long scar on his forehead.

"That's a nasty looking scar. What happened?"

"An accident when I was on the USS *Randal*."

Christine walks to her desk chair.

"Okay, let's sit and I will explain your assignment."

Christine sits down in her desk chair.

Rig sits down in a chair in front of her desk. He quickly scans the office and finds it typical of shipboard offices everywhere—navy-gray painted walls and bulkheads. The deck is green vinyl-tile. The heavy furniture is bolted to the deck. Cables run in groups throughout the overhead.

Christine explains, "You are the Leading Radioman for both USS *Antares* and COMSUBRON THIRTEEN. All communications resources of COMSUBRON THIRTEEN and USS *Antares*, including radiomen, are pooled. Captain of USS *Antares* is your administrative chain-of-command. Commander Submarine Squadron Thirteen is your operational chain-of-command.

Rig is somewhat surprised because usually there is a master chief radioman assigned to both a submarine tender and to a submarine squadron staff.

Christine observes Rig's expression of surprise. She explains, "Master Chief Parden transferred early because he was selected to be the COMSUBLANT Command Master Chief, and the COMSUBRON THIRTEEN billet that he had occupied remains unfilled. So, that makes you the senior radioman for both squadron and *Antares*."

"Who is my division officer?"

"I am, temporarily, until a Submarine Communicator LDO reports aboard in June."

"Who?"

An expression of concentration appears on Christine's face while searching her memory; then, she remembers. "Lieutenant junior grade Chester Hamilton."

Rig expresses amused resignation.

"You know him?" Christine inquires.

"Yes. I was his watch supervisor onboard USS *Proteus* - five years ago. I was a first class and he was a second class."

Christine says, "You looked amused when I mentioned his name. Is there a problem with him?"

"Oh, uh, no problem. I don't remember much about him. I am resigned to the fact that as I continue with my navy career, I will experience more situations where sailors who were once junior to me and then went LDO or warrant will be my bosses in the future."

"Rig, your stubbornness not to apply for LDO really bewilders me. Why won't you do it?"

"I have my reasons."

"Like what?!"

"Laziness, for one."

Christine shakes her head while exhibiting disappointment. "Okay, Rig, I respect your desire to be secretive."

After a few moments of awkward silence, Rig asks, "What are my specific duties?"

"You are the operations chief. You will be responsible for preparing all communications plans, supervising communications operations, and supervising all communications personnel. Also, you will be the Command Career Counselor for Squadron and the Department Career Counselor for the Communications Department."

Rig expresses displeasure at that Career Counselor assignment.

"Rig, you're the only one in the department with the Career Counselor NEC. Do you have one of those Navy Career Counselor badges for your uniform?"

"Yes."

"Start wearing the badge. Chief Jennings was the

21

Communications Department Career Counselor, but he transferred two weeks ago without a replacement. No one else in the Squadron or in the Communications Department has the NEC."

Rig nods understanding. Then, he asks, "How many chiefs in CR Division?"

"Including you—six."

"Any significant problems that require my immediate attention?"

"Only two—we have a morale problem and we have a high number of mishandled messages."

With sarcasm in his tone, he comments, "What communications department doesn't have those two problems?"

Christine casts an amused expression and responds, "I have come to understand that. Do you think you can fix it?"

"If you want me to fix it, I need one-hundred percent control over the communications department."

Christine chuckles. "I knew you would say that. I remember our long talks about leadership and problem solving. But I do not have one-hundred percent control of the communications department. So, I cannot delegate that authority to you. The Chief of Staff will not allow me to make personnel assignments or change communications department policy without his approval. The best that I can do is to give you one-hundred percent of my support."

Rig exhibits bewilderment, "What's with the Chief of Staff? You're the communications department head."

"I'm the temporary department head with no submarine experience. Chief of Staff does not want my non-qual ass causing chaos and inefficiency."

"Did he call you a non-qual ass?"

"No, but I have overheard him using that label regarding

Surface Warfare officers on this ship. He believes a lot of problems are caused by officers who do not understand submarine procedure and submariner culture."

Rig expresses understanding.

"Rig, you don't agree with him?!"

Rig shakes his head slightly and replies, "No, but I understand where he is coming from."

Christine adds, "He makes it clear that he does not trust Surface Warfare officers."

Rig changes the subject. "I was wondering how a Surface Warfare officer became a submarine squadron communications officer."

Christine explains, "About three months ago, the *Antares* Communications Officer and Radio officer were murdered. A request for temporary replacements went out to local commands. NAVCOMMSTA Rota offered me up."

"Murdered? Where? How? By whom?"

"Sedo Mare Pueblo—located about fifteen miles north of Rota—near the beach. A lot of Americans live there, military families, and a lot or retired Brits and retired Spanish citizens, also."

Rig already knows all that, but he cannot reveal his knowledge to Christine.

Christine asks, "I rent a condo in town. Can you make it for dinner tonight?"

Rig expresses doubt as he asked, "Anyone from the ship live near you."

"No. Just wear civvies."

"Okay."

"And bring your overnight bag," Christine orders in a seductive tone.

"Will do," Rig responds while grinning from ear to ear. He stands and prepares to depart the office.

Christine expresses amusement and says, "Oh, one more thing that I am sure you want to know."

Rig stares at Christine. Her amused expression makes him curious.

"Your friend, RM1 Sharon MacDill, was transferred last week. Suddenly, message orders arrived several weeks ago to transfer her within ten days to NAVCAMSWESTPAC Guam."

"Thanks for the info," Rig replies nonchalantly.

Christine chuckles lightly. Still casting an amused expression, she challenges in a friendly tone, "Come on, Rig, you two were lovers."

Rig attempts to express indifference. "Is that what she told you?"

"No. She didn't tell me. I didn't even know you two knew each other until her transfer interview last week. She told me she was stationed in Thurso after I left. She said the two of you were friends. I saw *lover* in her eyes every time she said your name. It's a woman thing. I man would not have notice."

Rig hopes that Christine will not make an issue about it. To get off the lover subject, he asks, "You said she transferred suddenly."

"Yes, 'Needs of the Service' the orders stated."

Rig stares caringly into Christine's eyes as he asks, "What you know about Sharon and me will not be a problem in our relationship, will it?"

"Of course not," she says pleasantly. "Now, get on with your check in, and I will see you tonight."

Chapter 5

Rig enters the Chiefs Mess. The mess is sparsely populated during the final fifteen minutes of serving the mid-day meal. He feels conspicuous in his Dress Blue uniform. After sitting down at a table with several unoccupied settings, he forks some roast beef from a serving dish and places the slice of beef on his plate; then, he uses salad tongs to place some tomatoes and cucumbers on his plate.

Several minutes later, a short, stubby master chief with a bald head sits down in the seat across from Rig. The master chief wears a submarine warfare pin—*dolphins*—above the left breast pocket of his Working Khaki uniform.

The Master Chief offers his hand to Rig. "Senior Chief Page, I'm Master Chief Quartermaster Bill Tollerson. I'm the *Antares* Command Master Chief and president of the Chiefs Mess. I want to welcome you aboard."

Rig takes the master chief's hand, shakes it, and says, "Thank you, Master chief, I am pleased to be aboard."

The master chief advises, "I assigned you rack 9C in Chiefs Berthing. I set your bags on the mattress. I had one of the mess cranks get you a set of bedding. It's a lower rack. All the middle racks are taken. Some of those middle racks are occupied by chiefs junior to you, and we can move one of them to get you a better rack."

Rig shakes his head, "No need, Master Chief. I will be living on the beach. My assigned rack is not important."

"As you want, Senior Chief."

Rig takes a bite of food. While he chews, the master chief stares Rig in the eye. Rig anticipates a flood of questions.

"You're a hero and a celebrity, Senior Chief, but you have a notorious reputation for attracting trouble. Command

25

leadership wants you to make a serious effort to avoid trouble."

Rig expresses contemplation. Then, he responds, "I'll do my best." He continues eating.

The master chief stares curiously at Rig's service stripes - hash marks. Then, his eyes move to Rig's ribbons and pins. He asks, "What boat and what year did you earn your dolphins?"

"USS *Jack*, 1969."

"I read about you being shot by your division officer when you were on the *Randal*. How did a radioman qualified in submarines get assigned to a destroyer?"

"It's a long story. Not one that I want to explain."

Master Chief Tollerson asks, "Did you earn your Surface Warfare pin on the *Randal*?"

"Yes."

"That must be the reason why you advanced to senior chief early … earning both submarine warfare and surface warfare pins."

"Could be," Rig responds.

"Do you have any college degrees?"

Rig cocks his head to the side, stares quizzically at the master chief, and comments in friendly tone, "You're asking a lot of questions. What's going on?"

"As Command Master Chief, I need to know the chiefs as well as I can. You're a paradox—a bundle of controversy, but the navy advances you early. I need to know your character."

Rig nods and expresses understanding. He asks, "What was your question again?"

"Do you have a college degree?"

"I have two associates—one in Electronic Engineering and the other in General Studies."

"Two! Well, now I am beginning to understand why you were early selected for senior chief."

"I guess," Rig responds mildly. "Selection boards never

advise as to why some are selected and why others are not."

Master Chief Tollerson asks, "What will be your job onboard?"

"I will be the leading radioman for both Squadron and CR division."

"Your immediate supervisor will be Lieutenant Hawthorne, right?"

"Yes."

"CLEAR THE MESS DECKS" is announced over the 1MC.

"I must go to a meeting," Tollerson sates. He rises and walks off.

Rig looks around the mess. He is the only chief remaining. Mess cooks are clearing the tables.

Chapter 6

Rig and Christine lie naked in Christine's bed. They are resting after their first sexual routine of the evening. The sequence of their first sexual routine was established during their initial affair in Scotland. First, they engage in short foreplay followed with Rig performing cunnilingus on Christine until she reaches orgasm two or three times. Then, Christine fellates Rig through ejaculation and beyond.

When they first met in Scotland and became lovers, Christine was hesitant to engage in oral sex. She had no experience with it and thought it somewhat unnatural. She had told Rig, "*I was raised as a lady and graduated from Brown University. Oral sex is perverted and I will not engage in it.*" Her love affair with Rig brought her down to earth and she lost her haughtiness.

Rig had introduced oral sex into their love making during their second night sleeping together. After several minutes of finger stimulation and Rig whispering into her ear that using his lips and tongue would intensify the pleasure, Christine reluctantly submitted to cunnilingus. She was shocked by the blinding, body-shuddering orgasm she first experienced under the control of Rig's experienced technique.

Minutes after she had recovered from those cunnilingus orgasms, she refused to fellate Rig. She feared Rig would disrespect her for performing such a disgusting act. Rig convinced her that it was a natural act of love making. She finally relented to Rig's persuasion and Rig coached her through it. After she saw how much Rig enjoyed it and how much Rig cherished her for performing the act, she became more willing, enthusiastic, and passionate when fellating him.

About six weeks into their affair in Scotland, she had said that she appreciated Rig's refrain of debasing the act by calling it a *blow job*. But after that, they both referred to fellatio as a blow job. *"You were the first to say it,"* Rig had reminded her each time; then, they would both chuckle.

Their second night sleeping together in Scotland set their sequence of sexual acts and became their established routine. They always started with a long session of foreplay, followed by oral sex, and then at least two acts of traditional intercourse during the night.

For Rig, no sexual act is more satisfying than for a woman he loves to freely, willingly, lovingly, and passionately fellate him through ejaculation and beyond. Christine is one of the few women he loves.

Although she thoroughly enjoys multiple orgasms during cunnilingus and thoroughly enjoys fellating Rig, Christine prefers traditional intercourse love making. For her, traditional intercourse is the act of love—the joining of two people who love each other.

Rig lies on his back. Christine rolls onto her side and faces him. She runs her fingers through his thick, rust-colored chest hair. She tells him, "Every time I read about you in the newspapers, I think of that night you fought off those terrorists in Thurso. When you were accused of being a mad bomber or hurting those union workers, I couldn't help but think that you are capable of those things."

"Are you asking me to reveal if those accusations are true?"

"Only if you want to."

Rig says nothing.

Christine snuggles up to him. He is aroused by her hot breath on his neck.

The moonlight coming in through the windows of the balcony door allows her to see Rig's naked body. He has an erection. His lean, broad-shouldered body takes her breath away.

After a few awkward moments, Christine asks, "Do you still feel the same way about me? The night before I left Thurso, you told me you loved me."

"I do love you, Christine, but I am not *in love* with you. Do you understand?"

"Yes, I understand. I know the difference. I am not the only woman you love, am I?"

Rig sighs deeply, attempting to convey annoyance. The other women who he loves, Sally Macfurson and Barbara Gaile, enter his thoughts. He believes in being honest with the few women he loves. He detests the idea of a romantic relationship based on lies. He also is somewhat disturbed by Christine putting him on the spot with such questions. But he also understands that Christine needs clarity in their relationship.

Rig answers, "There are other women in my life. Right now, you are the woman in my life; I have no plan to search for any other."

"I am seeing someone," Christine tells Rig in a guarded tone, not sure how he will respond. I want to keep seeing him, and I want to keep seeing you, too. Are you okay with that?"

Rig asks, "Are you engaged?"

"No."

"Then, I have no problem with that," Rig specifies without emotion.

"You're not jealous, then?"

"Of course I am jealous, thinking of another man sharing your bed. But I have no right to object and I won't."

"He is a navy cargo pilot stationed at the Rota Navy Air Terminal."

"Does he know about me?"

"No, and when he is in town, you and I cannot be together. I don't want him to know about you. This is the last time you can come to my place."

"I am okay with being the secret other man because life could become complicated if he knows about me."

Christine says, "Because if he becomes jealous and makes a fuss, he might complicate your undercover work with naval intelligence, right?"

Rig turns his head and looks at Christine.

Christine says, "That's why you are in Rota, right—some mission for naval intelligence?"

Rig responds with a quizzical stare.

"Come on, Rig. Remember that night before I transferred to Iceland. I told you that I suspected you were some kind of undercover agent."

"Yes, I remember."

"Well, during my first week in Iceland I was visited by two navy commanders who debriefed me and had me sign non-disclosure documents, committing me to never telling anyone what I suspected about you. They said because I have a top secret clearance there is no reason to take any further action regarding my knowledge about you. So, you must have told someone in your intelligence chain of command what I said."

Rigney sighs deeply and replies, "Yes. Standing orders require that I report anyone who suspects or comes to know my true status."

Christine responds in a supportive tone, "I am okay with that, Rig."

"Good. Then you know that I cannot answer questions about my off-ship activities." Rig pauses; then, he adds, "My naval intelligence work could take up a lot of my time."

"We'll work it out," Christine promises in a seductive tone. "Now, make love to me."

They wrap their arms around each other and kiss—a long warm kiss with lots of tongue. Then, Rig caresses her neck, and she nibbles on his ear. He moves his hand to her clitoris and massages it softly. Christine moans with pleasure. She spreads her legs.

"Now, Rig."

Rig moves on top of her. Christine spreads her legs more.

Rig enters her gently.

She gasps as she feels him fill her.

"I love you, Rig. No matter what happens or how long we are separated, I will always love you."

Rig does not respond with words. He rotates and pumps his hips in the repeated sequence that Christine likes best.

Two minutes later, Christine rasps in his ear, "Oh, Yes! That's it!" Her body quivers with the pleasure of orgasmic release for the third time this evening.

Rig continues to caress her neck. He increases the speed of his hip movements.

She tightens her arms around him and wraps her legs around his hips. She adjusts her hip motions to synchronize with his increased repetitions. Her breathing becomes deeper and faster. She senses that she will have another orgasm before Rig is finished.

Rig moves his lips to hers. Their tongues do not stop dancing until they both reach orgasm.

They separate and lie side by side on their backs. Their breathing is deep and rapid. Their bodies are exhausted. They both wonder if they can do that again one more time tonight, as has been their past sexual routine.

Ten minutes later, they are asleep in each other's arms.

Chapter 7

Rig stands in the outer officer of Captain Daniel Finney, Commanding Officer of USS *Antares*.

This is Rig's third day onboard and he has put away his dress uniform and now wears Working Khaki with garrison cap.

The captain's yeoman hangs up the phone; then, he turns on his swivel office chair and says to Rig, "You can enter, Senior Chief."

Rig opens the office door, enters, and closes the door behind him. He snaps to attention and states, "Senior Chief Page reporting, sir!"

"Stand easy, Senior Chief. Take a seat. We'll start in a moment."

Two minutes later, the captain of the USS *Antares*, sits opposite Rig at the captain's conference table. The captain shuffles some papers.

While waiting for the reporting-aboard interview to begin, Rig takes a quick look around the captain's office. The office is not the usual navy-gray office decor. Paintings of epic sea battles decorate the wood paneled bulkheads. Sound dampening tiles cover the overhead. A deep pile blue carpet covers the deck. The conference table is dark wood and matches the paneling on the bulkheads.

The captain advises, "The *Antares* Communications Department comes under the operational control of COMSUBRON THIRTEEN. For all other command functions and procedures, the Communications Department comes under my authority and responsibility.

"I understand, Captain. I have been in such situations before."

"I want you to make Communications Department

equipment readiness and operator training your number one priority."

"Will do, Captain."

"Good. Because the last time we went to sea, our at-sea communications systems performed poorly. Not all the radiomen knew how to operate those systems. I do not want to go through that again."

"I'll take care of it, Captain."

One hour later, Rig enters the office of Captain Theodore Crossman, COMSUBRON THIRTEEN Chief of Staff. Captain Crossman sits at his desk.

Rig steps to the center of the room, snaps to attention, and announces, "Senior Chief Page reporting, sir!"

Captain Crossman stands up from his desk; then orders, "Stand easy, Senior Chief." The captain offers his hand. Captain Crossman is a lean, medium-height man who projects a confident manner, as do all officers who have commanded ships at sea and have been successful in their careers. He wears both Submarine Warfare Officer and SSBN Deterrent Patrol insignias.

Rig and the Chief of Staff shake hands.

The Chief of Staff neither smiles nor exudes a welcoming smile. He motions for Rig to sit down.

Rig immediately notes the office has the same décor as the office of Captain Finney.

Crossman lays Rig's service record on the desk and opens it to the section that lists Rig's previous commands.

Crossman asks, "Are you checked in, settled in, and ready to go to work?"

"Yes, sir, except for the reporting aboard interview with the commodore. That's later today."

34

"Senior Chief, did you request this assignment?"

"Not specifically, sir. I asked to be assigned to Europe."

"You do not have a lot of submarine experience for a Senior Chief qualified in submarines. Your record shows that you earned your dolphins in 1969 while serving aboard the *Jack*. You were only on the *Jack* for five months. How did you earn your dolphins so quickly—takes most submariners a year?"

"I was half-way done with my quals when I transferred from *Barb* in 1968. *Barb* and *Jack* are the same class boats. So, the captain of the *Jack* allowed my quals signed on *Barb* to apply to quals on *Jack*."

Crossman glances down at Rig's *List of Assignments*. Then, he looks back up and says, "You have never served a full tour on a submarine and never served on a boomer, correct?"

"Correct, sir."

The captain closes Rig's service record, then, he asks, "What are your goals for your tour of duty onboard *Antares*?"

Rig answers, "Improve the morale and qualifications of each sailor in the communications department. Appears those are the two areas that need the most attention."

"What about operations efficiency? We get two or three complaints a week from boomers regarding message handling."

"That's about average for any message center processing eighteen-hundred message copies per day."

The captain expresses disapproval of Rig's response. He challenges, "Does that mean you do not consider improvement in operating procedures to be a priority?"

"My experience is that message processing mistakes are not caused by incomplete or invalid operating procedures. Those mistakes are caused by radiomen temporarily losing attention to detail for one reason or the other. Humans make mistakes. A few mistakes made when handling eighteen-hundred copies per day is inevitable.

"Senior Chief, I want your priority to be reducing the amount of complaints we get regarding message center service. Boomer sailors are burdened enough without having to deal with message center mistakes."

Rig expresses contemplation as he attempts to understand the meaning of Captain Grossman's order to reduce complaints against the *Antares* message center.

Crossman interrupts Rig's thoughts, "Here's an example, Senior Chief." Crossman picks up some stapled sheets of paper and hands them to Rig.

Rig becomes irritated but does not show it. *I'm being tested!*

Rig scans the message; then, he reports, "The last message page is missing—page four of four."

"Yes, and that is the way the captain of the *Woodrow Wilson* found it on his message board this morning. I estimate that one man-hour of boomer crew time was wasted solving that problem. Those boomer crews have 30 days to prepare their submarines for patrol. Boomer man-hours are valuable. Correcting preventable mistakes wastes a boomer sailor's time. Such time-wasting evolutions can snowball and can delay boomer departure times, which has a snowball effect on the schedule of all ships and commands involved in boomer schedules in the Atlantic and Mediterranean."

Rig responds, "Sir, the *Woodrow Wilson* radiomen pick up their messages at the *Antares* message center; then, back on their boat they prepare the message boards for the *Woodrow Wilson's* officers. The last page could have come off after they picked up at the message center. That message was shotgun distributed to all message users because it is addressed to ALLSUBLANT. No other users reported a problem. Is it not possible that the *Woodrow Wilson* radiomen lost that message page?"

"Senior Chief, I am not going to get into a finger-pointing contest with the captain of the *Woodrow Wilson* over who made the error. My order to you is reduce the number of complaints."

"Aye, aye, sir."

The captain moves on to another subject. "The U.S. Navy presence in Spain is based on a fragile agreement with the Spanish government. Spain is not a NATO country, so there is no NATO Status of Forces Agreement to anchor U.S. presence. U.S. Navy commanders in Spain are under orders to maintain a low profile. Any incident by naval personnel that might attract the curiosity of the Spanish press is quickly resolved by navy leadership. You are notorious for attracting trouble. I order you to present a low profile and avoid trouble before it becomes trouble."

"Aye, aye, sir."

Captain Crossman had attempted to have Rig's orders to *Antares* cancelled. He had made several phone calls to former submarine colleagues at NAVPERS, but his request was denied. Then, Captain Crossman asked a former colleague at NAVPERS if COMSUBRON THIRTEEN sent an official PERSONAL FOR COMNAVPERS message would it be effective in getting Page's orders cancelled. He was told the orders would not be cancelled because of needs of the service.

Captain Crossman tells Senior Chief Page, "Add to your list of priorities an action plan to increase first-term reenlistment rates in the department from forty percent to seventy percent."

"Aye, aye, sir."

Two hours later, Rig sits before Commander Submarine Squadron THIRTEEN, Commodore Kevin Weller.

Commodore Weller's navy rank is captain but has the title of commodore because he commands a submarine squadron. He is a short and wiry man with close-cropped brownish-gray hair. His Naval Academy ring appears oversized on his small hand.

The commodore's office is twice the size of the Chief of Staff's office and similarly decorated.

The introductions are complete, and the busy commodore gets down to business. "I am impressed with your rapid advancement to Senior Chief and with your Hero of Thurso status. Your record specifies high marks in leadership, management and professional performance.

"However, all that negative press you received last year is disturbing. Have your problems with that labor union been resolved?"

Rig replies, "That labor union is not currently attacking my family. I don't know if it will start up again."

"Did the police ever discover the identity of that so-called *mad bomber*?"

"I don't know, sir. My focus, now, is on my assignment aboard *Antares*."

The commodore nods and expresses approval of Rig's response. Then, he asks, "What is your assessment of the operational readiness and material readiness of the Communications Department?"

Rig responds, "Material readiness is excellent and in-port operations are effective and efficient with few complaints from communications users. I attribute that to having a chief in charge of each watch section. I will assess at sea operations when we go to sea."

The commodore advises, "At-sea operations needs some work, but *Antares* rarely goes to sea and only for a few weeks when it does. You should channel some of your attention toward training for at-sea ops. However, the *Antares* Communication Department already has enough chiefs subordinate to you who can train the troops.

"As the Squadron leading radioman, I want your number

one priority to be monitoring and verifying the material readiness of each boomer's radio room while they are in upkeep. I want each radio room to have zero items in the Equipment Status Log when they depart on patrol. I want you in the radio room of each boomer at least three times per week checking the status of maintenance actions. I trust my boomer crews, but I also know the value of frequent and direct Squadron attention onboard a boomer during upkeep.

"Lieutenant Hawthorne meets weekly with the communications officer on each boomer to discuss any difficulties with radio room repair and maintenance. Lieutenant Hawthorne provides me with weekly reports. I want you to provide her with input for that report regarding any problems that you see developing. If there are no problems, state so in the report."

The commodore pauses for a few moments while he casts an appraising stare at Rig. Then, he challenges, "Do you think you can handle that, Senior Chief?"

"Yes, sir."

"Good. Return to your duties."

Rig and Lieutenant Christine Hawthorne discuss the schedule for the next day. When the discussion is over, Christine asks, "How did your reporting interviews go?"

"I now have three number-one priorities."

Christine chuckles while she comments, "Nothing unusual about that, right?"

"Business as usual," Rig answers while expressing amusement.

Chapter 8

So that he blends in with the other lunchtime joggers, Rig wears sweat pants and a hooded sweatshirt. The hood is up and he wears dark sunglasses.

No one pays attention to him.

As he jogs up to the building, he notes a surveillance camera mounted near the roof. He arrives at the outside door. The sign on the door states: U.S. NAVY WEATHER SERVICE ROTA SPAIN. He presses the doorbell. Several seconds later a male voice says over the intercom, "Please state your purpose, sir."

"Rigney Page to see Mr. Rouston."

Several minutes later, the door opens and is held open by Arleigh Rouston. "Come in, Senior Chief."

Rig enters. He stands in a small lobby. On the wall opposite the building entrance is a heavy metal door with pushbutton cipher lock access. Like most navy buildings, the floor is sea-green colored vinyl tile and the walls are painted a light green.

Rouston advises, "I am not putting you on the unescorted access list because this will be the first and last time you will be in this building. In the future, we will meet off base."

Rig nods and expresses understanding.

Rouston enters the cipher code for the metal door. He leads Rig into the visitor waiting area where an armed marine sits behind a desk. A rack of M-16s and shotguns hang on the wall behind the marine.

The marine pushes the visitors log toward Rig.

"You must sign the visitor's log. Then, I will escort you. I will brief you in the conference room."

Several minutes later, Rig is seated at the conference room table and faces a portable movie screen. Rouston stands next to the screen and has a pointer in his hand. A slide projector sits on the center of the table top.

Rouston presses the FORWARD button on the slide projector control device. An aerial view of Sedo Mare Pueblo appears on the screen. Rouston uses the pointer as he explains. "Sedo Mare Pueblo is a community of American military, affluent Spaniards, and retired Brits. Twenty years ago, the Sedo Mare Valley was just grass and volcanic sand. Then, a developer bought the whole valley and turned it into a community of condo buildings and single-family houses. As you can see, the single-family houses were built through the center of the valley. Condo buildings are built at the base of the hills on the east end of the valley. A popular beach owned by the developer, with private access only for Sedo Mare Pueblo residents, is located on the west side of the pueblo along the Atlantic coast. There are lots of American sailors renting houses and condos. The housing office on base coordinates rental agreements between sailors and owners.

"Last year, the Rota Naval Investigative Office began forwarding investigative reports to ONI regarding erotic activities in the Sedo Mare Pueblo. Normally we would not get involved in non-espionage activities. But when sailors and their dependents involve themselves in inappropriate behavior, they can be blackmailed for classified information."

"What kind of erotic activities?"

"Wife swapping parities and naked people having sex in the streets."

Rig flinches and blinks his eyes. An expression of amused curiosity appears on his face.

Rouston continues, "Do you remember that wife swapping club that was exposed at that navy communications station in the Pacific several years ago?"

Rig nods and answers, "Yes, I remember that—about thirty radiomen and cryptology techs and their wives—big scandal.

All the sailors were disciplined. All the sailors and their wives were transferred back to the states to different commands."

"That's the one," Rouston confirms. "What is not widely known about that wife-swapping scandal is that classified material was found in the homes of some of those sailors during a surprise raid by the navy authorities. ONI concluded that some of those sailors were being blackmailed by enemy agents and classified material was used as blackmail payments."

Rig nods understanding and comments, "So, ONI is interested in activities in Sedo Mare Pueblo because of possible security leaks of classified information?"

"Yes. U.S. military personnel residing in Sedo Mare Pueblo include the full range of U.S. military operations in Rota area."

Rig asks, "Have you uncovered anything yet?"

"No, and without solid evidence, headquarters will not authorize a fully funded operation to investigate. Military budget cuts are severely hampering ONI counterintelligence operations. All we have are unsubstantiated claims by some Sedo Mare residents. But none of those residents can provide names or specified locations other than most of the activity occurs in the east end of the valley.

"After those *Antares* officers were killed, I made an aggressive effort to get headquarters to provide operatives and to fund an operation. When I reported to headquarters that one of the officers killed had previously scheduled an appointment with NIS for the day after he was killed and when I reported that classified material was found in the burnt rubble of that officer's house, headquarters allocated some money for my general fund and assigned you to Rota."

Rig asks, "Were those officers being blackmailed or selling classified material?"

"I don't think so. The classified material found in the rubble was XEROX copies of MARK 48 Torpedo Technical Manuals.

Those manuals were not scorched and were obviously planted after the fire. Plus, both officers were communications officers, not weapons officers. They did not have access to those manuals. Both officers were shot to death before the house was burned. So, whoever did it is sending a message. Intel analysts are not certain what that message is or for whom that message is intended.

"The whole incident is not making sense. Analysts say it might have just been an act of senseless violence. But if that is true, then, why the planted classified material? Yet, planting classified material may have been a diversion from something bigger."

Rig asks "What is my mission?"

"I have rented a condo in Sedo Mare Pueblo in your name. The condo is located on the top floor of a six-story condo building located at the southeast corner of the Sedo Mare Valley. I live in the same building on the second floor. From now on, briefings will be held in your condo or mine."

Rouston points at a building on the projected aerial slide of Sedo Mare.

"Your condo has a large walk-in closet off the master bedroom. I built a fake wall in that closet, providing you with a hidden compartment that has plenty of space for storage of surveillance equipment, code books, and weapons.

"Your condo has balconies facing east, west, and north, which will provide you with a view of the entire valley. At night, you are to use night vision optical equipment and night cameras to observe and record activities in the valley. You will focus on the eastern end of the valley because that is where reports tell us that all that erotic activity is taking place."

"Every night?" Rig questions.

"That file in front of you is everything we have on Sedo Mare. You'll see that reports of unusual activity occur mostly on weekend nights with occasional reports of nights during the week. Use your own discretion. The Sedo Mare Valley has an interesting history. I think you will find it fascinating."

"Can I take this file with me?"

"Yes, that is your copy. Store it in the concealed space in the closet."

"How large is the condo?"

"Fifteen-hundred square feet. We have furnished it and have stocked the shelves and refrigerator."

Rig smiles and expresses pleasure. "Sounds comfortable and luxurious."

"It is."

Chapter 9

Senior Chief Rigney "Rig" Page scheduled a meeting with other departmental chiefs in the Communications Department office. Rig sits in Lieutenant Hawthorne's chair. Sitting around the small office are five radioman chiefs and the Leading Signalman.

Four of the radioman chiefs are assigned to the position of Communications Watch Officer, CWO, and supervise communications operations during their rotating eight-hour watches. Each is the direct supervisor of the radiomen in their watch section.

The fifth chief, who is the senior E-7, fills the position of Communications Material System Manager, Physical Security Officer, Crypto Security Officer and a number of other administrative positions.

The Leading Signalman, a first class petty officer, supervises signals division operations and three other signalmen. Because the *Antares* seldom goes to sea, the signals division does not require a chief signalman.

Rig wears the COMSUBRON THIRTEEN uniform of the day, which is always the same as the USS *Antares* Uniform of the Day. He wears Dress Khakis, which includes his military ribbons, his Submarine Warfare Device, and his Surface Warfare device.

The other chiefs wear Working Khaki uniform. Senior Chief Page and Chief McBride are the only two in the room who wear the submarine warfare insignia—dolphins. All the other chiefs and the Leading Signalman wear Surface Warfare insignias.

Rig opens the dialog. "I spent most of my first week observing communications operations. For the most part, operations comply with applicable manuals and publications. Processing times are within specifications and traffic checkers

45

are finding mishandled messages quickly and taking corrective action within acceptable time periods. All work centers are complying with maintenance and cleaning schedules.

"The negatives that I observed are few but significant. Low morale is apparent in some of our sailors. Also, only a few of our sailors are compliant with uniform and grooming regulations. I also uncovered that many of our sailors hold submariners in contempt and call them prima donnas who are not held to regulations.

"I want every sailor compliant with uniform and grooming regulations, and no *on the borderline* crap. I want our sailors distinctively compliant. No doubts at a glance that a sailor is compliant. If you need to use rulers to measure hair and beard length to determine compliance; then, the sailor is not far enough inside the envelope to satisfy me. No more mixing uniform and civilian attire on watch, off watch, or on liberty. All uniforms are to be in good repair as defined in uniform regulations. If you are in doubt about a sailor's compliance, then he is on the borderline or not compliant.

"Regarding the open contempt for submariners, all negative comments against submariners shall stop immediately and vice versa. Just order your subordinates to stop. We do not have time to change their thinking, but we can immediately change their behavior."

"Regarding low morale . . ." Rig pulls several slips of paper from his breast pocket and hands them to each of the chiefs and to the Leading Signalman. "These are lists of those low morale cases that I have observed. Something in their lives is depressing them. Find out what is bothering each of them and see if you can do anything to help them resolve it." Rig glances at the calendar; then, he says, "I want a verbal report from each of you by Tuesday of next week. Your report should include the nature of the problem and what you can do to help resolve it."

Rig pauses and glances at each face. Then, he asks, "Any questions before we move on to my last topic?"

Chief Radioman Pete O'Conner speaks, "Rig, what if we cannot solve a sailor's morale problem? Like if a sailor's problem is living in Spain away from mommy and daddy? I know that is the case for several sailors on the list."

Rig glances at the First Class Signalman, SM1 Kelter. Then, Rig shifts his attention to Chief O'Conner. Rig considers if what he is about to say is appropriate for the first class signalman to hear. He decides that what he is about to say should not be heard by a sailor lower in rank than a chief. Rig says, "Petty Officer Kelter, please step out of the office for a few moments. I'll let you know when you can come back in."

"Aye, Senior Chief." Kelter exits the office and shuts the door behind him."

Rig specifies, "When we are outside the Chiefs Mess, I want you to address me as 'Senior Chief,' and I will address all of you as 'Chief.' Calling ourselves by our first names in front of the troops is not conducive to good order and discipline. And no more of chiefs addressing subordinates by first name and vice versa. We need to halt the first name addressing in the communications department."

Chief O'Conner responds, "Sorry, Senior Chief. First name use by chiefs to other chiefs and even junior chiefs addressing master chiefs by first name in front of the troops runs rampant on the *Antares*. I advanced to chief while onboard—six months ago. I just never thought to do otherwise."

Rig states, "So I have noticed. I spoke to the Command Master Chief about this issue. I think we will hear something official from him during the next all chiefs meeting."

After a short Pause, Rig looks at the chief sitting closest to the door and says, "Tell Petty Officer Kelter that he can come back in."

After SM1 Kelter is seated, Rig says, "Regarding Chief O'Connor's question about solving a morale problem not being within his power to solve, like homesickness. We probably cannot eliminate a sailor's homesickness, but we can improve his morale by getting the sailor involved in outside activities that will keep his mind off home. Come to me if you want assistance, and we will tackle the problem together."

Rig pauses for a few moments, waiting for addition questions. None are asked.

"The next subject I want to discuss is maintenance and cleaning schedules. I have been assigned as Department 3-M Manager. I have reviewed department 3-M procedures and I have only two changes to implement. First, forward all 3-M paperwork to me by placing it in my message box in the message center and not in the Communications Officer's message box like you did before. Second, when you reschedule maintenance or cleaning, I want to be informed. Just write me an informal note citing the equipment or space and why you rescheduled. Put the note in my message box in the message center.

"You can keep the practice of performing assigned maintenance and cleaning actions while your section is on watch. However, rescheduling an action to another day because the assigned person in your watch section was too busy while on watch is not a valid reason for rescheduling. If the assigned person is too busy on watch, then that person must stay aboard after watch to perform the action. You might recommend to members of your watch section that on a day they have assigned maintenance actions or cleaning actions that they come in early before watch to perform those actions."

Rig pauses; then, he asks, "Any questions?"

Everyone remains silent. Several shake their heads.

After a short pause, Rig states. "The last subject that I want to discuss is the Navy Physical Fitness Program. We have a lot of fatties in the department. When was the last time that the required annual physical fitness tests were conducted?"

Chief O'Conner, who has been onboard the longest, states, "Not Since I have been onboard."

Senior Chief Page orders, "All of you shall read the CNO directive on physical fitness. Then, within the next 30 days, I want everyone in your watch sections tested. Slot me a copy of your physical fitness test schedule. Make sure you follow the rules—like having a corpsman present. Those who fail the fitness test are to be retested within ninety days. Pass and fail details are to be included in performance evaluations."

"What about day-workers?" RMC Bremerton questions sarcastically. "Or are they exempt from the burden of regulations as usual?"

Rig casts a curious stare at Chief Bremerton and wonders where that burst of attitude came from.

Rig responds while still staring at Bremerton, "Include all day-workers in your watch section physical fitness schedule."

"Does that include the officers?" Bremerton challenges in the same sarcastic tone. "Or are they exempt, also?"

Page advises, "We won't concern ourselves with the officers."

After a pause, Rig inquires, "Do any of you have questions?"

Chief Bremerton is the first to respond. "Senior Chief, I understand that you were recently advanced, that *Antares* is your first tour as a senior chief. Is that correct?"

"Yes."

"How many years do you have in the navy and how long have you been a chief petty officer."

"I have been in the navy thirteen and a half years. I have been a chief for three-and-a-half years."

"Were you frocked?" Chief Bremerton asks with an inflected tone indicating that he is about to make his point.

"I was frocked. My official advancement date is April fifteenth—three months from now."

"Uh huh!" Chief Bremerton declares. "So, had you not been frocked, you would be junior to all of us except for Chief O'Connor."

Rig shakes his head slightly as he responds, "I am not grasping your point, Chief."

"My point, Senior Chief, is that you supervise five chiefs, and four of those chiefs have more time as a chief than you. Before you go making any big, morale busting changes, you should consult us."

Rig nods and expresses his understanding. He responds, "I do not plan on making such changes."

"Come on, Senior Chief! What the hell do you call making our department do physical fitness tests during our off time when the rest of the ship doesn't do physical fitness tests at all?!"

Rig glances at the faces of the other chief radiomen and the first class signalman—looking for confirmation that they feel the same as Chief Bremerton.

Chief Trenton stares at Chief Bremerton and states, "Actually, John, uh, Chief Bremerton, I think it is a good idea. It will get our people motivated to exercise. My section will do the test after the first day watch—should not take more than an hour, if that."

"Humph!" Bremerton utters toward Trenton. "No inconvenience for you, Chief Trenton. You're already an exerciser and big weightlifter and you're single with no kids that tie up all your off time."

After some moments of pause, Rig asks, "Any more questions?"

Everyone remains silent.

"Meeting over," Rig announces.

Chapter 10

At 11:30 PM on his third Friday in Spain, Rig sits in a patio chair on a balcony of his Sedo Mare condo. All lights are turned off and he sits in the dark. A high-power, night-vision telescope sits atop a tripod before him. Off to the side, a camera with a high magnification night-vision telescopic lens sits atop another tripod. A bottle of brandy and a snifter sit on a table next to him.

The chance of someone seeing Rig on his balcony is slim. His condo is on the top floor. His condo building sits farther up the hill than others in the neighborhood. Only someone located one-mile across the valley on a balcony of the same height and with night vision equipment could see him.

He has had the eastern end of the Sedo Mare Valley under surveillance for three hours and has seen nothing unusual. There are no street lights and the only illumination along streets comes from the windows of residences and front door lights.

Earlier in the evening, Rig observed a full parking lot near the beach restaurants and nightclub. Parties are in progress in many houses. He hears music, loud voices, and laughter coming from several houses close by. Balconies of some condos are full of partiers.

At 2:00 AM. He sighs deeply. He takes a sip of brandy.

A few minutes later, he notes increased activity on the streets. Through the night-optics telescope, he scans the eastern side of the valley. Then he moves his area of surveillance to the west—toward the ocean. The migration of partiers to their homes begins. Rig easily tracks the partiers by following car headlights and bobbing flashlight beams of those walking home. Rig logs the activity in his notebook.

Thirty minutes later, activity on the streets has thinned. Sedo Mare Pueblo is quiet and dark, and he logs so in his notebook. A glance at his watch reveals the time to be 2:30 AM. The brandy glass is empty. He decides to surveil for another thirty minutes.

Fifteen minutes later, parking lights of three vehicles appear in a dark area about five blocks away. Rig peers through the optics of the high-power, night vision telescope. Three, two-and-one-half-ton cargo trucks idle side-by-side inside the *Imperio Construir* fenced compound. A tarp covers the cargo area of each truck. The warehouse is the size of a jetliner hangar and could easily house a fleet of those trucks. The ONI file on Sedo Mare explained that *Imperio Construer* is the Spanish subsidiary of *Empire Construction*—the English land company that owns and develops the Sedo Mare Valley.

A fourth truck exits the warehouse garage door and parks behind the other three trucks.

Several men stand in front of the trucks. They carry clipboards and small low-yield flashlights and appear to be comparing the paperwork on one clipboard with paperwork on other clipboards.

The entire scene fires Rig's curiosity. He continues to watch. He records the license number of each truck. After ten minutes, the trucks move in single file toward the storage area gate. After exiting the gate, the trucks move south toward the Rota highway. Rig loses sight of the trucks as they move behind the hills.

Rig returns his attention to the construction company storage yard. Through the night-optics telescope, he observes one man with a thick beard moving about. The man holds a small flashlight that projects its beam to the ground. The man locks the doors to the warehouse. Then, he turns and walks across the compound to a small gate for yard workers. He walks through the gate; then, locks it. After crossing the street, he stops at a high-wall gate that allows access to the large courtyard of the house that is owned by the Sedo Mare Building Superintendent.

During the next thirty minutes, nothing of interest occurs. Rig disassembles his surveillance equipment and stores it in the secret compartment in the walk-in closet.

Chapter 11

Rig sits in the *Antares* Chiefs Mess. He just finished breakfast and is in the process of finishing his second cup of coffee. He glances at his watch—0723.

A chief electronics technician wearing Service Dress Blues sits down across from Rig.

Rig recognizes the tall, wiry, rugged looking chief. Bushy black hair contrasts the chief's deep blue eyes. The chief's face bears a few small scars that were not there the last time Rig saw him.

"Senior Chief Page, we have crossed paths before."

Rig nods affirmative and says, "Yes, I remember you—Clark Air Force Base Philippines, 1975. I was TAD to Mobile Communications Team Five. Sorry, I don't remember your name."

"Phil Heans."

Rig expresses recognition. "Phil, please call me Rig when we're in the mess. I have been onboard for several weeks. This is the first time I've seen you."

"Been on leave—just returned."

Rig nods; then, comments, "That assignment to MCT FIVE seems like yesterday. Time flies, as they say."

Heans says, "Every time your name appears in the newspapers you are the topic of conversion in the mess. The number of people who claim to know you rises with each new headline. You must be the most notorious chief in the navy."

Rig responds, "There are many stories circulating about me that are not true."

Heans replies, "I often tell the story of that time you saved me from a beating in that Angeles City bar, and that time you killed three Viet Cong guerrillas. People accuse me of an exaggerated sea story, but I keep telling it, anyway."

Rig speculates, "I am sure that each time the story is told, the body count rises."

Heans nods and expresses understanding. Then, he says, "When your transfer order to *Antares* was listed in Navy Times, you became the topic of conversation in the mess. Chief Benedict told us you and him were stationed together in Greece about ten years ago. He said you were always beating up on bullies there. He said you were court-martialed for punching out an officer. But you were found innocent, although over thirty people saw you hit the officer."

Rig shakes his head and expresses resigned frustration; he clarifies, "I was not court-martialed. It was an Article thirty-two hearing. The charges against me were dropped after the hearing."

"Whatever," Chief Heans declares. Then he adds, "Chief Plonter told us you were in the newspapers in California about bombing union buildings and beating up guys in unions."

"Lies," Rig responds. "If that were me, I wouldn't be here, right?"

"Chief Plonter said the papers called you a *mad bomber* and you were arrested for shooting someone."

"Charges were dropped because of lack of evidence," Rig responds.

Chief Heans chuckles lightly; then, says, "I must say that after watching you in action in Vietnam, I was never surprised about anything I heard or read about you, especially that time you were The Hero of something or other—when you stopped a terrorist attack. Uh, where was that?"

"Thurso, Scotland."

Heans nods acknowledgment; then, he says, "I must go to quarters. Great to see you again and glad you're aboard." Heans stands and walks off.

The bugle for quarters sounds over the 1MC announcing system: "ALL HANDS TO QUARTERS FOR MUSTER AND INSPECTION."

Rig is now the only chief in the mess. Communications Department does not hold quarters at the same time as the rest of the ship. Each communications watch section holds quarters before assuming the watch.

Several mess cooks move about the mess and clear away breakfast dishes.

Master Chief William Tollerson, the USS *Antares* Senior Enlisted Advisor, sits down across the table from Rig.

"Got a minute?" Tollerson asks.

"Sure."

Tollerson sits down next to Rig. Then, says, "You're assigned to the USS *Antares* Petty Officer of the Year selection board."

"Sounds exciting," Rig responds in an unenthusiastic tone. "When? Where?"

The master chief removes a sheet of paper from a clipboard. "Here is your assignment letter from the XO. The schedule and instructions are included in the letter."

Rig glances at the letter. He focuses on the names of the chiefs who make up the board. He inquires, "How did I get picked for this?"

"The board must be senior chiefs and master chiefs from departments other than the four candidates. The candidates come from Repair, Engineering, and Weapons."

Rig glances at the schedule. Interviews are four days away, and he must make time to read the four candidates' service records.

Chapter 12

Rig and Arleigh Rouston, OIC Naval Intelligence Office Rota, sit at Rig's kitchen table. Rig's condo is located on the top floor of the building. Rouston's condo is located on the second floor. Rouston briefs Rig on the Sedo Mare Pueblo construction company.

"Those trucks you observed departing the *Imperio Construir* compound are registered to *Imperio Construir*. The Spanish Naval Intelligence Office here reports that those same trucks delivered cargo to the civilian docks approximately four hours after those trucks drove out of Sedo Mare Pueblo. That cargo was loaded onto ships owned by *Saint Claire, Limited* and delivered to ports in Egypt, Syria, Israel, Saudi Arabia, Lebanon and Bahrain. Those ships did not make any stops to any port outside of the Middle East."

"Now, here it gets really interesting. The Chief Executive Officer and largest stockholder of *Saint Claire, Limited* is a Turkish billionaire with businesses all over the Middle East, primarily shipping companies."

Rig expresses curiosity as he asks, "What was the cargo?"

"*Imperio Agua* bottled water, according to invoices and shipping documents.

"Bottled water?!"

"Yeah, and according to our London office, *Imperio Agua* and *Imperio Construir* are owned by *Empire Construction* whose headquarters is in London.

Rig recognizes the *Imperio Agua* brand name. *Imperio Agua* bottled water is sold in stores, bars, and restaurants throughout Europe.

While expressing curiosity, Rig responds, "Why would a construction warehouse at Sedo Mare Pueblo store bottled water for shipment to the Middle East? I suspect some nefarious plot afoot. Is there an operation or mission developing from that discovery?"

"Yes. There is," Rouston answers. "We have been tasked to investigate that warehouse. Your mission is to get into that warehouse and discover what is going on in there."

Rig appears contemplative. Then, he states, "I will need additional equipment."

"Write out a list."

Chapter 18

One hour after sunset, Rig sits in the dark inside his car near a deserted beach to the north of Sedo Mare Valley. He glances at his watch and wonders why Rouston is thirty minutes past due for their rendezvous. He decides to wait ten minutes more.

Because of the cold winter wind blowing in from the Atlantic, he keeps the engine and heater on and the windows shut. His car headlights and parking lights are switched off.

Several minutes later, Rig sees headlights in the rearview mirror moving slowly toward him along the lonely, narrow, dirt road. When Rouston's car stops behind Rig's car and Rouston turns off his lights, Rig exits his car and gets into the passenger seat of Rouston's car.

Rig briefs Rouston on the hoodlum attack against the American couple.

"I have not received any reports on that," Rouston advises.

Rig expresses surprise. "Maybe the Policía or shore patrol has not forwarded their reports, yet."

Rouston explains, "The local Naval Investigative Service field office forwards a copy of local Spanish Policía reports and Shore Patrol reports to me every day. Those reports cover all communities within thirty miles of Rota. Nothing on that incident was reported."

Rig concludes that the American couple is too embarrassed to report what happened at the crime scene.

Rouston adds, "That couple should not be hard to find. If his wallet and her purse were stolen, their I.D. cards were probably stolen. I will send a query to NIS to check with the base Pass and I.D. Office for a list of names of couples who live in Sedo Mare Pueblo and both have requested reissue of lost I.D. cards."

"Let me know what you find out."

"Will do," Rouston promises. Then, he asks, "Are you ready to recon that construction compound?"

"Yes, I'm going in tomorrow tonight about zero-one-thirty. Not much has been going on in that compound in recent nights. The weather forecast calls for heavy rains for the next two days. That provides little chance that anyone will be moving about in the compound tomorrow night."

"How are ya gonna get in?"

"There are some ruts running under the fence in several locations. Some of those ruts are big enough for me to slither in."

Rouston questions, "And the locks on the warehouse door?"

"Chains with padlocks—my lock-pick set should defeat those."

"What if your lock-pick set doesn't work?"

"I will give it up. I do not want to destroy any locks to let anyone know that someone was there. But I don't think I will have a tough time getting in."

Rouston advises, "There is little security around that compound. Either there is nothing of value inside that warehouse or the owners want to portray there is nothing of value inside that warehouse. Too much security would draw attention."

"That's the way I see it," Rig responds.

"Do you still believe that you do not need backup?"

"Not this time."

Rouston responds, "I will be listening in on channel one, anyway. Give me an all clear when you are done and out of there."

"Will do."

Chapter 19

RM2 Robert Baylor sits across the desk from Senior Chief Page in the *Antares* Command Career Counselor's office.

Rig asks Baylor, "What would it take for you to reenlist?"

Baylor stares intently into the senior chief's eyes as he asks, "Can I talk honestly, Senior Chief, without later being harassed about it?"

"Yes," Rig answers.

Baylor explains, "During my enlistment, I did more than what was required of me. During my first eighteen months onboard, my wife was not with me. I lived onboard and I worked hard on radioman quals and surface warfare quals between watches—so that I would qualify quickly. When my wife arrived, I applied for navy housing. The waiting list was six months. So, we rented a substandard apartment in town. I have worked shitty hours for three years—half the time in three sections. Every leave request for more than seven consecutive days was denied. At every turn the radio gang is blamed for everything and never rewarded for anything. Many times, my watch section has been called in during our days off to chip paint and to participate in ceremonies requiring full dress uniform, while day-workers sit in their offices drinking coffee and are seldom required to come in on their weekends. But I never complained. I did my work and I performed well because it is my nature. Now, all of a sudden, the navy is willing to cater to me so I will reenlist. It's too late, Senior Chief. The navy cannot treat me like a slave for three-and-half years, then, be nice to me when the end of my enlistment arrives."

Rig asks, "What was your rank when you first reported aboard?"

"I was an E2—RMSA."

"When did you make RM2?"

"Two years ago. I am now eligible for accelerated advancement to first class. I took the RM1 exam last month."

Rig does a quick calculation in his head; then, he asks. "So, you made RM2 with less than two-years of service?"

"Yes, and when I made RM2 I had already earned my surface warfare pin and qualified in all Main Comm watch stations, except for Communications Watch Officer and Technical Control Supervisor."

"You qualified for Technical Control Operator, before you advanced to second class?"

"Yes, and I'm half-way complete on my quals for Technical Control Supervisor."

Rig is impressed. He inquires, "What motivated you to do all that?"

"I was married when I first arrived aboard *Antares*. I was told that I could not get command sponsorship to bring my wife over until I advanced to RM3 and had two-years of service. Like I said before, I lived onboard for the first eighteen months. Living onboard made it easy to complete all those quals and correspondence courses. I wanted that command sponsorship for my wife."

Rig casts a grin at Baylor and says, "Appears to me you were rewarded for your hard work."

In a raised, emotional tone, Baylor retorts, "I earned it! It was not given to me!"

"And now you can earn more in exchange for more years of service."

Baylor shakes his head, "No. My wife and I are going back to Kentucky and live a normal life—a life where I am home every night. A life when I am off work, I am not subject to the whims of incompetent chiefs and officers who order me to come back onboard within the hour because they forgot to post an off-watch work schedule. A life where I am not ordered during the last minutes of my watch to stay onboard for the next twenty-four hours because of some last-minute, whimsical project thought up by the commodore."

Rig asks, "What are you going to do when you get back to Kentucky?"

"My father-in-law has offered me a management trainee position in his auto sales company. He owns three car lots."

Rig asks, "Do you have any college degrees?"

"Before I joined the navy, I completed two years of college but ran out of money."

"Have you applied for an Associate's Degree under the Navy Campus for Achievement program? You definitely qualify."

That question catches Baylor off guard. No one had ever mentioned that before.

"Uh, no, I never heard of it."

"Have you attended any college courses offered by the University of Maryland at the Naval Base Education Center?"

"Yes, I have completed some Spanish Language courses— received an 'A' in all courses, although I missed a lot of classes because of my watch schedule. I am currently taking a European History course."

Rig expresses thoughtfulness for a few moments. Then, he asks, "What does your wife think of returning to Kentucky and leading a normal life?"

Baylor casts a curious expression that conveys he suspects the senior chief already knows and wonders how the senior chief could know. "With all due respect, Senior Chief, that is none of your business."

Rig expresses contemplation for a few moments. Then, he advises, "If there were ever anyone who is LDO material, you're it. There is no doubt in my mind that if you continue your level of achievement in the navy and you apply for the Limited Duty

Officer program, you will be selected."

Baylor expresses befuddlement. This is the first time anyone has talked to him about officer programs. He knows some of the LDOs onboard, and he believes that he could achieve what they have achieved. He considers that Senior Chief Page provided something new to consider, but then he states, "You cannot guarantee that, Senior Chief, can you?"

"No, I can't, but you can apply for advanced radioman training, followed by choice shore duty, as a reenlistment incentive. And, there is that hefty reenlistment bonus. During that choice shore duty assignment, you can further your technical education and your college education. At the end of that shore tour, you will have eight years in, which is the minimum eligibility time-in-service requirement for LDO."

Baylor blurts, "What?! I must wait for another four years to apply?! No way!"

Rig tries another approach, "The results from the first class exam will arrive before your enlistment expires. What will you do if you are selected for advancement?"

"I'll turn it down. I only took the test to prove that I can be selected for first class with less than four years of service."

Rig casts an understanding expression. Then, he says, "Okay, Baylor, you can go back on watch."

Baylor expresses curiosity. He wonders about the Senior Chief's motives. He asks in a curious tone, "Senior Chief, do you really care if I reenlist?"

Rig responds, "Yes, for the benefit of the navy. You're an achiever, and the navy needs achievers."

"But you would not lose any sleep over me not reenlisting, right?"

Rig chuckles; then responds, "The navy will survive your discharge."

"I'm sure it will," Baylor declares. Then, he asks, "Why did you stay in?"

"I enjoy the work and the lifestyle."

Baylor knows about the senior chief's notorious reputation: *Hero of Thurso*, shot by a navy officer who was a deserter, accused of blowing up union buildings in Southern California, accused of revengeful attacks against union thugs, and rumored to be a womanizer who has had affairs with women officers. Baylor has no doubt that the senior chief lives an exciting life. An admiring smile spreads across Baylor's face.

"What?" Rig inquires.

"Nothing, Senior Chief." Baylor stands; then, departs the office.

After Baylor is gone from the office, Rig analyzes his conversation with Baylor. He concludes that Baylor's mind is made up and that any further attempts to reenlist him would be a futile effort.

Chapter 20

Rig exits his condo—wearing civilian clothes and carrying a canvas seabag that contains his mission equipment. He drives his car to the Rota Naval Base; then, he drives directly to the storage area that is owned and maintained by naval intelligence under the cover name of U.S. NAVY WEATHER SERVICE ROTA. The perimeter of the storage area is protected by a twelve-foot-high chain link fence with rolled barbwire strung along the top of the fence. A sign on the chain link gate announces: AUTHORIZED PERSONNEL ONLY – CONTACT U.S. NAVY WEATHER SERVICE ROTA.

Rig unlocks the gate and walks to the Quonset hut that serves as a two-vehicle garage. He unlocks the padlock on the garage-style door and lifts up on the door handle.

Inside the garage and as described by Rouston, Rig finds an old model, dented and rusting panel van of European manufacture with Spanish license plates. He starts up the van and drives it outside of the fenced area and parks it next to his car. Then, he drives his own car into the Quonset hut. After locking up the area, Rig drives the van to Sedo Mare Pueblo.

He parks the van at a predetermined spot one block from the *Imperio Construir* compound. The predetermined spot is behind a high mound of topsoil that hides the van from view of anyone inside the *Imperio Construir* compound.

The area in which he is parked is a patchwork of small houses and undeveloped lots. The closest illumination comes from high wattage lights on the roof of the *Imperio Construir* warehouse one block away.

In the cargo area of the van, Rig changes into a black-colored, cotton fabric jumpsuit and black leather steel-toe, steel-heel work boots. Then, he buckles a utility belt around his waist that includes attached pockets for small tools, a flashlight, and his lock pick set. A holster holding his compact, short-barrel, nine-millimeter Beretta is also attached to the utility belt. In other pouches attached to the belt are the Beretta noise suppressor and two extra ammo magazines.

After applying black greasepaint to his face, he dons black colored rain gear that includes a rubber floppy rain hat and a full-length rubber raincoat.

Rig opens the van's cargo door and steps into the drizzling rain. His boots sink two inches into the muddy road surface. He can see five feet ahead. He knows that if he keeps the compound lights to his right, he will stay on the muddy road.

During a daytime surveillance of the compound, Rig had identified several ruts running under the fence that are large enough to provide him access to the compound. The nearest rut is ten feet north of the southwest corner of the compound.

He feels his way along the fence until he finds the rut. He lies on his back, grabs the fence with his hands and pulls himself halfway inside. Then, he finishes the task by using his feet to push his body the rest of the way.

Inside the compound, he stands and looks toward the warehouse and locates the sliding, garage doors. Lights mounted over the door reveal that the doors are locked together with an iron chain woven between the door handles and a large padlock holding the chain tight. He will be at risk of being exposed while he stands under those lights and defeats the door lock. The dark of early morning and the cold rain minimizes the chance that anyone will be out and about. He cannot smash the light because a smashed light will be evidence that there was an intruder.

The warehouse sliding door is one-hundred feet from the fence. As Rig walks toward the garage door, the rain washes the mud from his rubber rain gear. He becomes visible in the illumination of the door light when he is ten feet from the garage doors.

As he works to defeat the lock with his lock pick set, he becomes anxious with each minute that he stands in the light. After seven minutes, he opens the lock; then, he pulls the chain free of the handles.

He slides one door open wide enough to allow him to step inside. He drops the chain and lock on the concrete floor just inside the sliding doors, then closes the sliding door.

With the doors shut, he is engulfed in darkness.

He pulls out a low-power, short-beam flashlight; then, points it at the floor and slides the power switch to on. The area around him illuminates. The concrete floor is wet from rain that dripped through multiple holes and cracks in the roof. As expected, the concrete floor is covered with the muddy footprints of warehouse workers during the day. Therefore, Rig's muddy footprints will mix with the others.

The closest stack of construction materials is ten feet high and has a one-hundred-square-feet base. The stack is covered with a rain-proof tarp. Rig lifts the bottom of the tarp and discovers a stack of cement bags.

After fifteen minutes he has discovered a dozen tarp-covered stacks; all are stacks of construction supplies. He also comes across several small construction vehicles. All the construction vehicles are positioned so that there is a wide and clear path down the center of the warehouse to the sliding doors. He assumes that the path is parking space for those trucks that transport the bottled water.

After twenty minutes, he has investigated only half of the football-field-sized warehouse. He exhales deeply as he considers the amount of time it will take to complete his investigation of the warehouse.

Several minutes later, he comes upon a walled-in area in the northeast corner of the warehouse and speculates that office space is contained within. He searches for an entrance into the walled-in area and finds a locked cargo door. Defeating the lock with a lock-pick set takes five minutes. Then, he lifts up on the cargo door.

He does not immediately enter the space. First, he scans the space with his flashlight. Machinery occupies three-quarters of the room. The machinery is unfamiliar to him. The light switch is on the wall just inside the door. The room is self-contained within the warehouse and does not have windows. There are several air conditioning vents. Exhaust fans are mounted on the two walls that face the inside of the warehouse. There are no leaks in the ceiling of this room. The concrete floor is clean and dry. He is confident that if he turns on the lights with the door closed, no light will escape to the outside of the warehouse.

Rig removes his dripping rain gear and his boots and drops them just outside the door to the room.

In his stocking feet, he steps inside the room. He closes the garage-like door. After flipping the light switch, ceiling mounted florescent lights brightly illuminate the room. The space is approximately fifty-feet by fifty-feet and has its own roof about fifteen feet high.

He spends some time walking around the machinery. At first, he cannot determine its function. He has never seen a machine like this before. He walks to the far end of the machine. On the floor on the other side of the machine, he finds several pallets of empty bottles with no labels. Next to the pallet of empty bottles, he finds several open boxes that contain stacks of red-colored, wraparound bottle labels. The red-colored label includes the picture of a waterfall. The words *Imperio Aqua* are printed above the waterfall. Below the picture of the waterfall in smaller print are the words: *purificada y embotellada en España*.

Near the boxes of red labels, Rig discovers a six-inch

stainless-steel pipe coming up through a square-shaped shaft in the floor. The shaft opening is three feet by three feet. A protective, four-foot-high railing is installed around the opening. Rig leans over the protective railing. Cold, wet air flows in an updraft into Rig's face. The shaft and pipe descend farther than the reach of the flashlight beam. Running next to the pipe coming out of the shaft is a conduit of electrical cables. A ladder is mounted to the aluminum siding of the shaft. Rig considers going down the shaft; then, decides to finish his inspection of the machinery first.

He follows the electrical cables in the room. The electrical cables connect to a power panel control box with a large breaker switch on the front.

Two feet above the shaft opening, the six-inch, stainless steel pipe turns ninety-degrees; then, after a few more feet, the pipe connects to a floor mounted pump. The pump is currently not running. On the other side of the pump, the pipe runs for six feet and then enters a series of filtration screens. One foot after the filtration screens, a Y fitting splits the pipe into two, six-inch pipes. Each pipe has a lever valve with a sign. The valves are shut. The sign on the top pipe reads: PUEBLO. The sign on the bottom pipe reads: MÁQUINA DE EMBOTELLADO.

What the hell! A water bottling plant!

He decides not to investigate what is at the bottom of the shaft.

Twenty minutes later, Rig is back in the cargo area of the panel van. He turns on the hand-held radio and verifies the channel selector is set to position one. He presses the transmit button and speaks softly into the microphone, "Clear, over."

Two seconds later, rig hears Rouston's voice through the receiver. "Clear, out."

Several minutes later, Rig is driving the van back to the Rota Naval Base.

Chapter 21

Rig has just finished lunch and is about to stand up and leave the Chiefs Mess when Master Chief Tollerson and Senior Chief Hackett sit down on the other side of the table; they face Rig.

Master Chief Tollerson is the USS *Antares* Senior Enlisted advisor.

Senior Chief Hackett is the USS *Antares* Command Career Counselor.

Master Chief Tollerson says, "We need a few minutes of your time to talk about RM2 Baylor."

Rig glances at his watch, then responds, "Okay."

Senior Chief Hackett asks, "Did you tell Baylor that you would not lose any sleep over him not reenlisting?"

"No, I didn't," Rig responds.

Rig's response confuses Hackett and Tollerson. Rig tells the truth, but it is not what they expected.

After a few moments of awkward silence, Rig asks, "Anything else?"

Master Chief Tollerson asks, "What did you talk about?"

"We talked about his plans after the navy and I advised him of the LDO program."

Senior Chief Hackett asks with an edge of challenge in his tone, "You didn't talk about why he does not want to reenlist?"

"He told me why, but we did not discuss it."

"So, you didn't convince him to reenlist, then?"

"Convince him?" Rig shakes his head. "I am not a salesman. I told him what he could gain and accomplish in the future by staying in the navy. That's all. He must convince himself. The decision is his."

Senior Chief Hackett offers, "He hates watch standing. You could take him off watches and make him a day-worker."

"No." Rig states with finality. "Too obviously favoritism."

Hackett pushes. "But you do have a second class day-worker in Main Comm. You could substitute."

"No."

Hackett challenges, "Why not?"

"That day-working position is on six-month rotation and is filled by the senior second class who has not worked in that position. Baylor is too far down the seniority list."

"What are the duties of that position?"

"Division Supply Clerk – Berthing Compartment Supervisor – Division Laundry Petty Officer – Division Damage Control Petty Officer – Division Mail Petty Officer – and all-around *go-fer*."

Hackett declares, "Sounds like a lot of work and responsibility for one person."

Rig responds, "It is, but not enough for two people, and the Main Comm watch bill is already undermanned by twenty percent."

Master Chief Tollerson asserts, "Baylor hates watch-standing. Put him on days, and he will feel better about the navy. Working days will increase the chance he'll reenlist."

Rig responds, "That is your judgment, Master Chief, and a judgment that I disagree with."

Senior Chief Hackett explains, "The ship's first-termer reenlistment rate has been decreasing since we left the States. Both the CO and XO have expressed interest in Baylor's decision to reenlist. They both want to discuss reenlistment with Baylor. After that, they could order you to place Baylor on day work."

"That would be counterproductive," Rig states. "It would affirm Baylor's belief that the navy only shows interest toward sailors at reenlistment time, and he will not reenlist, anyway. The other CR Division watch standers will resent such an obvious incentive to reenlist and will hold the chain-of-command in contempt. The best thing to do is leave him on the watch bill. There is more chance that he will change his mind if he sees that the navy is not showing favoritism toward him."

Master Chief Tollerson tells Rig, "I think control of this situation is out of your hands."

Rig shrugs and comments in a resigned tone, "I am not surprised."

Master Chief Tollerson and Senior Chief Hackett stand; then, they depart the Chiefs Mess.

Chapter 22

Rig and Arleigh Rouston sits at the kitchen table in Rig's condo. Rig just finished a verbal briefing on what he found in the *Imperio Construir* warehouse.

Rig informs, "It's all in my written report." Rig passes his report to Rouston.

Rouston asks, "What prevented you from going down that shaft to discover what was at the bottom?"

"Not sufficiently equipped," Rig answers. "I think there is significant underground water flow at the bottom of that shaft, judging from the cold, damp updraft through the shaft."

Rouston directs, "You're going down that shaft next week. Make a list of equipment you'll need."

Rig nods acknowledgement. Then, he is quiet and exhibits contemplation.

"Is there something else?" Rouston asks.

"Yes," Rig confirms. "I did not make it part of my report because it seems irrelevant, although curious."

"What is it?"

"Remember I said that I found empty bottles and red-colored labels for *Imperio Aqua* in that bottling room?"

"Yes."

"I have the same size bottles of *Imperio Aqua* in my refrigerator, and the labels have the exact same waterfall picture and wording. But my bottles have green colored labels; not red labels like in the warehouse bottling room. Every market I've been in sells *Imperio Aqua* with green labels, even the navy commissary. The only place I have ever seen red labels for *Imperio Aqua* was in that warehouse bottling room."

"Include that information about label coloring in your report." Rouston hands the written report back to Rig.

"Okay," Rig says. "I will have the amended report to you by this evening."

Rouston directs, "When you go in next week, get a sample of that water. I'll send it to the lab in London for analysis."

Rig nods; then asks, "Anything else?"

"Just keep up your nighttime surveillance of Sedo Mare."

"Will do. Has anything surface regarding the attack on that American couple?"

"Been narrowed down to six couples. NIS is questioning them."

"What about the license number of the car those attackers drove?"

"Yes, did get a response to that. Car is owned by a young Spanish criminal who lives in Cadiz. He has been arrested a dozen times for burglary, assault, robbery, and one murder. He went to trial on a few but no convictions. He went to trial on the murder charge, but the prosecution star witness was found dead on the morning she was scheduled to appear in court. The report says his uncle is a crime kingpin with enough Policía and politicians on his payroll to keep his nephew out of jail."

Rig thinks on that. Then, he comments, "Obviously, that punk has become emboldened. Takes a lot of arrogance and audacity to drive your own car to a crime scene."

"You should forget about it," Rouston advises in a warning tone. "Let NIS handle it."

Rig wonders why Rouston did not name the thug and wonders why Rouston does not offer Rig the file to read.

Rig expresses resignation as he responds, "Okay. I'll forget about it."

After Rouston departs, Rig picks up the phone and dials a number that he committed to memory several months ago.

At the other end of the line in *La Línea da la Concepíon,* a male voice answers. "Si, digame."

"This is Rigney Page."

The other end is silent for a few moments. Then, the voice says in English, "Ah, yes. I was briefed that you might call while you are in Spain. What can I do for you?"

"I need some information. Can we meet?"

"What information?"

"I can only tell you that face-to-face."

"Where are you now?"

"Rota."

"You will need to come here. Do you know *La Línea da la Concepión?*"

"Yes, next to Gibraltar. I can be there tomorrow. When and where?"

The man provides directions to a restaurant on the *La Línea da la Concepión* waterfront and the time to meet. Then, he specifies, "Please dress like a European."

"No problem," Rig responds. "How will I recognize you?"

"I will recognize you. I have your description."

After hanging up the phone, Rig wonders if *The Guardians* will be as helpful now as they were back in the States.

The Guardians approached him last year with an offer to help him fight against union thugs and other domestic enemies who were threatening his family. The offer of help required Rig to join *The Guardians* and commit his skills and his knowledge to *The Guardians'* cause.

The Guardians is a secret organization whose existence is known only to the membership. The organization's purpose is to protect those individual liberties guaranteed by the Constitution. *The Guardians* hide their existence so that America's domestic enemies cannot find them. They operate on a cell structure to maximize anonymity and security. The organization was formed over one-hundred years ago;

originally, to fight against the powerful Democratic Party in the southern states that refused to comply with federal civil rights laws. During *The Guardians'* one-hundred-plus years, the organization has never been uncovered by government and has never been compromised by infiltrators.

Chapter 23

Senior Chief Page sits in front of Lieutenant Christine Hawthorne's desk. He briefs the Lieutenant on repair issues listed in the Communications Department Equipment Status Log.

Rig states, "2-Kilos have been initiated on all ESL items and repair actions are scheduled."

Christine expresses approval, "Good job, Rig. The ESL has fewer items now than any time since I've been onboard."

Rig responds with a pleased smile as he states, "If we take care of the small problems in a timely manner, the big problems will not occur."

Christine expresses agreement.

Rig glances at his watch. He stands.

"Wait," Christine orders. "I have one more thing for you." She hands Rig a sheet of paper and says, "I got this memo from the Chief of Staff this morning."

Rig quickly reads the memo. The Chief of Staff orders Lieutenant Hawthorne to assign RM2 Baylor to day-working duties.

While still looking at the memo, Rig says, "I will take care of this today."

Christine asks, "Do you know what this is about?"

"Yes. *Antares* CO, XO, Command Master Chief, and Command Career Counselor believe moving Baylor to day-working will motivate him to reenlist."

Christine expresses confusion as she explains, "I talked with Baylor this morning. He is firm on his plan to leave the navy and go back to Kentucky to live. He said there is nothing the navy can do to change his mind."

Rig responds, "Yes, I know. Baylor also told Master Chief

Tollerson and Senior Chief Hackett the same thing."

Christine looks down at her desk while she considers the situation.

Rig waits patiently.

Christine asserts, "We cannot protest this action. We must follow orders."

"I know. I will initiate the watch bill change today."

"What actions will you take?"

"I'll put Baylor under training with Crothers for a week. Then, Crothers will take Baylor's place on the watch bill."

Christine expresses in a concerned tone, "Crothers has only been day-working for a month. This action will not only affect Crothers's morale. It will also cause dissention in the ranks because of obvious favoritism."

"I know," Rig says while expressing uneasiness.

"There will be questions about the move. How will you handle it?"

"When asked, I will say that the Chief of Staff ordered it. I will deny knowing why."

"How can you say you do not know why?"

"Because the Chief of Staff didn't say why in his memo. We are just guessing that it is a reenlistment incentive. If I am asked why, I will say that the Chief of Staff did not explain why."

Chief Bremerton calls RM2 Baylor to the Communications Watch Officer's desk.

Baylor expresses curiosity as he arrives at the CWO's desk.

"You're going day-working starting tomorrow morning. Crothers will train you for a week. Then, you relieve him of his duties, and he will replace you in my watch section."

Baylor chuckles and expresses amusement. He says, "No thanks, Chief. I do not want my shipmates harassing me because

I am being favored over another sailor who earned his day-working position. My wife and I have already scheduled my days off during the week for some short trips around Spain. Transportation and hotels have been reserved and paid for. I prefer not to completely reschedule my last two months in the navy. My wife would become very upset, and I'll hate the navy more."

Chief Bremerton advises, "I will pass your rejection up the chain."

"Baylor has turned down the day-working job," Senior Chief Page tells Lieutenant Hawthorne.

"What?"

"Baylor told Chief Bremerton yesterday that he did not want the day-working job."

"Makes no difference," Christine declares. "Captain Crossman ordered it. He reminded me this morning that he wants it done immediately, without argument or discussion. At this point, what Baylor wants is irrelevant."

Rig questions, "Without argument or discussion were the Chief of Staff's words?"

"Precisely," Christine states while shrugging her shoulders and expressing resignation.

Rig knows and understands that approaching Captain Crossman regarding Baylor's desires would be futile. A navy captain has issued his order and he has declared that he does not want it challenged.

Rig states, "I'll take care of it immediately."

Senior Chief Page tells Chief Bremerton, "RM2 Baylor is off the watch bill as of now. He is to report to RM2 Crothers within the hour. Crothers will train Baylor for one week. Crothers will be assigned to your watch section next week as a replacement for Baylor."

"Okay, Senior Chief. Will comply."

"I want to see Baylor's reaction," Rig advises.

Chief Bremerton scans Main Comm and finds Baylor standing at the NAVCOMMPARS terminal printer. Baylor is processing incoming messages.

"Baylor!" Chief Bremerton calls out in a raised voice.

Baylor looks over his shoulder. He sees Chief Bremerton and Senior Chief Page standing at the Communications Watch Officer's desk. Both chiefs are staring at him.

Chief Bremerton motions toward Baylor to come to the CWO's desk.

Baylor senses that unpleasantness is about to come down upon him. He walks quickly to the CWO's desk.

"You're going day-working immediately. Crothers will train you. Then, you will relieve him next week, and Crothers will come back on the watch bill."

Baylor expresses disappointment as he says, "I do not want to go day-working. I am happy to stay on the watch bill for the last two months of my enlistment."

"Sorry, Baylor," Chief Bremerton responds in an apologetic tone. "You have no choice."

Baylor does not believe that this situation cannot be reversed. He asks, "Who does not provide me with a choice?"

"Chief of Staff—Captain Crossman," Rig advises.

"I want to talk to Captain Crossman," Baylor declares in a slightly demanding tone.

Chief Bremerton expresses surprise and questions, "Are you saying that you have not talked to Captain Crossman about your reenlistment opportunities?"

"I have never spoken with Captain Crossman—ever. The

only officer that I have had a conversation regarding reenlistment is Lieutenant Hawthorne."

Rig says, "Fill out a request chit to speak with Captain Crossman and give it to me. I will personally walk it through the chain-of-command."

"I will do that. Uh, what do I do now?"

Rig explains, "Crothers is down in Radio One storing supplies. He is expecting you. You will be in training under him for one week; then, you will relieve him and he will replace you on the watch bill."

"I will fill out that request chit, first, okay?"

"Okay," Rig answers.

Baylor walks off in search of request chit forms. He considers that at this moment in time he would sell his soul to be discharged immediately.

Rig and Bremerton exchange glances.

Rig comments, "The depth of absurdity in this situation has no limit."

Chapter 24

Rig walks along the Rota Naval Base pier towards the USS *Antares*. The submarine tender is Med-moored—stern to the pier. One boomer is moored alongside the *Antares* and two boomers are moored to the pier.

He is dressed in working khaki uniform with garrison cap. Passing sailors greet him with nods or "good morning, Senior Chief." His hero reputation and newspaper celebrity are known to most sailors assigned to the *Antares*.

After walking up the stern brow and performing the traditional ceremonial boarding procedures, he proceeds to Chiefs Berthing. In Chiefs Berthing he opens his locker and retrieves his daily-planner notebook and slips it into his back pocket. After departing Chiefs Berthing, he climbs the ladders to the 03 Level where the message center is located.

As he enters the Main Comm spaces, a ship-wide announcement comes over the 1MC. "DO NOT ROTATE OR RADIATE ANTENNAS WHILE MEN ARE WORKING ALOFT."

As Rig approaches the message center area of Main Comm, the Communications Watch Officer tells Rig, "Senior Chief, Lieutenant Hawthorne is looking for you. She said you are to go to her office as soon as you arrive."

As Rig enters Christine's office, she glances at her watch.

Rig glances at his watch—1045. Then, he sits down in front of the lieutenant's desk.

Christine assumes a professional posture, which tells Rig that they will not be discussing their next romantic hotel stay.

Christine informs, "Your banker's hours have caught the attention of the Chief of Staff. He wants to know if you have a valid reason for arriving to work mid-morning most days."

"Yes, I do," Rig replies. "My mission in life is to protect the American people from the red menace. Sometimes, that mission causes me to arrive onboard late morning."

Christine raises an eyebrow. "Chief of Staff says he wants you to be onboard during scheduled working hours."

Rig sighs deeply and expresses resignation. "Okay. I will—"

An announcement over the 1MC interrupts Rig.

"DO NOT ROTATE OR RADIATE ANTENNAS WHILE MEN ARE WORKING ALOFT."

Rig asks Christine, "Did you know about antenna work aloft today? There is nothing on the ship's work schedule about it."

Christine explains. "An upgraded NAVSAT antenna system arrived last night from NAVELEX with a written order from CNO. The CNO order directs replacement of the old antenna system as soon as operational conditions permit. It's an immediate navy-wide upgrade. The commodore ordered the NAVSAT replacement to take place this morning. That's how the Chief of Staff noticed you were not here when working hours started. He wanted you to assign two radiomen as augments to Repair Department because all of the Repair Department antenna teams are committed to boomer work this morning. Also, Chief of Staff wants you to personally supervise the operational test after the antenna system is installed—all to be completed by thirteen hundred. I called the Communications Watch Officer and told him to find two radiomen to assign."

Rig questions, "Why is the Communications Department involved in a navigation satellite replacement? If any department should be augmenting the Repair Department in a NAVSAT antenna replacement, it should be Operations Department, specifically quartermasters."

With slight irritation in her voice, Christine advises, "I don't know, Rig. I did not question his order. There was no valid reason to question his order."

Rig responds in an apologetic tone, "Okay. It just gets a bit tiring that the Chief of Staff uses CR division as his labor pool for every last-minute, poorly planned project that comes along. Every time this happens, CR division must adjust and delay work that we already planned and scheduled."

Christine asks, "Do you know how to operate and test a NAVSAT receiver?"

"Depends on the model. I will get one of the quartermasters to assist. When we're done here, I will go topside and find out how far along they are with the antenna replacement. Is there anything else?"

"Yes. Petty officer performance evaluations were due yesterday. Do you have them?"

"I sent them back to the chiefs who wrote them—too many grammatical errors."

"But they are due to me today and due to the XO and Chief of Staff five days from now."

Rig responds, "You would send them back."

"No, I would rewrite them—would only take me a day."

"No need for that," Rig states. "Chiefs who have been getting high marks in writing skills for years should know how to write sentences and use punctuation correctly."

"When will I get those evaluations?" Christine's tone becomes agitated and insistent.

"I told each chief to go to the base library and check out books on grammar. I ordered them to turn in the corrected evaluations to me within three days."

"Corrected?"

"I circled and identified their errors as syntax, spelling, or punctuation. I told them to go to the library, find books on grammar, and fix the errors."

"But that only gives me two days to review and edit and

make my own changes." Christine exhibits frustration."

Rig cast a questioning expression at Christine as he comments, "Christine, when chiefs are originating evals, there is no reason for anyone up the chain of command to spend a lot of time editing them. If we stand firm on this now, the next evaluation cycle will be easier on you and me."

Christine express thoughtfulness for a few moments, then, asks, "Does the base library have the texts they will need to correct their errors?"

Rig expresses irritation and does not answer.

Christine is about to ask another question when an announcement is broadcast over the 1MC.

"ALOFT RESCUE TEAM REPORT TO THE FORWARD MAST. ALL OTHER PERSONNEL STAND CLEAR."

The announcement is repeated.

Rig jumps to his feet and starts toward the door.

Christine states, "Rig, the announcement said for all other personnel to stand clear. Deck division provides men for that rescue team with a chief boatswain mate in charge."

"My radiomen are aloft?! I am going topside!"

"I'm coming with you."

But Rig does not hear Christine. He is halfway up the ladder going to the next level. Ten seconds later, he arrives at the bottom of the forward mast.

Rig quickly appraises the situation. At the bottom of the mast, two sailors tend the loose end of a line and are staring toward the top of the forward mast. Rig's eyes track the line upward. Then, he sees RM3 Wagner hanging at the end of his safety harness lanyard from the starboard yardarm. Wagner appears to be unconscious. The line tended by the two sailors at the bottom of the mast hangs from the yardarm and passes within a foot of Wagner.

Another sailor stands on a ladder rung near the top of the mast, and he points at Wagner and yells, "His buckle came loose! He is slipping out of his harness!"

Rig quickly scans the deck for the rescue team. He sees three sailors who wear dungarees and a chief who wears khakis come over the top of the ladder and step onto the deck. They are carrying safety harnesses and a tool bag.

Rig concludes that time is of the essence. He calculates that the rescue team, who has not yet donned their safety harnesses, will not get to Wagner before Wagner slips out of his safety harness and falls to the deck.

Rig steps quickly to the two sailors tending the line and asks them, "What is the purpose of this line?"

"To pull tools up to the yardarm," one of them answers.

"Step away from the line," Rig orders.

The two sailors let go of the line and take several steps backward.

Rig grips the line with both hands and yanks hard. The line remains secured to the yardarm. Then, while still gripping the line with both hands, Rig lifts his feet off the deck. The line holds his weight.

The sailor standing high on the mast yells frantically toward the rescue team, "Hurry, he's slipping out of his harness! Please hurry!"

Rig takes one more glance at the rescue team. The team is not ready.

The emergency medical team comes on deck carrying medical bags and a stretcher.

Lieutenant Hawthorne, the Chief of Staff, and the *Antares* Commanding Officer come over the top of the ladder and onto the deck.

Without a word, Rig tucks the end of the line under his belt. Then, he begins his climb up the line hand over hand. His feet swing from side to side as he climbs.

Rig ignores orders shouted at him by the *Antares* CO and Squadron Chief of Staff to come back down to the deck.

Within seconds, Rig reaches Wagner—who is still unconscious. Wagner has a swollen, bleeding cut on his forehead and his breathing is shallow.

While hanging on to the line with his left hand, Rig uses his right hand to pull the end of the line from under his belt; then, he coils twenty feet of the line around Wagner's chest and ties it off between Wagner's shoulder blades.

Rig climbs the additional six feet up the line to the yardarm. He sits on the yardarm and pulls in the slack of the line between him and Wagner. Then, he ties the line to an antenna base that is welded to the yardarm. The stress of Wagner's body weight is now on the line and not Wagner's safety harness lanyard. The lanyard is now slack.

The rescue team is just starting their climb up the mast ladder.

The crowd at the bottom of the mast now number more than thirty sailors—a mixture of white hats, chiefs, and officers. The crowd glances back and forth with excited anticipation at Rig and Wagner.

Rig estimates that another thirty minutes will elapse before the rescue team executes its safety-saturated procedures to get Wagner down to the deck where the medical team waits.

Wagner's breathing was shallow when Rig reached him, and the line coiled around Wagner's chest restricts his breathing.

Rig considers that Wagner could die from lack of oxygen before the rescue team gets to him.

After quickly assessing the risks, Rig disconnects Wagner's safety-harness lanyard from the yardarm. Rig locks his legs between two steel bars that are part of the antenna base. He unties the line from the antenna base.

Wagner drops slightly before Rig reacts to holding Wagner's weight.

Wagner is now swinging slightly at the end of the line.

Loud gasps of horror come from the crowd below.

Rig lowers Wagner using hand under hand movements to control the speed of descent.

Several times, the line slips a few inches through Rig's sweaty hands, causing painful and bloody rope burns to his fingers and palms. The angle of his body to the weight on the line is awkward and causes sharp jabbing pain to the middle of his back. He ignores the pain and continues lowering Wagner.

Fifteen seconds later, Wagner is on the deck.

Six and a half minutes have elapsed from the time Rig started his climb up the line to the time Wagner was lowered to the deck.

The crowd moves back and clears an area for the medics to work.

The medics remove the line coiled around Wagner; then, they hover over him and take his vitals. They strap an oxygen mask to Wagner's face.

One minute later, one of the medics announces, "He is alive - weak pulse but steady - getting stronger and he is breathing easier."

The crowd lets out a loud sigh of relief.

Rig stays aloft, watching the actions below.

One of the medics motions to the stretcher bearers. The medics and stretcher bearers carefully lift Wagner from the deck to the stretcher; then, they strap him into the stretcher. One minute later, six stretcher bearers are maneuvering Wagner down the starboard ladder.

With the injured man gone, the crowd looks toward Rig.

Rig lowers himself down the line hand under hand. When his feet land on the deck, he notices that Lieutenant Christine

Hawthorne stands close by with other officers and a few chiefs.

Rig walks over to Lieutenant Hawthorne, shows her his hands and says casually, "I got some rope burns. I'm going to sickbay for treatment."

Christine responds, "Okay, Senior Chief. Come to my office when you're done in sickbay."

"Aye, aye, ma'am." Rig turns and walks across the deck toward the ladder.

The First Division chief boatswain mate stands among the group of officers, chiefs, and white hats at the bottom of the mast. He stares after Rig and declares admiringly to no one in particular, "I have been working the decks of navy ships for more than twenty years and I thought I had seen everything that can happen, until today."

The *Antares* CO turns to the Deck Department head and orders, "I want a complete report on this incident, including why that sailor's harness was coming apart. I want that report by the end of the week. We are required to submit an incident report up the chain of command to Squadron and to the Naval Safety Center."

"Aye, aye Captain," the Deck Department head responds.

The crowd begins to disperse. The COMSUBRON THIRTEEN Chief of Staff, Captain Theodore Crossman, motions to the *Antares* Commanding Officer to wait. When he is certain that he can speak privately, the Chief of Staff advises, "Dan, I want to be informed as the investigation into this incident progresses. Send a copy of each draft report to me for review."

"Aye, aye sir."

Twenty-minutes later, Christine Hawthorne sits at her desk and sips coffee. She recalls Rig's action of saving RM3 Wagner from falling to his death. She focuses on the chief boatswain mate's summation of Rig's actions as something he had never witnessed before in twenty years in the navy.

Christine knows about Rig's physical abilities. She had observed that extraordinary strength one stormy night two-years ago on a desolate, single-lane Scottish road when Rig's rental car experienced a flat tire. They found the combination lug wrench and jack handle in the boot, but the jack itself was missing. After Rig loosened the lug nuts on the flat tire, he raised the back of the car while Christine replaced the flat tire with the spare tire.

Christine had asked Rig about his strength. Rig had tried to deny his extraordinary strength with a shrug and nonchalant comment, *"It's a small car—a Mini. What man of normal strength could not lift up a rear corner of such a lightweight car?"*

Christine did not buy it and continued to pester Rig about hiding his strength.

Rig eventually caved and told her. *"I am stronger than most men,"* he had told her. *"It's genetic in males in my family. Normally, the trait skips a generation. We don't know why. Like my paternal grandfather had it, but my father does not. I first discovered my growing strength during the early stages of puberty. Family lore says the strength is linked to the amount of body hair on Page men. My grandfather had the same heavy coat of reddish-brown body hair like me. But my father has a moderate amount of body hair. Not that my father isn't strong and tough, but not to the extent I am."*

At Rig's demand, Christine had promised to never reveal what she knows about him.

Christine also knows about Rig's fearlessness. She was present that night in Thurso, Scotland when Rig led other chiefs in a *Repel Boarders* attack against terrorists who invaded the base. They killed some terrorists and captured the rest. She is not surprised by what Rig did on deck today.

Christine's remembrance of Rig's past exhibitions of power stirs an aching emptiness in her loins. She sighs deeply and her heart beats faster as she gazes with anticipation at the symbol on her calendar that specifies the date of their next rendezvous at the Cadiz hotel.

Chapter 25

The drive from Rota to the *La Línea da la Concepíon* marina takes nearly two hours. Night has fallen when Rig parks his car in the marina parking lot.

Lights shimmer over the water of the marina. A dozen yachts lie at anchor in the harbor.

After exiting his car, he slips into the coat of his tailor-made suit. His total image reflects that of a Northern European athlete in an expensive Italian suit.

He enters the marina restaurant, which is rated three-stars in the Michelin Travel Guide. The light-blue ceramic-tile floor shines and sparkles. All the tables have white tablecloths with quality dinnerware in place.

A Spaniard in a well-maintained black suit and bow tie approaches with menu in hand. Rig assumes the Spaniard to be the maître d'. The Spaniard says, "Bondadoso tarde señor."

"Good evening," Rig responds.

The maître d' asks in perfect English, "Would you like to sit near the window or on the patio overlooking the water?"

Rig thinks the temperature is too cold to sit outside. He notices a man at a window table waving at him.

Rig tells the maître d', "I am joining that gentleman." Rig points toward the man at the window table.

As Rig approaches the table, the man stands to greet him. The man is middle-aged with a trim build and light-brown hair.

The man stretches out his hand to Rig and says, "My name is Jack Tacker. Please call me Jack."

Rig shakes Jack's hand and says, "Call me Rig."

The two men sit down at the table. They face each other across the table. The position of the table provides a dazzling view of the harbor.

A waiter who wears the standard white shirt, black bowtie, and black trousers arrives at the table to take their drink orders.

Rig orders, "Just a Perrier with a side dish of six lemon slices."

Jack orders a glass of white wine.

After the waiter departs with the drinks order, Jack advises, "To save time I ordered the sea bass dinner for both of us—my treat. I have another appointment at eight o'clock. So, let's get down to business. What can I do for you?"

Rig looks around the restaurant. Only four other tables are occupied and no one sits closer than thirty feet. The dinner hour in the Spanish culture starts around 8:00 PM.

"Can we talk in here?"

"Yes—softly."

Rig hands Jack a folded piece of paper.

Jack comments, "Those bandages on your hands. Nothing serious, I hope."

"Rope burns," Rig advises. "Shipboard hazard—should heal quickly."

Jack opens the paper and reads a Spanish vehicle license number. He casts an inquisitive stare at Rig.

Close to whispering, Rig says, "I believe the owner of that car is a criminal. I would like a complete dossier on him and his closest friends and his closest relatives. I believe his uncle is a criminal kingpin in the Rota area."

"I can do that," Jack responds "Anything else?"

"I need some untraceable weapons."

Jack stares questioningly at Rig.

"I need a custom-made automatic rifle with night scope and suppressor that is ranged for a minimum of five-hundred yards and one-hundred rounds of ammunition. I also need a nine-millimeter automatic pistol with suppressor, two magazines, and 200 rounds of ammunition.

Jack responds, "I must obtain authorization from my superior before I can issue weapons. He will want to know your plan for using those weapons."

The waiter arrives with drinks and dinner.

Jack says, "After we eat, we will go to my car where I can record your complete brief on what you have experienced and why you need those weapons.

During the next thirty minutes, Rig and Jack engage in small talk that includes American politics and the more interesting areas of Spain that are off the tourist path. They are politically compatible.

After they finish dinner, Rig and Jack go to Jack's car and Jack records Rig's full account of what he has observed in Sedo Mare Pueblo. He provides details of that night the two hoodlums assaulted and robbed the American couple.

Jack turns off the recorder; then, says. "Unusual place for a water bottling plant. *The Guardians'* leadership will want the details of that operation.

"My naval intelligence controller has directed that I discover what is at the bottom of that shaft. After my next recon into that plant and down that shaft, I will call you and arrange a meeting."

After a few moments of silence, Jack opines, "I must tell you that am neutral on your justification for those weapons. Your explanation alone on tape must successfully sell your cause as beneficial for *The Guardians* to support."

Rig expresses thoughtfulness; then, he asks, "What is your experience with such a request? Is it normally approved?"

Jack responds, "Situations involving *The Guardians* are infrequent with me. I have been the contact in Spain for five years, and I have never received a request like yours before. Eliminating the local criminal population is not an objective of our organization."

"How long before I know?"

"A week at most. I will call you."

Two hours later, Rig arrives at his condo in Sedo Mare Pueblo. Fifteen minutes later, he has set up his surveillance equipment on the patio and is scanning the Sedo Mare Valley for unusual activity.

Chapter 26

Rig boards the USS *Antares* at 0948. He proceeds to Chiefs Berthing and retrieves his daily planner. He did not eat breakfast before leaving his condo; so, he decides stop by the Chiefs Mess for a muffin and a cup of coffee.

He picks a table away from the other chiefs.

One minute later, Master Chief William Tollerson, USS *Antares* Senior Enlisted Advisor, sits down across the table from Rig. The master chief expresses that he intends to engage Rig in conversation.

Rig asks in an enthusiastic tone, "Good morning, Master Chief, what's up?"

"The captain tasked me to investigate the situation surrounding an inquiry about your character. The captain received a letter from a local boat broker. The boat broker asked the captain to vouch for your trustworthiness regarding a six-month rental contract for a sailboat. The letter specifies that you paid a two-thousand-dollar deposit, paid for the first month's rent, and specified that you qualified as an excellent sailboat handler."

The master chief stares curiously into Rig's eyes.

Rig asks, "I have met all the broker's requirements, except a trustworthiness endorsement. Is there a problem with getting an endorsement from the captain? The captain's endorsement is the only requirement holding up my access to the sailboat."

"I don't know," Tollerson responds. "The captain wanted me to investigate your financial situation and give him a report before he responds to the letter."

Rig advises, "Do not worry about the money. I have the money."

"Really," Tollerson says in a sarcastic tone. "I calculate that after taxes you're paid about one-thousand dollars a month. I checked on that condo you rent in Sedo Mare. According to the rental agency, those top floor condos with a spectacular view rent for four-hundred a month. And that car you rent costs you one-hundred sixty dollars per month. So, just in rentals alone—with the sailboat—your monthly cash outlay is eight-hundred-sixty dollars. That leaves you one-hundred-forty a month to live on. I am concerned and I know the captain will be concerned that you're living outside your means and are headed for financial trouble."

Rig advises, "My navy pay is not my only source of income. My other income exceeds the amount of my military pay."

Tollerson flinches, blinks his eyes, and expresses surprise at Rig's claim. He expected Rig to come up with irrational reasoning as to how easy it is to live ashore on one-hundred-forty dollars a month.

"So, I have no money problems," Rig states. "How soon can I expect a positive response from the captain to the boat broker? I am looking forward to going sailing."

Tollerson casts a doubtful stare at Rig. He challenges, "How do you earn other income that is more than your navy pay?"

"None of your business!" Rig's tone becomes raised and defiant.

Chiefs across the room turn their heads in Rig's direction.

Master Chief Tollerson warns, "Look, Senior Chief, a positive endorsement relies on proving to me that you can afford it."

"Do you think I am lying?"

"The captain will ask me if I have proof that you can afford it."

Rig is silent while he considers the value of telling the master chief to *fuck off!* But his calmer, more sensible side prompts him to say, "I have proof in my locker. Will you wait a minute while

I get it?"

The master chief nods affirmative.

Rig returns three minutes later with a thick envelope. Instead of sitting across the table from Tollerson, Rig sits beside him. He removes a multipage report from Fidelity Investments and hands it to the master chief. "This is my yearly statement from Fidelity Investments."

Tollerson scans the front page; then, he scans the other pages. He looks up from the pages and says, "I do not understand all of the financial jargon. Please tell me what I am looking at here."

Rig takes the report, then, points to the 1978 totals, "This is the total at the beginning of 1978 and this is the total at the end of 1978. And this number is the total increase in my portfolio for 1978—twenty-four-thousand dollars."

Rig turns to the back page; then explains, "This is the history of my account for the previous five years. As you can see, each year my account value increased; and for the past three years, the yearly increases were more than double my navy pay."

Tollerson's eyes are wide and he expresses astonishment. For clarification, he questions, "Five years ago you started with eighteen-thousand dollars and now you have a total of one-hundred-and-twenty-one thousand dollars?"

"Yes," Rig responds.

"How did you do that?"

"I didn't. My stock broker at Fidelity did it."

"What did he do?"

"Mostly by trading in gold and oil futures."

"How does that work?"

"Buying on margin. For example, he puts up ten-thousand dollars in my account to buy fifty-thousand-dollars-worth of futures. If the price on those futures has increased by the time I sell, then I make the profit on the total fifty-thousand. If the price decreases, I lose. Fortunately, I have a good broker and I have never had to pay up for a margin call."

"That sounds risky," Tollerson declares.

"In the beginning, it was very risky—the higher the risk, the higher the reward. Last year, I decreased the margin percentage. So, if the price goes down, I am not required to come up with thousands in a margin call."

Tollerson asks, "Why gold and oil?"

"When Jimmy Carter was elected President, my broker predicted that Carter's policy would drive up the price of gold and oil, and my broker advised that I should shift from stocks and bonds to gold and oil. As you can see, his advice was accurate."

Master Chief Tollerson expresses thoughtfulness for several moments; then, he asks, "Where did you get the original eighteen-thousand?"

"Regular savings from my paycheck and savings from two reenlistment bonuses."

"And what motivated you to risk your savings in the stock market?"

Rig explains, "I looked into the future and realized that I would never become financially independent by saving a portion of my paycheck each month. So, I spent a year researching how to better my financial future, and all research said the same thing. Take risks or I will never prosper. So, I took risks. Now, it's not as risky because I reduced the margin percentage, like I said before."

Tollerson nods and expresses that he accepts Rig's explanation. Then, he asks, "Do you have quick access to that money?"

"Yes," Rig answers. "I can write a check on the account anytime. I already cashed a check on that account at the navy exchange for two thousand dollars—for the security deposit on the boat."

Tollerson chuckles while he comments, "Your shipmates, including me, have been comfortable with just buying U.S. Savings Bonds through automatic paycheck deductions."

"Yes, I know," Rig responds, taking care to ensure his tone does not express sarcasm.

"Looks to me like your finances are covered. I will tell the captain that he should endorse your trustworthiness."

"Great." Rig stands.

Tollerson inquires, "Can you give me the contact information on your broker?"

"Sure." Rig rips off the corner of the report's first page that includes his broker's contact information and hands it to Tollerson.

Chapter 27

Rig uses the same process and path as he did last week to gain access to the *Imperio Construir* warehouse. This time, he does not use a flashlight or turn on the lights in the bottling room. He wears night-vision goggles.

He checks his watch—2:15 AM. He leans over the protective railing of the shaft opening where the water pipe disappears into darkness. A steady cool and damp updraft hits his face.

Rig is dressed the same as last time, except no rain gear on this dry, moonless night. He wears the same utility belt with tools and his pistol. He removes the night-vision goggles and dons a miner's helmet. He flips on the helmet's battery-operated lamp. He climbs over the railing; then, begins his descent.

He descends slowly and inspects the interior of the shaft, looking for items of interest that he will need to investigate. The lower he goes the louder the sound of running water and the more intense the updraft. He counts the ladder rungs as he descends so that he can later calculate the depth of the shaft. Eighteen inches separate each rung.

At approximately one hundred and twenty feet, Rig exits the bottom of the shaft and the light on his helmet reveals that he might be a cavern. He looks down to see what is at the bottom of the ladder and he discovers a wooden bridge with an iron-rod safety railing. The bottom of the ladder is ten feet away.

At the bottom of the ladder, he finds an electrical distribution box with a lever switch on the side. He pulls down on the lever. Several dozen lights come on and illuminate the cavern, a tunnel actually. Rig turns off his helmet lamp to conserve the battery.

He studies the area and finds that he is in a natural lava

tunnel about one-hundred feet in diameter. He stands on the wooden planks of an arch bridge built on a metal-rod frame. The arch bridge spans a river thirty feet wide. The water of the river moves at a steady rate from east to west.

Because of the sharply curved bottom of the tunnel, wood-plank walkways have been constructed between the bridge and various sets of machinery installed on level platforms.

Rig looks to the east for a few moments; then, he looks to the west. The lights rigged in the tunnel do not allow viewing of the tunnel past fifty yards in either direction. He uses a compass to ascertain the exact east to west bearing of the tunnel.

The water pipe routes along the bridge surface to the north side of the river. He walks off the bridge to the north side of the river. The water pipe routes through several machines before dipping below the surface of the river. Rig inspects the machines and identifies them as pumps and filters.

He slips off his backpack and retrieves a quart-size thermos. He removes the cap; then, he dips the thermos beneath the surface of the flowing river. The water is cold to the touch.

After filling the thermos and putting it in his backpack, he considers exploring the dark areas of the tunnel to the east and west. Then, he concludes that such an exploration would be reckless. He should not chance being trapped and later discovered by the bad guys.

Ten minutes later, Rig is standing in the bottling room. His helmet lamp catches a water case with several, capped, red-label water bottles. He takes one bottle so the lab can compare water at the river source to the water after processing.

He swaps his miner's helmet for night-vision goggles. Then, he makes his way out of the warehouse, out of the compound, and back to the panel van.

Chapter 28

Rig dials Jack Tacker's telephone number.

Jack's phone in *La Línea da la Concepíon* rings five times before Jack answers.

"Si, digame."

"I have the information you requested," Rig advises.

Jack responds, "Good, and I have the items you requested.

"Shall we meet at the same place?"

"No," Jack answers. "I will come to your home."

"I will be home after eighteen-hundred."

Jack asks, "Any problem with me observing your surveillance actions and spending the night?"

"No problem. I have a spare bedroom."

"I'll be there at nineteen-hundred.

Rig opens his condo door.

Jack enters. He is dressed in casual clothes *fabricado por España*. He carries a small leather suitcase in his right hand and has a golf bag slung over his left shoulder.

"Follow me to the guest bedroom and drop off your gear. Then I will take you on a tour of the place."

After the tour, they are sitting in the living room sipping American whiskey. The golf bag stands in a corner near to the balcony door.

"Nice place," Jack comments. "I assume that naval intelligence is paying for it, right?"

"Right."

Jack glances at the golf bag; then, looks back at Rig and says, "Let me show you what I brought."

Jack pulls a long and narrow leather case from the inside of the golf bag; then, he lays the case on the coffee table. He opens the case. A rifle lies in a contoured pocket. The suppressor lies in a contoured pocket under the barrel. He lifts out the sniper rifle and suppressor and hands them to Rig.

Rig studies the rifle for a few moments. He notes that the weapon has a six-round cylinder like a revolver but elongated to accommodate rifle size bullets. He casts a quizzical expression at Jack.

"Custom made," Jack informs. "It is untraceable. Custom made bullets, similar in size to AK-47 bullets and with a special mix powder for distance. Meets all the specs you asked for. The night-scope has already been ranged for eight-hundred yards. The revolver technology has the advantage of no ejected shells left behind should you need to move quickly after firing."

"Let me see the ammo."

Jack hands Rig a cigar-box-size metal case. "I could only get fifty rounds. I placed an order for fifty more."

Rig checks the rifle's safety switch to ensure it is set. He loads the cylinder with six-rounds. Then, he props the rifle against the coffee table.

Jack hands Rig two spare cylinders for the rifle. He explains, "For quick reloading. A single spring-loaded clamp holds the cylinder in place. You need to practice swapping cylinders. The faster you can swap, the less you risk being compromised."

Rig loads the two spare cylinders; then, places them on the coffee table. He picks up the rifle, then, screws on the twelve-inch-long suppressor. After verifying the suppressor is properly installed, he lays the rifle on the floor.

Jack hands Rig two nine-millimeter Beretta automatic pistols, each in their holster. The larger Beretta is a heavy long barrel with a fifteen-round magazine and its holster is made for wearing on a belt. The smaller Beretta is a short barrel with an eight-round magazine and its holster is made for wearing on the ankle.

Rig loads both weapons and verifies their safeties set to on. He doesn't screw on the suppressors.

Jack hands Rig three knives—one is a combat knife in its leather sheath—one is short switchblade with a leather wristband for wearing under the cuff of a shirt or jacket—one is a throwing dagger in its leather sheath.

Rig inspects each knife and nods his approval. "They match my request, perfectly."

"Where will you keep those weapons?"

Rig picks up the sniper rifle and pistols and says, "Follow me. I'll show you."

In the master bedroom closet, Rig points to the back wall with built in shelves that hold sheets and blankets; he explains, "That's a false wall."

He gets on his hands and knees and removes the hidden panel under the bottom shelf. Rig removes his surveillance equipment from the hidden space. Then, he stores all the weapons that Jack gave him.

Jack comments, "You said your controller lives in this building. Aren't you afraid he might discover your private stash of weapons?"

"A risk I am willing to take. But even if he does find them, he would not be surprised that I have private weapons."

Jack and Rig sit on patio chairs in the dark on Rig's surveillance balcony. They sip American beer from bottles while looking out over the night-time view of the Sedo Mare Valley. Most of Sedo Mare Valley lies in their view. Lights are clustered at the beach around the shops and cafés. High street lights are placed around the perimeter of condo building parking lots. In the single-home areas, there are no street lights; patio lights and front door lights provide the only illumination.

Jack hands Rig an envelope.

"What's this?"

"Report on that license plate number. The car belongs to one Cristóbal Dario, the nephew of local crime boss Marcio Dario. That report includes dossiers on Cristóbal and his closest friends. They're all criminals."

"Okay, thanks, I'll read the entire report in the morning," Rig leans forward and looks through the tripod-mounted, high-power, night-vision telescope.

Jack raises night-vision binoculars to his eyes.

Rig explains his surveillance routine in detail.

Jack asks, "Those nights that you saw residents dancing naked in the streets—did you observe other unusual events that might be related somehow?"

"I thought about that each time, but I could not come up with anything."

After a few minutes of silence and beer sipping, Jack asks, "Where do I find the *Imperio Construir* compound?"

Rig points to the northeast as he says, "Six-hundred yards in that direction. It will be the largest lighted area in the direction."

Jack asks, "May I look through the big eye?"

"Sure," Rig stands. "I'm going to the kitchen to get more beer. Do ya want anything?"

"Yeah. Do you have any chips?"

"Yes, I'll bring 'em."

Jack slips into the chair behind the high-power, night-vision telescope.

As Rigney returns to the balcony with several bottles of beer and potato chips, Jack looks up from the telescope toward Rig and says, "My lucky night. There is activity in the *Imperio Construir* compound, and several dozen people are parading naked through the streets—appears to be a mix of Americans and Spanish. Take a look."

As Rig and Jack shift places, a small table with open beer

125

bottles tips over and spills beer over Jack's shirt and pants.

"I'll wash up and change clothes." Jack departs the balcony.

Rig looks through the night-vision telescope and sees exactly what Jack said was happening. He notes that the naked parading is focused in the northeast section of the pueblo. Rig turns his focus to the *Imperio Construir* compound. He sees only two men standing near the sliding door of the warehouse. A worker wearing coveralls is locking the sliding door. The other man is the *Imperio Construir* superintendent who lives in the villa across the street from the construction compound. Rig recognizes the superintendent by his manner, clothes, and full black-colored beard.

Arleigh Rouston, Rig's naval intelligence controller, has ordered Rig to obtain daytime photographs of all the compound workers. Rig has yet to catch the superintendent outside during daytime.

Chapter 29

Rig sits in front of Lieutenant Christine Hawthorne's desk onboard the USS *Antares*. He watches the lieutenant read the petty officer evaluation forms. Her expression never changes and she writes edits in red ink.

Christine lays the evaluation forms aside on her desk. She states, "Too many grammar and syntax errors. I cannot forward those evaluation forms as they are currently written. I thought you told the chiefs to rewrite them."

"I did," Rig responds. "That is what they gave me as rewrites."

Christine responds, "Evals written by Chief Trenton and Chief McBride need only a few, minor edits. I will make those edits and have my yeoman type them up and forward. But those evals written by Chief Bremerton and Chief O'Conner need to be rewritten. We are out of time; so, I want you to rewrite them and handed to me by thirteen-hundred tomorrow." Christine passes those evals needing rewrite to Rig.

Rig stands in preparation to exit the office.

Christine states, "I have another subject to discuss with you."

Rig sits back down.

"Chiefs performance evaluations are due next month. I have been working on yours. I feel awkward. I cannot evaluate you objectively. I wanted to know how you feel about it. I was hoping you would write your own evaluation."

"No problem. I will do that, but I will not be objective about me either."

Christine casts an amusing smile as she says, "I know, but I also know that I will not need to rewrite it because of poor grammar."

Chapter 30

At 1:00 AM Sunday morning, the parties around Sedo Mare Pueblo are breaking up. People are walking the streets. Most of the cars departing parties are exiting Sedo Mare Pueblo. Rig logs what he sees.

At 2:00 AM, Rig identifies the car of those two criminals who assaulted the American couple two months ago. Thanks to Jack Tacker, Rig knows that car belongs to Cristóbal Dario—the nephew of the local crime lord. The car moves slowly in a square pattern around the center of the pueblo. Rig assumes they are hunting for prey. Rig changes his search pattern to the street just ahead of the car.

Several minutes later, Rig sees a young American couple walking along a dark deserted street.

Dario's car speeds up and passes the couple. The car turns right at the next street. The car stops behind a courtyard wall. The car is hidden from the American couple's view.

The custom-made sniper rifle provided by Jack Tacker of *The Guardians* lies on a folded blanket alongside Rig's chair. Two fully-loaded ammo cylinders lie on the blanket next to the rifle. He picks up the sniper rifle and places the stock of the rifle to his right shoulder. The barrel of the rifle points in the general direction of Dario's car. He has never fired this sniper rifle and depends on Jack's promise that the rifle's components are fully functional, have already been ranged, and the weapon is ready to fire.

Rig peers through the rifle's night-vision scope. He estimates 300 meters distance to the hoodlums' car. He adjusts the scope optics for 300 meters. The green hue produced by the night-optics does not distort his view of the scene. The roof of Dario's car comes into clear focus in the cross hairs. Rig's intention is to scare off those criminals with close, well-placed shots that break car window glass, chip off portions of a wall, or kick up dirt and concrete.

Both thugs turn the corner with guns in hand and wearing ski masks like last time.

The American couple blocks Rig's aim on the thugs by ninety percent. Taking the shot is too risky. He waits.

The two criminals force the couple around the corner in the same direction as Dario's car.

A few seconds later, Rig sees one of the criminals from shoulders up above the roof of the car on the driver's side.

They are going to abduct them!

That courtyard wall blocks most of Rig's view of Dario's car. Rig assumes that the other hoodlum is forcing the couple into the back seat. Rig concludes that once the couple is in that car their death is certain.

Rig makes a split-second decision. He shifts the crosshairs of the sniper scope to the hoodlum's nose and pulls the trigger. Through the scope, Rig sees blood, bone, and brain spurting through the nose and eye holes of the ski mask.

A few moments of desperation flood Rig's mind. He knows that the one remaining thug cannot drive the car and hold the couple hostage at the same time.

Then, Rig observes the American couple running away from the car. At the same time, the other thug comes running around the corner of the courtyard wall. He runs along the street toward Rig's general direction. The American couple is running to safety in the opposite direction.

Rig speculates that the thug erroneously thinks that the shot that killed his compadre came from the same side of the street where the car is parked.

Rig has a clear shot on the thug. He hesitates to pull the trigger because the thug is no longer a danger to the American couple. The thug stops, raises his gun, and fires at a target that Rig cannot see.

Fearing that the thug is firing at an innocent bystander, Rig places the crosshairs on the thug's heart. He pulls the trigger. The thug drops.

Rig picks up the night vision binoculars and searches for the American couple. He sees them running away, hand in hand. A minute later, the couple is running through a more densely populated area of Sedo Mare Pueblo. They turn a corner. Rig loses sight of them.

He moves the binoculars to view the area where he dropped the second thug, looking for the person that the second thug was firing at. Rig finds no one about.

He returns his focus to the *Imperio Construir* compound where trucks are being prepared for dispatch.

Rig shifts to the night-vision telescope. He writes down the license number of each truck.

At 0300, Rig tumbles into bed. He falls asleep quickly while thinking about the events that will follow the discovery of two men who were shot-to-death on the streets of Sedo Mare Pueblo.

Chapter 31

Rig does not wake until he hears his bedside phone ringing at 0900.

"Hello."

Christine Hawthorne says, "Good morning, Rig. We're going sailing today, remember?"

"Oh, yes. I remember," Rig responds in a voice fogged with sleep.

"Are you ready?" Christine asks—her tone edged with impatience.

"Where are you?"

"I am in the lobby of your building."

In a concerned tone, Rig asks, "We agreed that I would pick you up."

"You were supposed pick me up at seven-thirty. When you weren't there by eight, I figured you were sleeping in from another late night of doing whatever it is that you do into the late of night. So, I came here to wake you."

Has anyone seen you?" Rig inquires in a concerned tone.

"No," Christine responds. Then, she asked, "Are you ready?"

"Give me ten minutes to dress and bush my teeth."

Twenty minutes later, Rig arrives in the lobby dressed in khaki pants, boat shoes, and a black windbreaker. He carries a gym bag that contains extra socks, underwear, shaving kit, and several bottles of sunblock. He exhales a sigh of relief when he sees Christine dressed in casual clothes and lightweight jacket with her hair down and covered with a scarf and wearing sunglasses. No one would recognize her as Lieutenant Hawthorne during a casual glance.

They get into Christine's car.

Rig drives toward the pueblo's south exit. Two Spanish Policía cars speed by going in the opposite direction.

Christine comments, "When I drove into Sedo Mare, there were Policía everywhere. I saw a couple of U.S. Navy Shore Patrol cars, also. Something big must be happening."

Rig doesn't say anything.

Christine stares curiously at Rig; then comments, "Looks like you didn't have time to shave and shower."

"I will do that on the boat, after we are anchored in that secluded cove I told you about."

"Your boat has a shower?"

"Yes, and a bathroom and a kitchen and six bunks."

"Must be a large sailboat. Must have cost you a lot."

"I didn't buy it. I rent it and the slip from a boat broker. The agent told me that the owners live in Ireland and rarely come to Rota for a visit."

"They are not afraid that you might disappear with the boat, never to return. Or, maybe wreck it?"

"I had to give them information where I was stationed, and I had to demonstrate my competence to handle the boat. They consider me a good risk."

"How much does it cost you?"

"A two-thousand-dollar deposit. Rent for the boat, slip, and slip utilities are three-hundred per month total."

"You must really like to sail!"

"Yes. I love it."

"Where is your boat docked?"

"Chipiona Marina."

By 3:00 PM, the Policía crime technicians had completed their investigation of the crime scene and departed the area.

Policía Lieutenant Jorge Conrado stands by his car in

the eastern area of Sedo Mare Pueblo. He glances at his watch; he becomes impatient waiting for his appointment to arrive. The dead bodies were removed hours ago, and all the crime scene technicians departed twenty minutes ago.

Several dozen Sedo Mare Pueblo residents linger around the perimeter of the crime scene waiting for the last Policía car to depart.

Finally, the black-colored, late-model Mercedes limousine turns the corner and comes to a stop next to Lieutenant Conrado's Policía sedan. The passenger side rear door opens. A heavy-set man in his fifties who wears an expensive Italian suit and shoes exits the vehicle.

Lieutenant Conrado expresses surprise at the presence of the Rota crime lord. He was expecting one of the crime lord's underlings.

Marcio Dario offers his hand to Lieutenant Conrado. "Thank you for contacting me, Jorge. I have not yet notified my brother of his son's death. I need to know the details so I can answer his questions."

The Policía lieutenant responds, "Señor Dario, the Policía will not notify your brother until you give permission. Your brother will need to identify the body."

"May I perform the identification? I want to spare my brother the grief."

Conrado explains, "The identification will be difficult. Most of Cristóbal's face is distorted."

"Cristóbal has several tattoos that I can identify."

"Then, yes, you may do the identification."

"Thank you, Jorge. You have always been a friend and compadre to my family. Your consideration will be remembered. Now, please tell me what happened."

"Please follow me," the Policía Lieutenant says politely.

Marcio follows Conrado to a car parked at the corner of an intersection. Marcio notes the white outline next to the parked car that shows where a body had lain. Dried blood lies within the chalk outline. The chalk outline also shows that the body was holding a handgun.

Lieutenant Conrado points to the chalk outline and explains, "Your nephew, Cristóbal, was found here. He was wearing a ski mask when the bullet entered his head. The bullet passed through his head and lodged in the pavement there." The lieutenant points to a small chalk circle ten feet away. He adds, "High caliber bullet. The other bodies were found around the corner."

Dario and Conrado walk to the corner; then, they turn east and walk the half-block to where the other two bodies were found. Marcio's limousine follows.

The Sedo Mare Pueblo residents who remain on the scene do not follow the policeman and the other man who they believe is a high-level policeman of some kind. The residents had been warned not to follow the Policía around the crime scene and to stay more than fifty feet away.

There are two chalk body outlines—one on the north side of the road and the other on the south side of the road. Two feet from the body outline on the north side of the road is a white outline of a handgun.

Lieutenant Conrado points to the body outline on the north side of the street and informs, "That was your nephew's friend, Sandalio Ramos. The body over there was an American sailor who lives in Sedo Mare Pueblo and worked at the American Naval Base in Rota."

The Rota crime lord appears thoughtful for a few

moments; then he asks, "What do you conclude from what you have found?"

Lieutenant Conrado explains, "We only have preliminary findings. More detail will come later. This is what we conclude so far." Conrado takes a deep breath; then continues. "Your nephew and his friend arrived on scene during early morning. They both wore ski masks and carried automatic handguns. We believe they were engaged in a crime when they were shot and killed. When your nephew was shot by persons unknown and fell to the ground, your nephew's friend, Sandalio, ran around the corner and ran eastward where he encountered the American sailor. Sandalio shot the American. Then, Sandalio was shot by someone unknown.

"Because of the location of bodies and locations of the deadly bullets that have been dug from the road, we believe the shots that killed your nephew and his friend came from the east. The angle of the bullets in the road and the angle of the entrance and exit wounds on Sandalio's body lead us to believe the shots came from the east at a high angle."

Marcio looks eastward. He notes that the only high places are the upper floors of six condo buildings. Marcio turns his attention back toward Lieutenant Conrado and questions, "You think the shots came from one of those tall buildings?"

Conrado nods, "Yes. One of those condo buildings within a ninety-degree range. That is our initial conclusion. After all the ballistic tests and calculations are complete, we will have the angle of fire narrowed."

Marcio glances to the south side of the road. Then he asks, "What is your conclusion as to why Sandalio killed the American?"

"Must have thought the American was a threat. We can only speculate at this time."

Marcio glances back toward the tall condo buildings to the east. A bewildered expression appears on his face, then he comments, "But it was dark. How?"

"Had to be a high-power rifle with both night-optics scope and a silencer."

"A professional assassination?" Marcio wonders aloud.

"Could be," the Policía Lieutenant responds.

"Keep my informed."

"Of course, Senior Dario, my pleasure to do so."

After Marcio Dario returns to his Mercedes, he tells his driver, "Take me to the residencia of Señor Orrantia."

Several minutes later, Marcio Dario's limousine stops at the driveway gate for the home of the *Imperio Construir* superintendent for Sedo Mare, Jacinto Orrantia. The limousine driver rolls down his window and presses the attention button on the intercom.

A few seconds later, a voice sounds over the intercom, "State your business."

The driver says into the intercom, "Señor Dario to see Señor Orrantia."

The gate opens.

The limousine stops under the portico at the front door of the house.

Jacinto Orrantia meets the limousine and opens the back door.

After exiting the limousine, Marcio Dario offers his hand to Jacinto Orrantia and says, "Cousin, I apologize for the unannounced visit. Might we speak for a few minutes?"

"No problem," Jacinto states. "Come inside and we will have a glass of wine while we talk."

Several minutes later, Jacinto and Marcio sit in Jacinto's den. Marcio who takes no care of his body is mildly envious of his lean and healthy cousin. As young boys they played together on Rota's beaches. Their fathers were first cousins but are no longer among the living.

"Have you heard about Cristóbal's death? He and his friend were killed in Sedo Mare Pueblo early this morning."

"Yes," Jacinto acknowledges. "My men mingled with residents where the bodies were found. I received reports throughout the day."

Marcio takes a sip of wine. Then, he states, "I will have Leoncio Pinero investigate this assassination. I ask that you provide him with any information and assistance he requests."

"No problem, Marcio. I know Leoncio and his reputation for uncovering truth."

"You should expect a visit from him tomorrow."

The two men stand and shake hands.

Jacinto escorts Marcio to the limousine.

Chapter 32

The thirty-six-foot-long sloop with the name *"mistress de el mar"* sails southward across the calm ocean one mile off the coast of Sedo Mare Pueblo. Rig and Christine sit side by side with the tiller between them. Rig controls the tiller and has his eye on the jib and thinking he may need to trim that sail.

Christine stares up at the sunny, cloudless sky; she comments, "What a pleasant day this has been—cool and sunny. Great lunch in that secluded cove. Sailing is an exhilarating experience. I could come to love it."

Rig smiles and says, "Sailing tests man's skills against the power of the sea. I think that's why I like it so much."

Christine points eastward and says, "Sedo Mare Pueblo looks so small from here."

Rig stares toward Sedo Mare Pueblo. His expression turns reflective.

Christine notices Rig's expression. After a few moments, she asks, "How do you like living there? Lots of rumors about violence and naked dancing in the street. Do you see any of that?"

Rig turns his attention away from Sedo Mare Pueblo and stares into Christine's eyes. His expression turns to one of concern.

Christine returns a smiling, curious expression and asks, "What is it Rig?"

"Do you remember in Thurso when those Scottish terrorists threatened your life?"

"Yes," Christine answers. "The navy transferred me to Iceland because of it."

"They threatened you because of your close relationship to me."

"I know that," Christine responds with nod.

"I worry about your safety, now," Rig informs.

Christine flinches. She exhibits alarm.

"My after-hours intelligence activities could draw the attention of some violent criminals."

"Criminals?!" Christine responds in a high-pitch questioning tone. "I thought you were a spy?!"

"I often encounter violent criminals."

"Uh huh, and now you want to dump me because you are concerned for my safety."

Rig stares caringly into Christine's eyes. "Yeah. Something like that."

"Can you tell me what has happened that makes you so concerned about me?"

"No."

"I won't accept that. Can't we add secrecy protocols to hide our relationship?"

"Yes," Rig answers, "but our secret relationship could still be compromised."

Christine's eyes are misty as she casts a pleading expression at Rig. "I don't want to stop seeing you. What can we do to better hide our relationship?"

"Are you sure, Christine? Remember Thurso. You were on their hit list that night."

"I'm sure."

He explains, "Okay, then. We cannot visit each other's home. We must always meet at remote locations that require travel over open roads where we can determine if we are being followed. We travel to those locations separately. We check into separate hotels."

Christine nods acceptance. Then she asks, "What about sailing? I really like it. Can we still go sailing together?"

"Yes, but never at Chipiona Marina where I keep the boat.

You will go to a remote dock somewhere and I will pick you up and drop you off there."

Christine reflects thoughtfulness. Then she asks, "Who is after you?"

"No one is after me. They don't know who I am. They might not discover who I am. I am just being cautious."

Christine exhales a sigh of relief.

"After we dock, you should drive back to Rota. I will take a taxi to my condo."

Rig stares through one of the darkly tinted windows in his condo. Tinted film covered windows are not an uncommon feature because they are used to block the summer sun. However, the windows in Rig's condo are covered with a thicker and darker tint than what is normal in other condos. The tinted films that cover the windows in Rig's condo are designed to prevent viewing from the outside to the inside and provide a clear view looking from the inside to the outside.

Rig glances at his watch—5:30 PM. Then, he returns to looking out the window. He stares toward the northwest at the street where the body of those thugs fell. An unusual number of people walk along the street. He raises binoculars to his eyes. Onlookers stare at the bloodstained chalk outlines of two bodies.

This window gives Rig a different angle of view to that street than the balcony from where he fired the sniper rifle. The chalk outlines are directly across the road from each other. He now knows he was correct in his actions to blow away the thug because the thug was firing at another person.

The chalk outline of the first thug he shot is hidden behind a property wall. The thugs' car is gone.

Rig knows that the Policía will calculate the angle of the

140

shots he fired at those thugs. *They'll get it within thirty to forty degrees,* Rig concludes. He knows that there will be investigators out there at night scanning condo buildings for someone on a balcony or on a roof with night-vision equipment and weapons. He also understands that investigators will be tracking down the shooter. *Just a matter of time before they knock on my door.*

He decides that he must cease his surveillance activities from the balcony.

Chapter 33

A Policía forensic technician stands on the spot where Cristóbal Dario was shot to death by an unknown sniper three nights ago. The time is late afternoon and the sun is to his back. The Technician looks eastward through a surveyor's scope mounted on top of a tripod. He holds a clipboard in his left hand—under the clip are copies of a photograph that present a view of the Pueblo to the east of where he stands.

Policía Detective Lieutenant Jorge Conrado stands behind and to the left of the forensic technician.

Leoncio Pinero stands behind and to the right of the forensic technician. Pinero is a licensed private detective and a confidant of crime boss Marcio Dario. Two days ago, Pinero started his private investigation of Cristóbal Dario's death. Marcio Dario's influence with the local Policía allows Pinero unlimited access to information gathered by the Policía.

Both Conrado and Pinero stand quietly and patiently while waiting for the technician's conclusions.

The forensic technician moves his eye off the scope and studies the photo on the clipboard. He draws a line on the photograph to complete a rectangle. Then, he draws a rectangle of the same dimensions and location on three identical copies of the photograph. He hands one copy each to Leoncio Pinero and Jorge Conrado.

The forensic technician advises, "The shooter was somewhere inside that box when he killed Dario and Ramos."

Pinero and Conrado study the photograph for a few moments. Then, they look to the east and study the area specified in the photograph. They both come to the same conclusion. The shooter most likely fired his rifle from an upper floor or roof of one of those six condo buildings.

The technician packs up and departs the area.

Detective Lieutenant Conrado advises that he must start questioning the residents of those buildings. He gets into a patrol car with the patrolman driver. The car moves off to the east.

Pinero walks across the intersection and climbs into the rear of a panel truck that has front and rear windows but no side windows. The Spanish Telephone Company logo CTNE is painted on both sides of the panel van. The interior of the van is stocked with cameras, telescopes, binoculars and all the night vision optics to cover a range of surveillance situations. Two men who wear misappropriated CTNE uniforms sit in the front of the van.

Pinero shows the photograph to the two men and explains their surveillance routine.

Both men express confident smiles in acknowledgement of Pinero's orders. Both men have years of experience at such surveillance and are sure they will discover activities out of the ordinary.

Chapter 34

Two days later, after arriving at his condo from a day's work onboard *Antares*, Rig goes directly to the window from which he has been surveilling Sedo Mare. He no longer uses the balcony for fear that Policía and others might be watching the balconies of his building from afar.

Using binoculars, he scans the crime scene again. Some residents still walk the crime scene and point and stare at the chalk outlines on the road surface. There are several unoccupied automobiles parked along the road, including a panel van parked next to the high courtyard wall where Cristóbal Dario's body was discovered. Several people move about but none act like investigators.

When Rig conducts his third scan of the street, he stops and focuses on the panel van. Only the rear and left side of the van are visible. The rear doors of the van have windows that are darkly tinted. The letters CTNE with a picture of a telephone under the letters is painted on the side. Rig remembers that is the logo for the Spanish telephone company.

Telephone poles and telephone lines near the van are clear of technicians. So, Rig focuses on the van.

Several minutes later, the van shakes slightly from side to side, revealing that someone moves about inside the vehicle. The door on the passenger side opens. A man who appears to be in his thirties, thin in stature, Spanish features, and wearing casual clothes exits the van. A camera with a telescopic lens hangs on a strap from his neck. The man looks back toward the van and says something, revealing that one or more people remain in the van. The man takes hold of the top of his pants zipper and pulls it down. Then, he steps behind the trunk of a tree. About a minute later, he reappears and enters the van. The van shakes slightly from side to side as people inside the van shift their positions.

Rig reasons that they are not the Policía, and they must have sophisticated optical equipment inside that van, including night-vision binoculars and night-vision cameras with telescopic lenses. And the windows in the rear give the people in the van full view of Rig's condo building.

They are looking for me, Rig speculates. He writes down the van's license number.

After several moments of thought, Rig realizes that he needs to know who those men are. He places the binoculars on the table to the side of the window. He turns and walks toward the secret closet while mentally forming a list of equipment that he will need.

Three hours later in the dark of an overcast moonless night, Rig walks, undetected, along a road that parallels the crime scene road. He is dressed totally in black and wears a black ski mask. The nearest street light is blocks away. He wears night-vision goggles so that he will see those moving about before they see him.

He turns left, then, walks toward the intersection where the van is parked.

He stops twenty feet away from the intersection. He stands next to the west side of a seven-foot-high courtyard wall. The van is parked out of Rig's sight on the road next to the courtyard's south wall.

Rig's plan is to climb the west wall, walk across the southwest corner of the courtyard, climb the south wall and come down on the other side of the wall next to the van.

Ninety seconds later, Rig's feet land on the ground between the courtyard wall and the van's driver's side panel. There are no windows on the van's side panels. He hears men speaking Spanish inside the van. He removes the radio-beacon device from his pocket. He extends the antenna and places the device on the underside of the van. The device's built-in magnet holds the device to the iron frame of the van.

Rig climbs the courtyard wall.

Twenty minutes later, he is back in his condo chugging down a bottle of cold *Aqua Imperio*.

After emptying the half-liter water bottle, Rig sits down at the kitchen table. An open metal briefcase holding a battery-operated, radio-beacon receiver sits on the table in front of him. He turns on the beacon receiver. Beeping sounds emanate from the receiver, and a flashing blip on the screen tells Rig that the beacon transmitter lays west of his position.

Rig prepares for a night of surveillance. He stuffs a few apples and several bottles of water into his backpack. He also packs a night-vision monocular and a night-vision camera with telescopic lens. He hesitates for a moment and engages in thought as to what else he will need. Then, he packs one of the nine-millimeter automatic handguns and an extra magazine.

Fifteen minutes later, Rig sits in his parked car several blocks out of sight of the van with CTNE markings. The beacon receiver sits on the passenger seat and emits low-volume beeps at constant intervals, indicating that the distance between the transmitter and the receiver remain at a constant distance.

The nearest street light is blocks away. Still dressed in black and slouching down in his seat, he is undetectable to any casual observer. As the hours pass, manmade sounds in the Sedo Mare Pueblo diminish. He yawns frequently. Cricket sounds drown out the beeps coming from the beacon receiver. Rig increases the receiver's volume.

At 11:20 PM a long beep tells Rig that the beacon transmitter is no longer stationary. The van is moving southward towards

Rota.

Thirty minutes later, the van pulls into a parking lot in Rota that is adjacent to the *Aureo Orilla* nightclub—located one block from the beach.

Rig does not enter the parking lot. He drives two more blocks, turns around, and drives back toward the nightclub. He parks along the street away from street lights and among other cars one-half block away from the nightclub. He has a clear view of the nightclub entrance and the parking lot entrance.

A camera with a telescopic lens rests on Rig's lap.

A black-colored Mercedes limousine is parked near the entrance to the nightclub. Rig records the license number in his notebook.

During the next thirty minutes, half a dozen partiers exit the night club. Then, three men wearing suits exit the club. Two of the men station themselves six feet apart, providing a guarded path to the Mercedes limousine. The third man enters the driver's side of the Mercedes and starts the engine.

The two guards continuously shift their eyes to different locations on the street and sidewalk.

Rig brings the camera to his eye and snaps some pictures of the men who are obviously guards of some kind. He keeps the camera lens pointed in the direction of the nightclub.

Several minutes later, two men exit the club. One is heavy-set, wears a suit, and appears dignified. The other man wears casual clothes and portrays a common manner. Rig recognizes the man in casual clothes as the one who exited the panel van in Sedo Mare Pueblo to take a piss.

Rig snaps five pictures of the two men as they walk to the Mercedes limousine.

The man in casual clothes opens the back door on the passenger's side of the Mercedes for the distinguished man in the suit. Then, the man in casual clothes walks around the back of the limousine and enters the rear door on the driver's side.

Rig decides to follow the Mercedes. He knows he can find the van anytime he wants.

Because of the hour, few vehicles are driving the streets. Rig stays back far enough not to lose the limousine's tail lights,

Fifteen minutes later, the Mercedes enters a walled compound on the *Avenida Punta Candor*. Rig passes the compound as the motorized gate closes. He notes the house number on the gate.

Concluding there is nothing more to accomplish tonight, he drives back to his condo in Sedo Mare Pueblo.

Chapter 35

Rig and his naval intelligence controller, Arleigh Rouston, sit at Rig's kitchen table.

Rouston asks, "Do you know about the shootings in Sedo Mare Pueblo last week?"

"Yes, but don't know the details."

"About 2:00 AM, two local criminals were killed and so was an American sailor assigned to the Rota Naval Base. One of those criminals by the name of Sandalio Ramos shot and killed the American sailor before he himself was shot and killed by a person or persons unknown. Naval Investigative Service has provided us with Spanish Policía reports that link the handguns of those two dead criminals to the murder of those two *Antares* officers last October.

"The Policía do not know who shot those two criminals, but they have plenty of leads. For example, they know from which direction the shots were fired. They have narrowed the range down to upper floors or roofs of one of several condo buildings that includes ours."

Rig asks, "So it was long distance shots with a rifle?"

"Yes, but they cannot identify what type of rifle because the caliber of the bullets does not match any known rifle. The Policía conclude that the rifle had a suppressor and night scope because residents in the area say they only heard one shot—the shot from Ramos's gun that killed the American sailor."

"Sounds like a professional hit," Rig suggests.

"Could be," Rouston responds in an agreeing tone. "The Spanish Policía will concentrate the investigation along a forty-degree range. They will be looking for someone with night optic equipment.

Rig knows that Rouston knows standard Chinese sniper

bullets such as those Rouston issued Rig would be easily identified. So, Rig is confident that no one will connect him to the death of those criminals.

Rouston states, "You must cease your surveillance."

Rig feels relieved that he need not come up with an excuse on his own to cease conducting surveillance from his balcony.

Rouston advises, "I've read your surveillance logs for that night. You did not report anything unusual. Thinking back, is there anything you saw, no matter how insignificant, that might link to those killings."

Rig casts an expression of contemplation for a few moments. Then, he says, "No—nothing."

After a few moments of silence, Rig hands Rouston a slip of paper. He says, "Some more license numbers for which I need names and addresses and everything we can find out about the people connected to those license numbers."

"What caused you to gather these license numbers?"

"Two nights ago, I saw what I believe to be a private surveillance operation. Could be a link to those criminals who were shot and could lead to discovering the motives for killing those two American navy officers.

Rouston nods understanding as he says, "Give me a couple of days to get these traced."

Rig glances at his watch; then asks, "Anything else?"

"Yes." Rouston responds in an enthusiastic tone and with a satisfied smile on his face. "We have received more intel on that water being shipped from the *Imperio Construir* warehouse."

Rig raises his brow and expresses interest.

Rouston explains, "Lab analysis of that water from the underground river shows concentration of a tasteless, natural hallucinogenic from a mushroom known to grow only in caves. Comparison of the sample you took from the underground river and the sample from the after-processing bottled water show that the concentration of hallucinogenic is reduced only slightly during the filtering and bottling process.

"*Imperio Aqua* bottles with green labels contain water from lakes in the Pyrenees. Red labels go only on bottles containing water from the Sedo Mare underground river. Obviously, *Imperio* wants someone to easily identify the funny water. Our investigators conducted a quick check around Europe and could not find any *Imperio Aqua* with red labels. Our initial analysis is that red-label bottles are being shipped only to the Middle East.

Rig suggests, "That could account for occurrences of strange behavior in Sedo Mare Pueblo, like the occasional naked parties. Some of that underground river water must be getting into the water supply."

Rouston informs, "I checked on the Sedo Mare water supply." It comes from a reservoir about five miles to the east. The water from that reservoir is pumped into water tanks on the hills above the Sedo Mare Valley."

Both men are silent while evaluating what it all means.

Rouston says to Rig, "You said there was a valve in the bottling room that routes water to the pueblo, but it was shut, right?"

"Yes," Rig affirms. "Both times I was in there that valve was shut."

Both men have their heads bowed and are silent while they attempt to connect the dots.

Then, Rig's head snaps up and his eyes widen. He says, "During my first few days here, you gave me a file to review. It included the history of Sedo Mare from Roman times to the present and included some aerial photographs of Sedo Mare at different times over the past thirty years. Do you have those photos with you?"

"Yes," Rouston digs through his leather satchel. He pulls out the photographs and passes them to Rig.

151

Rig lays out the photos on the table in date order. After a quick scan of the five photographs, he nods and expresses satisfaction that he found what he was looking for. He explains, "That earliest photo is 1951 and shows the Sedo Mare Valley with no buildings.

"In the 1958 photo, there is one small building at the same location as where the *Imperio Construir* warehouse is now.

"The next photo, 1962, there are about one-hundred single-family houses and some two-story quadraplexes scattered over the valley—no high-rise condo buildings, yet. Note the increase in size of the *Imperio Construir* construction compound from 1958 to 1962. Also, the warehouse was replaced during those four years with the current, larger warehouse. And the building superintendent's house was built during those four years.

"The most recent picture taken in 1970 shows that mass construction took place during the previous eight years. In the 1970 photo, you can see high-rise condo buildings at the base of the hills on the north, east, and south. And look here." Rig points his finger at two water towers on the summit of the eastern hills. "Those water towers were not there during the early years of the pueblo's existence. So, before the water towers were installed, that underwater river must have been the water supply for Sedo Mare."

Rouston nods agreement and says, "Makes sense, but there must have been a water treatment facility—probably located in those early buildings inside the construction compound. If that underground river was Sedo Mare's drinking water supply during the early years that would account for the frequent reports of odd behavior in that area, including those crazy naked parties.

Rig expresses doubt as he comments, "No one I know in Sedo Mare drinks from faucets. Everyone drinks bottled water. At Sedo Mare's beachside cafes, only bottled water is served.

The water from faucets is only used for showers, washing clothes, and washing dishes. I mean, that is true in most places in Southern Europe, right? So, occasionally, people unintentionally consumed underground river water, which must be the cause for those occasional naked parties?"

Again, silence overcomes the room while they consider possible answers.

Moments later, Rouston asks, "Are you all caught up on your report dictations for Marie?"

"Yes."

"Okay, give me your tapes and I will take them in."

Rig hands Rouston three mini tape cassettes.

Rouston informs, "Washington has ordered me to increase resources on this operation. Linking those Spanish criminals to the murder of those officers stirred ONI desire to see how deep it all goes. They want to know why classified material was found in the burnt-out house where those officers were murdered. I am placing another operative in Sedo Mare. One of his first tasks will be to discover the connection of those two murdered officers to the two criminals who were assassinated."

"Assassinated?" Rig asks in a high questioning tone. "Is that the official line? Those two criminals were assassinated?"

"Yes," Rouston answers.

"By whom?"

"Another agency is working on whom."

"What do you want me to do?"

"Nothing for now. Just take a break."

Rig exhibits confusion. He asks, "But if I am doing nothing, why do you need to send in another operative?"

Rouston smiles, chuckles, then responds, "Because, Rig, everywhere you go you draw stares and attention. This other operative will be mixing as much as he can with the residents, especially longtime residents. He is of Spanish descent, speaks the language fluently, and has a sociable personality. He is the opposite of you, which will work to our benefit. In other words, you are good at what you do and he is good at what he does."

Rig smiles as he nods acceptance. He thinks about maximizing his time sailing in his *mistress de el mar*.

Chapter 36

Rig and Jack Tacker sit at Rig's kitchen table. They sip cognac brought to the meeting by Jack.

After some small talk about the pleasures and adventures of living in Spain, Jack Tacker tells Rig, "I have the information you requested."

Rig stares with wonder into the face of the sophisticated Jack Tacker. "Wow! That was quick!" Rig declares in a surprised tone.

Jack utters a sarcastic chuckle and responds, "Not difficult to track down notorious people. You are trespassing on dangerous ground."

Jack passes a large manila envelope to Rig.

Rig opens the envelope and pulls out the photographs he took in front of the *Áureo Orilla* nightclub. Typed biographies of the people in the photographs are attached to the photos.

"Interesting people you're tailing." Jack comments. "The man in the casual clothes is one Leoncio Pinero. He is a former Policía detective who had a reputation as an excellent crime solver. He discarded his twelve-year policeman career and opened a private detective agency. One of his most influential and powerful clients is Marcio Dario—the crime boss in this area.

"The heavy gentleman in the suit is Marcio Dario. He controls crime in both Cadiz and Huelva provinces. Anytime Dario wants something investigated, he hires Pinero. Dario's power backs Pinero's investigations and every person in authority knows it. That power includes obtaining information by any means; torture included. Pinero has the nickname *The Inquisitor*, and that nickname accurately describes his methods. According to my sources, Pinero never fails. He's brutal, Rig. You need to be cautious and stay out of his way."

"He won't find me," Rig asserts. "The rifle cannot be tracked to me. No one but you and my controller know I was on my balcony that night."

Jack considers Rig's assertion; then, he states, "Sooner or later, the Policía or Pinero or both will come to your door during the normal course of their investigation. When they do, they will be evaluating your every word and every gesture. They are trained to detect lies."

"Don't worry, Jack. I have a lot experience lying successfully to the police."

"There is something else in that report that you should find interesting."

"What's that?"

"The Sedo Mare Valley is owned by the Dario crime family. They also own *Imperio Construir* and *Imperio Agua*.

Rig expresses surprise and responds, "I've read in naval intelligence documents that a British company owns all that."

"At one time, a British company did. However, when that British company, *Empire Construction*, began construction in Sedo Mare Valley, the Dario family moved in with its protection racket. When *Empire Construction* attempted to fight back, the Dario family used its influence with local labor and local authorities to halt construction. Vandalism of buildings and equipment became rampant and costly.

"Anyway, and to make a long story short, Marcio Dario made an offer to buy all *Empire Construction's* businesses, assets, licenses, and permits in Spain including the company names *Imperio Construir* and *Imperio Agua*. The offer was generous and *Empire Construction* accepted."

Rig expresses curious astonishment as he states, "I wonder

how naval intelligence missed that sale. It must be recorded."

Jack advises, "There are ways to camouflage such a sale. My operatives discovered it by following some company address changes in local provincial files."

Rig considers the significance of this new information. Then, he says, "This puts the Dario family dead center in everything going on here in Sedo Mare. They have found Middle East buyers for Sedo Mare's hallucinogenic laced drinking water. We must find out why that water is going to the Middle East. I must relay this information to my ONI controller. He will want to know how I came to know this information. I will need to be creative."

Chapter 37

Rig sits in the commanding officer's conference room along with other chiefs, department heads, XO USS *Antares*, and CO USS *Antares*. His dog-eared copy of the yardarm incident report lies on the table before him. Everyone waits patiently for the Chief of Staff.

Rig suspects that the yardarm incident occurred as the result of bad decisions on the part of the Commodore and the Chief of Staff. His suspicion began that same day as the incident when Rig was eating the evening meal in the Chiefs Mess. His bandaged hands were fumbling with eating utensils when Senior Chief Machinist Mate Jerome Cleveland had sat down across the table and started up a conversation.

"Rig, nice job today with saving that sailor."

"Thanks, Cleve," Rig had responded in a short, unenthusiastic tone meant to halt the conversation. People had approached him all day with comments admiring his courage. He was annoyed with being in the spotlight, and he wanted to quash another conversation before it got started.

Then, Cleveland had said something that sparked Rig's curiosity. "I am not surprised that evolution ended in near tragedy—no scheduling—no planning—hastily formed team with sailors who are inexperienced and untrained."

"Not scheduled? Hastily formed?" Rig had questioned; his tone turned enthusiastic in an attempt to prompt more information.

"Yeah, the NAVSAT antenna replacement was not scheduled for this morning, and both antenna repair teams were previously committed to boomer work. Plus, the pier crane was committed all day for boomer antenna replacements in the morning and weapons loading during the afternoon. The Repair Officer, Commander Packard, explained all that to the Chief of Staff. But the Chief of Staff told Commander Packard that the order came from the commodore and that Commander Packard was to find a way to comply with the commodore's order without delaying work on the boomers. The only way to do that was to form a temporary antenna team of inexperienced sailors from other departments."

Rig had asked, "How do you know about that conversation between Commander Packard and the Chief of Staff?"

"I was in the Repair Office updating the repair schedule when Commander Packard was on the phone with the Chief of Staff. That was about 0900. When I left the office, Commander Packard was still on the phone with the Chief of Staff.

"Next I heard on the subject was when the Aloft Rescue Team was called to the forward yardarm. Then, this afternoon, I heard that the radioman who went aloft had not gone through the Aloft Safety Course."

For days to follow, the yardarm cluster fuck was the topic of scuttlebutt conversation throughout the ship.

The draft report of the yardarm incident was distributed one week ago.

Rig became curious as to why the report did not disclose that the NAVSAT replacement task was a last-minute verbal order from the commodore. He decided to conduct his own, low-profile investigation into the yardarm incident.

As part of his investigation, he read the entries leading up to the incident in the Command Duty Officer Log and Repair Department Duty Officer Log. Additional information was gained by listening to conversations in the Chiefs Mess, and by personally questioning the two radiomen in the Communications Department who were assigned to the antenna replacement.

RM3 Wagner, the sailor that Rig saved from falling, revealed that he volunteered to go out on the yardarm, although he had never been aloft before and had not attended the Aloft Safety Course. Wagner said that he did not know that the Safety Aloft Course existed.

Rig smelled a cover-up.

He needed to collect more information on the incident but knew he could not question witnesses outside of his own department without the chain-of-command noticing. He concluded that the next best thing was to read those witness statements that should be attached to the report but are not. The only way he could read those witness statements was by breaking into the investigating officer's stateroom.

Junior officers do not have offices. They use their staterooms to do paperwork and keep their division files. Rig concluded that he would find the witness statements in Ensign Rolland's stateroom. Ensign Rolland and another ensign share a stateroom. However, both ensigns reside off ship with their families. So, Rig figured an early morning *incursion* into Ensign Rolland's stateroom would be low risk of being caught, although an enlisted man passing through Officers Country during the early morning would not go unchallenged if noticed.

During the early morning hours four days ago, Rig lock-picked Ensign Rolland's stateroom door, entered the stateroom, and locked the door behind him. He lock-picked Ensign Rolland's file drawer and found the witness statements. After conducting a quick scan of eleven witness statements, Rig knew he needed to make copies. He took the file to Main Comm and copied each statement. After stowing those copies in his locker in Chiefs Berthing, he returned the original file to Ensign Rolland's stateroom. His two treks through Officers Country, thirty minutes apart, went undetected.

Rig spent the next two hours lying in his rack behind his closed privacy curtains and studied every detail described in witness statements.

The order to replace the yardarm SATCOM antenna that morning originated from the commodore at approximately 0630. The commodore gave a verbal order to the Chief of Staff, Captain Crossman, to have the yardarm antenna replaced and made operational by 1300. Rig gained this information from the Chief of Staff's statement. A witness statement by the commodore was not included in the witness statements held by Ensign Rolland.

Rig constructed a timeline based on all the information he read.

0650 – The Chief of Staff relayed the order via telephone to the *Antares* Command Duty Officer (CDO), Lieutenant Commander Spiel.

0710 – *Antares* Command Duty Officer relayed order to *Antares* Repair Duty Officer (RDO), Lieutenant Laddner.

0740 – The RDO called *Antares* Command Duty Officer (CDO) and advised that both antenna crews were committed that morning to replacing antennas on two boomers. Also, the pier crane was committed all day to scheduled antenna replacements onboard both boomers and SUBROC loading for both boomers. Those boomer antenna replacements and SUBROC loading for both boomers were JCS priority because both boomers were scheduled to depart for patrol five days hence. The RDO explained to the CDO that he did not have the authority to reschedule JCS priority boomer work. The RDO advised that he must refer the issue to the Repair Department Head who should arrive onboard shortly.

0830 – The Repair Department Head, Commander Packard, called the Chief of Staff, Captain Crossman, and reported that all antenna repair resources were committed that morning, and that the yardarm NAVSAT antenna replacement could be scheduled for three days hence. After all, the yardarm NAVSAT antenna is only needed at sea, and *Antares* currently had no sea period scheduled.

According to Commander Packard's statement, the Chief of Staff explained that the commodore had issued an order to have it done by 1300. The Chief of Staff said he would not ask the commodore to reconsider when no effort had been expended to get it done. The Chief of Staff said he would supply two radiomen from the Communications Department to augment the Repair Department effort.

0840 – Repair Department Head, Commander Packard, went to the Electronic Repair shop in search of anyone who was not committed to work on the two boomers. He found ETN2 Bristol. Bristol advised that he was the only person from the Electronics Repair Division onboard and that the Electronics Repair officer was already onboard one of the boomers supervising antenna replacements and the senior chief ET was already on the other boomer supervising antenna replacements. Commander Packard assigned Bristol to lead the team effort to replace the NAVSAT antenna.

0905 – The two Communications Department augments, RM3 Wagner and RMSN Hollart, reported to the Electrical Repair Shop.

Neither Wagner nor Hollart had completed the Personnel Qualification Standards, PQS, for working aloft; but, then, no one had asked them. They did not know that *USS Antares Regulations* required completion of *Working Aloft PQS* before going aloft. A three-day safety course for working aloft is part of the PQS process.

The Communications Watch Officer, in his statement, explained that the order he was given to assign two radiomen to the task did not include a requirement to assign radiomen who

162

completed the PQS for going aloft.

The order coming down from the Chief of Staff to assign two radiomen to the repair department for NAVSAT antenna replacement did not specify two radiomen who had completed the *Working Aloft PQS*. During the frustrating rushed effort to comply with the commodore's reckless order to perform a routine task that could be properly planned for another day, no one in the chain of command ever considered the *Working Aloft PQS* requirement.

ETN2 Bristol had completed the PQS for working aloft but never considered asking RM3 Wagner or RMSN Hollart if they had completed the PQS. Assigning non-qualified personnel to an aloft task just isn't done. Bristol had never led an aloft team before, and it never entered his mind that seniors would assign non-qualified personnel to an aloft task.

The electronics repair division officer and the electronics repair division chief have checklists for aloft tasks which include a check on PQS completion, but the division officer and chief were busy on separate boomers and were unaware that a third, temporary antenna team was formed and tasked.

The Repair Department Head, Commander Packard, never considered that required checklists would not be followed by ETN2 Bristol, and ETN2 Bristol had no idea that such checklists existed.

0920 – The four-member, temporary antenna repair team arrived in the electronic repair division gear locker in search of tools and safety harnesses. They found industrial-size wrenches that ETN2 Bristol guessed would be needed to loosen the bolts that hold the currently installed NAVSAT antenna in place. However, all the safety harnesses were gone.

Knowing that no one can go aloft without wearing a safety harness, Bristol decided he must go in search of the Department Head and tell him of the problem. He told the rest of the team to standby in the gear locker until he returned.

0925 – Bristol entered the Repair Department Office looking for the Department Head, but the office was empty. He quickly glanced around the room, looking for a sign that might announce where the Department Head was. Then, Bristol saw two safety harnesses hanging on hooks behind one of the three desks in the office. He stared at the harnesses for a full minute while wondering if he had the authority to just take the harnesses without permission. Finally, he rationalized that he was assigned this task by the Department Head; so, he must be resourceful in getting it done. Bristol took the harnesses.

Bristol did not know that those two harnesses on that hook were destined for refurbishing because they had failed their last preventative maintenance checks. Everyone who works in the Department Office and all repair department officers and all repair department chiefs know that hook was for faulty harnesses destined for refurbishing. But none of those officers and chiefs was around to tell Bristol; they were all on boomers supervising planned work.

When Bristol returned to the gear locker, he found another sailor, a seaman apprentice compartment cleaner who was added to the team by Commander Packard.

At that point, the foundation had been laid for a classic, tragedy-ending, navy cluster-fuck.

0945 – The four-man team arrived at the bottom of the forward yardarm. ETN2 Bristol had seen antenna technicians lifted to the yardarm in a crane bucket to work on antennas. Bristol assumed the crane bucket was not applicable in this case because Commander Packard would have advised about a crane if it applied.

Instructions from Commander Packard were clear. *"Loosen the bolts at the antenna base; then, stop your work and come find me. I will give you further instructions, then."*

Commander Packard's intention was to halt the NAVSAT antenna work once the bolts were loosened; then, request services of the pier crane to lift out the old 170-pound antenna and put in place the new 180-pound antenna. He anticipated that the crane would not be available until late afternoon and the commodore's deadline for completing operational testing by 1300 would not be met.

ETN2 Bristol concluded that RM3 Wagner was the strongest of the four team members, and Wagner said he had no problem with going aloft to loosen the bolts. Bristol decided that he and Wagner would go aloft, and the other two members of the team would stay on deck as line tenders and runners for tools and equipment.

1000 - 1100 – For more than an hour, ETN2 Bristol and RM3 Wagner attempted to loosen all ten mounting bolts. They pushed together and they pulled together and they kicked together, but they were successful at loosening only four bolts. Bristol had concluded that the unmovable bolts were rust frozen and a cutting torch and a qualified cutting-torch tech was needed to accomplish the task. Bristol decided to go find Commander Packard and ask for instructions.

1102 – ETN2 Bristol had descended two rungs on the mast ladder when he heard RM3 Wagner say, "I am going to give this bolt one more try."

Wagner straddled the yardarm. He placed the wrench around the bolt, then, pushed hard in a forward motion. The wrench slipped off the bolt. With no resistance against his body weight, Wagner fell forward. His head hit the base of the antenna, which knocked him unconscious. His legs slipped away from the yardarm. The lanyard of his safety harness prevented Wagner from falling to the deck. He was dangling, unconscious, from the yardarm with a safety harness that was coming apart.

The draft incident report reduces all statements and log entries to these basic safety violation facts:

a. *When attempting to loosen the bolt, RM3 Wagner assumed a physical position specifically identified as dangerous in the Working Aloft Safety Course.*

b. *RM3 Wagner went aloft before completing the Working Aloft PQS.*

c. *RMCS Page ignored safety regulations in his actions to save RM3 Wagner from falling to the deck. Senior Chief Page also ignored verbal orders from both the USS Antares CO and the COMSUBRON THIRTEEN Chief of Staff to cease his actions and wait for the Aloft Rescue Team.*

d. *Safety belts used by ETN2 Bristol and RM3 Wagner had failed preventative maintenance checks but had not been labeled as unsafe.*

In other words, Rig concludes, the whole evolution was a cluster fuck because competent supervision was sacrificed in attempts to compete a task that wasn't operationally necessary. But the task was attempted anyway because no one wanted to stand before the commodore and challenge his order.

Some attendees to the meeting express impatience. The Squadron Chief of Staff is now fifteen-minutes late to the meeting.

Rig stares at his wrinkled, dog-earned copy of the draft incident report lying on the tabletop before him. The list of four safety regulation violations were derived from the sequence of events listed in the report, but the report sequence of events starts with ETN2 Bristol being assigned as team leader by the Repair Department Head. None of what happened before that is included in the report. Rig concludes that the powers in authority have decided that all actions before Commander Packard appointing ETN2 Bristol as team leader are irrelevant to the end result of a sailor's life being placed in danger.

Commodore Weller, Commander Submarine Squadron THIRTEEN, enters the conference room.

All rise to their feet and stand at attention.

Captain Crossman, the Commodore's Chief of Staff, does not accompany the Commodore.

The Commodore advises, "I will be sitting in for Captain Crossman today. Please be seated."

After all are seated, the Commodore looks at the *Antares* CO, Captain Finny, and says, "As I understand it, the purpose of this meeting is to develop conclusions and recommendations for the incident report; is that correct?"

"Yes, Commodore, that is correct."

With a friendly expression on his face, the Commodore, specifies, "The report can be wrapped up with me, Captain Finny, and the Repair and Deck Department Heads. Everyone else can return to their duties."

Just before exiting through the conference room door, Rig looks over his shoulders at the four officers sitting at the table. Those four officers will decide on who or what was at fault and why. Two line-officer captains and two mustang limited-duty officers sit at the table. The Deck Department Head is an LDO lieutenant with nineteen years in the navy and who spent ten years as a boatswain mate. The Repair Department Head is a LDO lieutenant commander who spent nine years as a nuclear power machinist mate. Rig already feels sympathy for the two mustangs.

Chapter 38

At 7:15 PM on a Wednesday evening, Rig opens the front door of his condo in response to the front door bell. Two men stand on the landing. One is a middle-aged man who wears a suit and tie, has a slim build, and is dark skinned with dark hair and thinly trimmed mustache. The other man who wears a Spanish policeman's uniform is younger and taller and has an athletic build. Both men have binoculars hanging from straps around their necks.

"You are Mr. Page?" the man in the suit asks.

"Yes. I am."

The man who wears a suit explains, "I am Detective Lieutenant Conrado." He shows his badge and identification to Rig; then, he nods toward the man in a policeman's uniform and informs, "This is policeman Prospero."

"How may I help you?" Rig asks in a polite tone while exhibiting a friendly smile.

"We are investigating a crime. I have questions I must ask. May we enter?"

Rig opens the door wider. "Yes. Please come in."

After the two policemen enter, Detective Conrado informs, "First, we must look around your apartment. Then, we must check the view from the balcony facing west."

Rig stares at Conrado for a few moments; then, he comments, "I have always been impressed by the number of Europeans who speak English as compared to most Americans who only know English."

"Thank you, Mr. Page. English is required study in our schools from the earliest years. Do you speak Spanish?"

"Not very good. I cannot carry on a fluid conversation. I

read Spanish pretty good, though, and I can understand short verbal phrases."

Conrado's friendly smile turns to a slightly impatient expression. "Now, we must look at your apartment. Then, I must ask you some questions."

"I will follow you," Rig offers.

The two policemen make a quick inspection of the condo. During the past few days, Conrado and Prospero have inspected over fifty condos and have come to expect nothing unusual. Every condo has a walk-in closet and when they glance into Rig's cluttered walk-in closet, they do not notice that it is fifteen inches shorter than the closets in other condos.

Conrado leads them to the west-facing balcony.

Conrado and Prospero raise their night-vision binoculars to their eyes. They have a clear view to the location where the two hoodlums and American sailor were shot. But, then, so do dozens of other condos they have checked.

They go to Rig's living room.

Prospero pulls a small notebook and pen from his pocket.

Conrado asks, "Mr. Page, you are an American sailor, yes?"

"Yes."

"Where is your work?"

"The USS *Antares*."

"I know of it. What do you do on the USS *Antares*?"

"I am the senior radioman. I supervise ship's communications operations and personnel."

"Do you own any rifles?"

Rig shakes his head slightly and responds with an even-toned, "No."

Prospero is recording Rig's answers.

Conrado asks, "Where were you three Sunday mornings ago around 2:00 AM?"

Rig responds, "Ah. When those three people were killed,

correct?"

"Yes."

"I was here—in bed asleep."

"You did not hear shots fired around 2:00 AM?"

"No."

Detective Conrado expresses thoughtfulness for a few moments. Then, he says, "Thank you for your cooperation, Mr. Page. We will exit now. I might come back with more questions."

With a friendly tone to his voice, Rig responds, "You are welcome anytime, detective."

Several minutes later, Detective Conrado and policeman Prospero stand in the lobby of Rig's condo building.

"That is all for today." Conrado tells Prospero. "Add Mr. Rigney Page to the list of those we will check with Interpol. How many on that list now?"

"Six—three Spanish men and three American men."

"Your first priority tomorrow morning is to initiate those Interpol checks."

Rig stands on his balcony and looks down toward the courtyard.

The two policemen walk across the courtyard to the parking lot. They enter a Policía car and drive away.

Rig returns to his living room and picks up the phone. He dials Rouston's night number.

"Hello," Rouston answers.

"We need to meet."

"Come down to my place. The door will be unlocked."

Ten minutes later, Rig sits in Rouston's living room. Rouston's wife busies herself in the kitchen preparing drinks.

Rig briefs Rouston on the visit by the Policía.

"Are you a suspect?" Rouston asks.

"They didn't say."

"If they suspect you are involved in any way, they will query Interpol for information on you. They will learn about your heroics in Scotland and about you being shot in Sardinia. They might also discover your arrest regarding those attacks last year against that labor union."

"I was never charged or *booked* in that labor union thing. So, that should not show up in an Interpol inquiry."

"That Thurso incident will reveal that you know how to use firearms and are willing to engage in violence. Do the Policía know about your boat?"

"I doubt they know about my boat," Rig says with confidence. "The boat isn't registered to me, and I doubt that boat rental agreements are registered with government."

Rouston explains his concern. "I hope they catch that killer soon. We can't have the Policía on your tail while you are on missions. We won't take any chances. After you depart for work tomorrow morning, I will send someone to your condo and remove all your ONI issued equipment and weapons. Is there any ONI equipment on your boat?"

"No," Rig responds, which is the truth because the two Beretta handguns and custom-made sniper rifle hidden on his boat were provided by *The Guardians*."

Rouston's wife delivers two chilled mugs of San Miguel. Then, she departs the living room and goes back to the kitchen.

Rig tells Rouston, "I need verification that no one is watching my condo, my boat, or following me. If someone is watching me, I need to know who it is."

"I will assign someone," Rouston promises.

After returning to his condo, he walks out onto the balcony that gives him the best view of the courtyard and parking lot. Dozens of cars sit in the parking lot. He cannot use any of his surveillance equipment to help identify a tail. If he uses surveillance equipment or surveillance methods, he would reveal too much about himself to any experienced operative.

Chapter 39

Every eighth day, Rig stands duty as COMSUBRON THIRTEEN Duty Chief. His duty desk is located in the COMSUBRON THIRTEEN Staff Office.

The time is 0215. The duty officer went to bed at midnight. The staff yeoman's locked file cabinet stands in the corner behind the staff yeoman's desk. The duty key ring hangs from Rig's belt.

Eleven days have passed since the meeting to finalize the Aloft Incident Report. Curiosity about the finalized report nags at his gut.

Rig goes to the office door and locks it. Then, he goes to the staff yeoman's file cabinet and unlocks it. He finds the Aloft Incident Report. He sits at the staff yeoman's desk and scans the document.

The report is typed on USS *Antares* letterhead paper. The report is addressed to Naval Safety Center with copies to COMSUBRON THIRTEEN and COMSUBLANT. The first part of the report is the same as the draft he previously read.

Added to the final report are *Conclusions* and *Recommendations* written by the Commodore, the *Antares* Captain, and the *Antares* Deck and Repair Department heads.

> *Conclusions:*
> *1 - Multiple procedural and safety regulations were violated because of the inexperience of the antenna team leader.*
> *2 - Conflicts with scheduled tasks and the Repair Officer's commitment to follow orders and get the job done compelled the Repair Officer to appoint an inexperienced antenna team leader.*
>
> *Recommendation:*

Update ship's instructions and regulations to:
1 - Specify that all safety harnesses must be tagged UNUSABLE within thirty minutes of failing preventative maintenance checks.
2 — Specify that all personnel working aloft for the purpose of removing, mounting, or replacing antennas must work from a crane bucket. NO EXCEPTIONS.
3 — Specify that no one goes aloft without an authorized Working Aloft Chit that must be signed by both the Repair Department Head and Deck Department Head. Both Officers are responsible for ensuring that each member of the aloft team meets all qualifications standards and that aloft checklists are being used and verified by a chief petty officer or higher rank.

The report's recommendations convey that the cause of the incident was lack of detailed safety procedures in the ship's regulations manual. There is no mention in the report that the NAVSAT antenna replacement task was a last-minute, reckless order from the commodore that required bypassing normal planning processes. Therefore, the commodore's reason for issuing that order is not explained.

Rig shakes his head and expresses disgust. He concludes that because there was no real harm, there was no real foul. Therefore, there is no need to enter negative comments in anyone's fitness report or performance evaluation. The vague brevity of the report is declaring: *No big deal here. The only reason this report exists is because regulations require it.*

Rig visualizes copies of the two-page report arriving in the mail at the Naval Safety Center, COMSUBLANT, and JCS. He visualizes mail bags full of reports in envelopes being dumped on the desks of bureaucrats who will open the envelopes of hundreds of daily reports and place those reports on reading boards. Then, Assistant Chiefs of Staff will review those hundreds of reports and decide which reports are important enough to get their superior's attention. Rig visualizes FILE WITHOUT ACTION stamped on the *Antares* Aloft Incident Report by every Assistant Chief of Staff who reads it. Thereby, burying a valuable lesson learned.

So, in the end, the report of an event that the *Antares'* chief boatswain mate categorized as *never been seen by him during twenty years on deck* will be filed away in cabinets of the great bureaucracy—never to emerge again.

Rig sighs deeply as he closes the file. He contemplates, then, accepts the order and nature of things in the organization to which he has committed his life.

Chapter 40

Detective Lieutenant Conrado stands before a whiteboard in his office at the Rota Policía Headquarters. During the weeks that he has been investigating the shooting homicides of Cristóbal Dario, Sandalio Ramos, and the American sailor, Conrado has been linking events and facts to people he has interviewed.

This morning, he received the Interpol reports on five people that he interviewed. Only one of them had an Interpol file—Mr. Rigney Page. The Interpol report provided details on events of a terrorist attack on a U.S. Navy installation in Scotland three years ago. The report describes Mr. Page's role in suppressing the attack. The report reveals that Mr. Page is a skilled marksman who was decisive in saving the lives of over thirty people.

Conrado writes Rig's name at the top of the list of those whose balconies or windows are aligned with the firing zone of the crime and who have a background with guns.

Conrado hears someone entering the office behind him. He turns and sees his old friend, Leoncio Pinero.

After they exchange pleasantries, Pinero gets down to business, Pinero asks, "Have you narrowed down your suspects."

Conrado explains, "All I have is a list of people who might be capable of such actions and have experience with guns, and their condos provide a line of fire to the crime scene. But none have a motive. The evidence so far points to a professional assassination."

"What about ballistics?"

"During our inquiries, we collected nine rifles. None

176

of them match. The murder weapon was custom made."

"May I see your list of possible perpetrators?"

"Yes." Conrado points to the white board.

Pinero scans the board and becomes familiar with its layout. Then, he concentrates on the list of five names written inside the drawing of the line of fire. Three names are Spanish and two are American. Each name has a number written beside it in reference to their condo location on the drawing.

"You were adding Mr. Page's name when I entered. What did you discover about him?"

Conrado answers, "He is a warrior and a hero and no stranger to firearms."

"But?"

"But he has no motive and no murder weapon."

"Any weapons at all?" Pinero questions.

Conrado explains, "We searched his home. No weapons found."

Pinero glances at the list of names on the white board. Then, asks, "What about the rifles that belong to the other American on the list?"

Conrado says, "Ballistics tests clear his rifles. Those five names are like smoke. There is nothing there other than their condos providing a clear line of fire to the killings and my judgement that those five men could kill without hesitation, without emotion."

Pinero expresses thoughtfulness for a few moments. Then, he asks, "Where does Mr. Page work?"

"On the ship *Antares* at the Rota Naval Base."

Pinero expresses surprise; then, he expresses suspicion. He comments, "So the only two Americans on the list both work on the *Antares*. Is that a coincidence?"

Conrado casts a quizzical stare at Pinero and states, "So you already know about the other American, Curtis Anderson."

Pinero nods confirmation. He states, "My old friend, you know that I am conducting my own investigation—for our mutual friend, Marcio Dario."

Detective Conrado asks in a friendly tone, "What have you uncovered that I do not know?"

Pinero responds, "If your white board represents all that you have uncovered, then you have uncovered more than I. Should I learn anything, I will share it with you."

Detective Conrado casts a doubting look at Pinero because Conrado knows that Pinero's allegiance is to his clients and not to criminal justice.

Chapter 41

Rig sits at the chart table in the control room of the ballistic missile submarine USS *Lafayette*. He has the boat's Equipment Status Log open to the Radio Division page. The *Lafayette* is five-days into its thirty-day upkeep period prior to departing on patrol.

Eleven maintenance items are listed for Radio Division. Each line item includes the sequence number of the related OPNAV FORM 2-Kilo (SHIP'S MAINTENANCE ACTION FORM). All eleven maintenance actions are assigned to the *Antares* Repair Department for action. The last status written in the ESL for all items is that the 2-Kilo forms were submitted to *Antares* five days ago when the *Lafayette* arrived in Rota for upkeep.

Rig closes the ESL binder and places it back on the shelf above the chart table. He exits the control room through the forward door and proceeds to the radio room.

Senior Chief Radioman David Bornadas answers Rig's knock on the radio room door.

Rig looks down into the face of the chubby, medium-height senior chief whose most notable features are his receding, jet-black hair and his bushy mustache.

Rig asks, "Senior Chief Bornadas?"

"Yes," Bornadas answers as he glances at Rig's COMSUBRON THIRTEEN STAFF security badge.

"I'm Senior Chief Page. I'm the COMSUBRON THIRTEEN Leading Radioman. I wanted to introduce myself. I hope you don't mind me showing up unannounced."

Bornadas casts a confused expression at Rig. Then, he appears distracted and looks over his shoulder at something in the radio room. "Uh, let me lock up what I am working on. We

179

can go to the crews mess. I'll buy ya a cup of coffee, and we can talk."

Five minutes later, Senior Chief Page and Senior Chief Bornadas sit down at the chiefs' table in the crews mess. Each hold a coffee cup filled to the mark with lifer juice.

Bornadas asks, "Did Master Chief Parden transfer?"

Master Chief Parden was Rig's predecessor, who had transferred before Rig arrived.

"Yes," Rig answers. "He was selected for COMSUBLANT Command Master Chief and transferred several months ago."

Bornadas stares at Rig for a moment; then, he asks, "What brings you aboard, Senior Chief?"

Rig Responds, "Please call me Rig when we are out of earshot of juniors."

"Okay, Rig, and please call me Dave."

"Okay, Dave. I came aboard to introduce myself to you with the intention of establishing a working relationship. I wanted you to know that should you have any issues with *Antares* message center services you are welcome to contact me for assistance. Also, I ask that you advise me of any situations in maintenance delays that might affect *Lafayette*'s patrol schedule. My duties require that I monitor boomer radio room maintenance actions for any problems that might threaten patrol schedules. So, I will probably be coming around two or three times a week. My boss and your boss have already established a similar working relationship."

Bornadas nods and expresses understanding. He informs, "Master Chief Parden and I had the same working relationship, and I am very satisfied with how it has worked. This is my fourth upkeep in Rota with COMSUBRON THIRTEEN. I have no complaints."

"No problems with message service, then?"

"No real problems. Now and then there is the occasional

poor message copy or a missing message page. Your message center always fixes it in a timely manner. I have nothing to complain about."

"What about the eleven maintenance actions listed in the *Lafayette* ESL?"

"In progress. I do not anticipate any delays and neither do the leading chiefs in the Electronics Repair Department on the tender."

Rig asks, "May I review your division 2-Kilo file?"

"Yes. Anytime. If I am not aboard, ask the duty radioman to let you into Radio."

As Rig departs the *Lafayette*, he performs the required and traditional salutes on the topside deck of the boomer. Then he walks up the gangway between the *Lafayette* and the *Antares*. As he steps onto the deck of the USS *Antares*, "Knock off ship's work" is piped over the 1MC. He goes directly to Main Comm to get an update from the Communications Watch Officer.

The Communications Watch Officer, Chief Radioman McBride, reports, "Just routine, Senior Chief. No communications outages occurred and message traffic flow is at the normal pace. The weekly NAVMACS test was successful. We picked up the *Sam Houston's* communications guard at twelve-hundred. She is scheduled to moor alongside at eighteen-hundred."

"Any personnel problems that I need to know about?"

"Nope."

"Any material problems?"

"One teletype machine and one receiver failed today. All the 2-Kilo work orders have been submitted to the repair shop and the equipment has been tagged."

"Anything I need to know?"

"Chief Benedict called twice this afternoon looking for you."

"Did he say why?"

"No."

Rig nods, then, turns and walks to the *message copy and distribution* area. He grabs his stack of message copies and memos from his slot box. He glances through the stack and finds nothing of action for him. However, there are two messages of some interest. Last night, an *Antares* petty officer was placed in shore patrol protective custody after Spanish Policía spotted the petty officer's vehicle speeding through Rota while being chased by a car with people shooting at the petty officer's car.

Before exiting Main Comm, he checks the weekly preventive maintenance schedule posted in the tech control area. All scheduled maintenance is up to date.

As Rig exits through the Main Comm front door, he comments under his breath, "This senior chief shit is easy." Actually, Rig knows that he is fortunate to have five chiefs working for him that keep the department running well. He knows his navy workload will not always be this light.

Rig decides to track down Chief Benedict before going home for the day.

Chapter 42

Rig enters the Chiefs Mess Dining Room. He scans the room looking for Chief Benedict. The evening meal is being served. Only half the tables are occupied. Those chiefs are either in the duty section or have priority work to be completed on one of the boomers. He does not see Chief Benedict. Rig decides to eat a light dinner before starting the drive to his condo in Sedo Mare Pueblo.

After transiting the steam line, Rig selects an empty table. He sits down with his plate of roast pork and raw veggies topped with vinaigrette dressing from the salad bar. Halfway through his meal, Gordon Benedict sits down beside Rig. Gordon wears dress blues and carries his cover. Rig concludes that Gordon just came aboard. Rig also concludes that he and Gordon are about to engage in a private conversation. Otherwise, Gordon would have sat down across the table facing Rig.

Rig and Gordon first met at Naval Communications Station Greece back in 1968. They were both second class petty officers then. Rig worked in the communications trailers and Gordon was one of the duty cooks in the galley. Rig likes and respects the selfless and friendly Gordon Benedict—now a Chief Mess Management Specialist who supervises both the enlisted galley and the chiefs galley.

"Hey, Gordon, what's up?" Rig asks while casting a friendly smile.

"I have a big favor to ask of you."

Rig keeps the friendly smile as he responds, "Gordon, if it is within my power to provide, I will do so."

A sense of relief comes over Gordon. He asks, "Do you know Quartermaster First Class Curtis Anderson?"

Rig appears thoughtful for a few moments; then, he says,

"Not personally. I read several messages this afternoon about him being in shore patrol protective custody."

"He's my brother-in-law. He's in *deep kimchi* with local criminals. They have threatened to kill him and his entire family, including in-laws. They broke into his condo in Sedo Mare and stole all his personal papers, including addresses and names of all relatives. I just sent my sister a telegram with instructions for all my family and all Curtis's family to go into hiding."

Rig's eyes are wide and his mouth is open. He expresses disbelief. He asks, "How did your brother-in-law get involved with local criminals?"

"Curtis is too scared to talk to anyone, except me. But he did not tell me much. He won't tell the Spanish Policía or the shore patrol. Local Naval Investigative Service agents are trying to intimidate him into talking, but he is silent so far. I don't know what he did."

After Rig considers all that Gordon has said, he asks, "What is the *big* favor you want from me?"

"I need your help in killing that gang of criminals."

Rig flinches and casts an astonished, disbelieving stare into Gordon Benedict's eyes.

Incorrectly interpreting Rig's response, Gordon advises, "Curtis and I have some money saved. We can pay twenty-five-thousand dollars."

Rig is stunned speechless. While still casting an incredulous expression at Gordon, Rig shakes his head to convey that he cannot believe Gordon would ask him to kill.

"Rig, please help us. We are desperate. Killing that gang is the only way to save all our lives."

Rig finally speaks. "I am not a hired killer. I am offended that you think I am."

Gordon pleads. "But you know how to kill people. You killed those criminals in Nea Makri, right? You killed those

184

terrorists. I don't know how to kill and neither does Curtis. At least, you must know people who do, right?"

Rig scans the Chiefs Mess. Only three other chiefs remain.

Again, in a pleading tone, Gordon begs, "Please, Rig, help us. We can't depend on the American government protecting us for the rest of our lives. Killing that gang is the only solution." Gordon shivers. Tears flow from his eyes.

Rig asks, "Where is your brother-in-law, now?"

"In the brig."

"Is he allowed visitors?"

Gordon releases a deep sigh of relief. Rig's question about Curtis's location tells Gordon that Rig might help. "Yes, he is in protective custody, not charged with anything."

Rig stands. He looks down at Gordon and says, "Let's go see him."

Gordon jumps up. His expression has changed to jubilation.

Noting Gordon's change of mood, Rig states, "I am not promising anything. I just want some details from Curtis."

"I understand," Gordon responds. His mood changes to somber anticipation.

Senior Chief Rigney Page, Chief Gordon Benedict, and Petty Officer Curtis Anderson, sit at a table in the brig exercise yard. They are the only people in the yard.

Anderson has the physique of a football lineman but not the confidence. He exhibits fear.

Gordon opens the conversation. "Senior Chief Page can help us. You must tell him everything."

Curtis expresses doubt. He knows Senior Chief Page's reputation as a tough and brave person. He has observed the senior chief jogging long distances around Sedo Mare and coming and going from the condo parking lot a few buildings to the south of his own. Curtis was on deck when the senior chief saved RM3 Wagner from falling to his death. But Curtis is convinced that nothing less than killing his pursuers is the solution to his problem.

Curtis responds, "No offense, Senior Chief, but you're just a senior chief. How can you possibly help us?"

Gordon offers, "Curtis, Senior Chief Page and I have been friends for a long time. He knows people who can help us, and he has skills that he can teach us."

Curtis shakes his head. "There is only one solution to our problem." His tone expresses desperation.

Rig advises, "I don't know if I can help unless you tell me everything."

"If I tell you what I know and what I have been doing, you will report me to the captain."

With a sincere and compassionate expression on his face, Rig promises, "I assure you that I will not inform the chain of command."

Curtis is moved by the Senior Chief's sincerity. "Okay, I'll tell you."

Rig pulls a notepad and pen from his khaki shirt pocket.

Rig says, "Start at the beginning, and no lies."

Curtis nods, indicating his acceptance of Rig's guidance. Curtis tells his story. "It began about six months ago, right after we arrived in Rota. We rented a three-bedroom condo in Sedo Mare Pueblo. I have a wife and three kids. We bought new furniture and bought a new car. We had to take out loans from the Navy Credit Union. We were living beyond our means. Then, one of my Spanish neighbors, Herberto, asked me to sell him American cigarettes and gasoline coupons and American liquor. He was willing to pay double what I paid in the Navy Exchange. I heard the rumors about him being a criminal black market trader. I refused. But, then, I found out that other sailors living in my building were selling to Herberto. I agreed to Herberto's requests because I needed the money. My wife and I do not drink alcohol or smoke and we only used a third of our gasoline rations. The extra money we got for selling Herberto helped us a lot.

"Several weeks later, Herberto gave me a list of items for me to buy at the Navy Exchange and Navy Commissary, and he offered to pay double what I paid. The list included jewelry and cosmetics and children's toys and food items like steak and some spices. I agreed. It got me even with my monthly bills. When I was short on money to buy those things Herberto wanted, Herberto would give me American dollars to buy them.

"Except for one time, all transactions took place in my condo. We had a scheduled time each week—Thursday evenings at nineteen-hundred. In the beginning, only Herberto came to my condo. Then, he started bringing two mean-looking Spaniards with him—Cristóbal and Sandalio. Ya know the type—hardened, street-fighter-scarred faces and lean-muscled.

"Then, about two months ago, Herberto told me he wanted the monthly schedule of arrivals and departures of boomers. He said he would pay me two hundred dollars for each list. At first, I said no. Then, Herberto showed me pictures of my wife and kids with Cristóbal and Sandalio in the background. My wife and kids did not know they were being followed. Then, Herberto showed me some pictures of me giving him American goods and of him giving me money. He must have used a hidden camera that one time we did the transfer in his condo.

"Herberto tried to convince me that giving him boomer schedules would do no harm to anyone because once the boomers arrive or depart, the information is known by everyone anyway.

"Those schedules are classified, and I told Herberto no. Herberto picked up one of the photos of my family shopping in Rota and handed it to Cristóbal who made a sinister face while looking at the photo.

"I caved, and agreed to give him the schedules. After that, Cristóbal and Sandalio were at every meeting. Then, Herberto asked for the local area operating procedures for boomers. That included dive and surface coordinates and communications frequencies. I was too afraid to say no. I just told him I would try because I did not have access to those publications, but that is a lie. Those publications are stored on bookshelves in CIC.

"I was afraid for my wife and kids, so I sent them back to the States.

"Then, one night I came home from the ship and discovered my condo had been broken into. The only thing taken was my private paperwork including my address list of everyone back in the states.

"Soon after that, Cristóbal and Sandalio were murdered. You know; those two who were found dead with that sailor in Sedo Mare Pueblo, I was questioned by the Spanish Policía about those killings. I think I am a suspect."

Rig asks, "Why are you a suspect? Does the Spanish Policía know about your black market dealings with Herberto?"

"I'm not sure," Curtis answers. "Detectives questioned everyone in my building. But those detectives kept coming back to my place. They never ask questions about Herberto. They set up distance measuring equipment on my balcony. I saw the Policía at your building a couple of times. Didn't the Policía talk to you?"

"Yes. They questioned me," Rig states. "Then, they came back a few days later and searched my place."

"They were looking for guns, right?" Curtis questions. "The Policía took my hunting rifles."

"Hunting rifles?" Rig asks—his eyebrows rise.

"Yeah. One is a thirty-aught-six bolt action with a scope and the other is a thirty-thirty lever action with a scope. I'm a hunter—have been all my life. I've gone on several special services hunting trips to the Pyrenees since I've been here. The Spanish Policía knows that about me. That's why I think I am a suspect in Cristóbal's and Sandalio's murders."

Rig directs, "Okay, continue."

"After the killings and after the Policía weren't around so much, Herberto knocks on my door and forces his way in. He said his associates believe I am the one who killed Cristóbal and Sandalio. He demanded I give him my rifles. He was surprised when I told him the Policía had already taken them."

Gordon interrupts, "Ballistics should clear you, right?"

"All I know about that is I didn't do it. Herberto insisted I get him a copy of the Rota Operating Area Procedures. I told him that security procedures were too tight for me to do that. I told him those publications were inventoried every day and that I am never alone with those publications. He told me to find a way or I would learn the penalty for not being innovative. He gave me until Thursday, yesterday, to bring him a copy. Then, he asked me where my family was. I told him they are in America on vacation. He warned me not to try and run because his people were watching me. He told me I can be found anywhere including the Rota Naval Base.

"I actually made a concentrated effort to make an opportunity to be alone in CIC. I stayed aboard Wednesday night and went to CIC at three in the morning, but there is always someone on watch in CIC.

"Yesterday afternoon when I arrived at my condo building and got out of my car, I saw two of Herberto's people walking quickly toward me. I got back in my car and drove away. They followed me in their car. They tried to force me off the road, but I kept driving toward Rota. They started shooting at me. Bullets were zipping by my head. Bullets shattered my car windows. I did not know if they were just trying to pull me over or if they were actually trying to kill me.

"I was speeding through downtown Rota when Policía cars with sirens blaring showed up beside me. One of the policemen yelled at me to pull over. The bullets had stopped flying. I looked in my rearview mirror and saw that those shooters were no longer chasing me.

"After several hours of interrogation in the Rota Policía Station, they turned me over to U.S. Navy shore patrol who brought me here."

Rig asks, "What did you tell the Policía?"

"I told them that I was driving from Sedo Mare to the Rota Naval Base when a car with two men I did not know tried to force me off the road and shot at me. That's all I told them."

Rig asks, "What did you tell the shore patrol?"

"The same thing I told the Policía. Shore patrol did not ask me much. It was the NIS agent who asked me the most probing questions. I told him the same as I told the Spanish Policía."

Gordon states, "They're not going to keep you in here indefinitely."

"They're going to release me tomorrow morning. I will stay on the *Antares*, but I need to get some stuff from my condo."

"No." Rig declares. "That Herberto will be watching your condo. Don't go near it."

"They'll trash my place and steal all my valuable stuff and they might find my tapes."

"What tapes?" Rig asks.

"Audiotapes. My meetings with Herberto in my condo are recorded on audiotapes."

While expressing both surprise and interest, Rig asks, "Why did you tape your meetings with him?"

"Not just him," Curtis explains. "I tape just about everything in my life. It's my journal—my diary. I have radio microphones mounted around my condo that are voice activated and feed my tape recorder. I also keep a portable tape recorder in my car. When I am driving home from work, I record a recap of the day's events."

Rig asks, "Are the microphones out in the open?"

"No. I place them behind furniture and behind hanging pictures."

"Where's the tape recorder?"

"It's in the bottom cabinet of the bar—behind some Spanish wine bottles. Unless you get down on your hands and knees and look into the cabinet, you wouldn't know it was there."

"Where do you keep the tapes?"

"Current ones—last six months—are in a box next to the tape recorder. The ones for past years are sealed up in a box in the closet."

Rig expresses thoughtfulness for a moment; then, he asks, "So your recorder and tapes were not touched when they stole your personal papers?"

"Correct."

After a few moments of thought, Rig asks, "Have you seen these criminals anywhere other than your condo? Like, where do they hang out?"

"I saw Herberto's car at the house of the Sedo Mare construction boss. Ya know; the house next to that fenced in warehouse. And I saw Cristóbal and Sandalio walking around outside that warehouse."

Rig writes some notes; then, he asks. "Is there anything else you know that might connect the construction company to criminal activity?"

Curtis stares curiously at the Senior Chief as he asks, "You think that is important?"

Rig answers, "We need to learn as much as we can about their activities. That means we need to get close to them without being detected. We need to know where they have eyes."

Curtis informs, "I never told Herberto that I can speak Spanish—fluently. Herberto and his friends would speak Spanish, thinking that I could not understand them. They often talked about a man named Marcio Dario. He's some kind of big crime boss. Herberto and all his friends pay tribute to that Marcio and they take orders from him."

Rig casts an impressed, eyebrow-raised stare at the blond-haired, gray-eyed Curtis Anderson. He asks, "How did you come to speak Spanish fluently?"

"My father was a navy officer. When I was six, he was assigned to the U.S. Embassy in Madrid. We lived in a Madrid suburb with Spanish families. All my friends were Spanish. I picked up conversational Spanish quickly. Actually, all the Americans kids who lived in Spanish neighborhoods picked it up quickly. It's a human trait. The younger you are the quicker you pick it up. The American school I went to in Madrid also taught conversational Spanish. We lived in Madrid for four years. I was totally fluent in conversational Spanish when we left. Later, I aced high school Spanish and college Spanish."

"Did you graduate from college?"

"I quit after two years. Wasn't for me. I joined the navy. I never regretted that decision."

"Did you ever hear Herberto and his pals talk about other Americans who were involved in black market trading or selling classified information?"

"Yes, several times. Once, they complained about not being successful at entrapping some navy officers. I think they were talking about those *Antares* officers who were murdered last year."

"We need to get those tapes," Rig declares with determination.

"Why? And you said I couldn't go there."

"I'll get the tapes," Rig states.

"But why?" Curtis asks while expressing bewilderment.

"I have my reasons."

Curtis's tone is skeptical when he asks, "Why are you helping us? You're risking a lot."

Rig does not hesitate with his response. "Like I said, I have my reasons."

Curtis expresses surprise, "You're going to help us, then? I mean in the way we want you to help us?"

"Possibly," Rig answers. "But I do not want you two doing anything until I get back to you."

"So you're okay with the money, then?" Curtis questions.

Rig expresses annoyance, "I am not doing it for the money! I don't want your money!"

"I'm sorry, Senior Chief. I misunderstood. I don't know you."

Gordon places his hand on Rig's shoulder and says, "Thanks, Rig."

Rig casts a serious expression at Gordon while he says in a warning tone, "You might not want to thank me when this is all over. Any plan I devise will deeply involve you and Curtis killing your enemies."

Gordon nods acceptance of Rig's words. His skin pales and his eyes reflect trepidation.

Rig and Arleigh Rouston's sit at Rig's kitchen table. Rig just completed briefing Rouston on the meeting with Chief Gordon Benedict and Petty Officer First Class Curtis Anderson. Rig omits that Benedict and Anderson plan to kill all the criminals involved.

Rouston asks, "Why did Anderson tell you all of that? What does he gain?"

"They want my help. Chief Benedict believes I can use some influence to get them orders back to the States ASAP. If they go through normal channels, they know the chain-of-command will investigate."

Rouston expresses surprise. "What special influence do they think a Senior Chief Radioman has?"

"Chief Benedict and I go back ten years. He suspects that I am more than just a Senior Chief Radioman."

"You need to file a report on that," Rouston reminds.

"I'll do it ASAP."

After a short pause, Rouston inquires, "Do you think Anderson is the one who killed those two Spanish criminals?"

Rig fakes thoughtfulness before he responds. "I don't know, but I think there is a criminal organization that believes he did."

Rouston asks, "How do you want me to proceed."

"Use Director of Naval Intelligence influence to transfer them stateside."

"I'll work on that," Rouston promises. "Anderson must undergo a thorough debrief by ONI analysts before he transfers. He must cooperate fully—providing every detail he knows about the Dario crime family extorting classified documents from U.S. sailors."

"I will tell him that," Rig responds.

Rouston asks, "Do you have a plan for getting those tapes?"

"I need to get into Anderson's apartment without anyone noticing."

"That might be difficult," Rouston informs. "Which building does Anderson live in?"

"Second building to the north of us."

Rouston nods his head. "That follows. The parking lot of that building is under constant watch. One of my operatives noticed the same car with different people sitting in it over several days. I traced their license number—registered to a private detective agency. They must be waiting for Anderson's return."

Rig nods and conveys his understanding of the danger. "That means I need to go in during early morning when even the most vigilant watchdog is nodding off to sleep. I will need a backup team for extraction should I run into trouble."

"No problem," Rouston confirms. "I can arrange that."

Chapter 43

Rig spent two nights surveilling Curtis Anderson's condo building and parking lot from the bedroom window of his own condo. His surveillance revealed that there is always one man with a handheld radio sitting in a car at the entrance to the parking lot. The operative in the car has a clear view of the condo building's front entrance.

On four occasions, Rig observed a second man exiting the building, crossing the parking lot and getting into the passenger seat of the observation car. He concludes that the second man watches Anderson's condo from inside the building.

The time is 0245 and Rig stands on the rain-soaked grass on the east side of Anderson's condo building. Anderson's balcony is three floors above Rig's head. Rig plans to enter Curtis's condo through the balcony above, which is out of view of anyone in the parking lot.

Dark clothing, heavy rain, and an overcast sky conceal his presence from anyone more than ten yards away. Rig wears night-vision headgear; the optics cover his eyes. He easily sees through the night.

He twirls the end of a rope with a rubber-covered grappling hook attached. He twirls the rope in a clockwise rotation. On the fifth approach toward eleven-o'clock position, he releases the rope. The grappling hook travels in an upward arc toward the side of the condo building. The grappling hook hits the side of the building just above the Anderson's balcony; then, it falls ten feet to the balcony's deck.

Rig hears a light *thud* when the rubber coated grappling hook hits the deck of the balcony. Anyone asleep should not have heard the *thud*.

For the next five minutes, he observes the windows and

balcony of Anderson's condo and adjacent condos. No one comes to investigate the source of the *thud*.

Rig pulls on the rope and two of the grappling hooks claws grab hold of the balcony's iron railing. He grips the rope and lifts his feet off the ground. The rope holds his weight.

Rig speaks into the voice activated microphone of his VHF radio headset. "Climbing the rope."

"*Roger.*" Rig hears Rouston's voice in the headset. Rouston sits in a panel van parked on a side street two blocks away. Rouston is Rig's back up and extraction team. Rouston is dressed the same as Rig.

The rain-soaked rope is knotted every two feet. Although the surface of the rope is wet and slippery, the knots make it easier for Rig to climb.

After climbing over the railing of Anderson's condo balcony, Rig reports into the microphone, "On the balcony."

"*Roger,*" Rig hears through the headphones.

Rig tests the balcony door handle. No lock—as Curtis Anderson had briefed. Rig opens the door, steps inside, and shuts the door behind him.

Leoncio Pinero sits in the dark at Curtis Anderson's kitchen table. He forces himself to stay awake. He has been here every night for a week waiting for Curtis Anderson to return. He purposely does not wait in the living room where comfortable seating is available for fear of falling asleep. Abducting Curtis Anderson is priority and earns him a bonus from Marcio Dario.

Pinero detects an increase in the volume of the rain— as if a door opened; he feels a change in air pressure. He thinks he hears the click of a latch bolt—a signal that a door closed. He moves quietly from his chair and crouches alongside the refrigerator. The refrigerator easily hides his thin and medium height physique from view of the kitchen doorway.

Inside the balcony door, Rig finds himself inside the master bedroom—as Curtis Anderson had briefed.

Rig has the floorplan memorized. The bar is in the living room. He moves to the bedroom door. He pulls his suppressor-equipped, short-barrel nine-millimeter Beretta and brings it up to firing position. He steps into the hallway and moves toward the living room. He keeps his weapon raised in firing position.

At the kitchen doorway, he quickly scans the kitchen and sees no threat. He continues along the hallway. Area rugs muffle his footsteps.

Most of the living room can be seen from the hallway. The bar stands on the opposite wall from the living room entrance. Slowly and cautiously he enters the living room; then, he conducts a quick scan and detects no one.

Rig places his Beretta on the bar top; then, he stoops to open the bottom cabinet. He removes wine bottles to get to the rear of the cabinet where the audiotapes are located.

He can't get to the tapes while stooped. He gets down onto his hands and knees. Then, suddenly, he catches a whiff of aftershave, dirty ashtray, and body odor. *Someone is behind me!*

His pistol is on the bar top and out of his immediate reach.

In one powerful, fluid move; Rig pulls his combat knife, jumps to his feet, turns, and swings the knife upward in a forty-five-degree angle. The knife blade slashes a deep cut into Pinero's right forearm, chest, and left shoulder.

Pinero instinctively drops the gun because nerves and muscles in his right forearm no longer function. Pinero's attention shifts to his bloody injuries. He expresses incredulous horror at what just happened to him. He had assumed that the person on hands and knees to be Curtis Anderson—no threat.

While Pinero is distracted by his injury, Rig delivers a powerful kick to Pinero's groin. When Pinero bends forward to hold his genitals, Rig knees him in the face. Pinero falls backward to the floor—screaming in pain.

Knowing that the screams will draw attention, Rig kicks Pinero in the temple. His steel-toed boot cracks Pinero's skull.

Pinero becomes silent.

Rig sheaths his knife. He stoops over Pinero and assesses the damage. The man is dressed in black and has black greasepaint on his face and back of his hands.

With his left hand, Rig grabs hold of Pinero's hair. With his right hand, he grabs hold of Pinero's chin. Then, he jerks Pinero's head to the side more than 140 degrees. The crunching sound affirms the man's head and spine are now separated.

Quickly, Rig retrieves the box of audiotapes next to the tape recorder. He stows the tapes and Pinero's revolver into his backpack; then, he holsters his own handgun.

Rig stares down at the dead man. Even through the green hue of the night-vision goggles, he easily recognizes Leoncio Pinero from the photos he took in front of the *Áureo Orilla* nightclub, later identified by Jack Tacker. Blood spreads out on the flokati area rug under the body. The wool in the rug soaks up the blood like a sponge.

He rolls up Pinero's body in the flokati rug. He secures the roll with duct tape that he found in a kitchen drawer. Rig slings the rolled-up rug with the body inside over his right shoulder—like a sailor carries his sea bag. Through his night vision goggles, he inspects the floor for traces of blood. No blood is evident.

When he arrives on the balcony, he tosses the rolled-up rug over the railing. When the body hits the rain-soaked grass, the *thud* is only slightly audible.

Rig speaks into the voice activated microphone. "Two for extraction."

"Two?"

"Me and one deceased."

"Roger."

Rig removes the grappling hook from the balcony railing and drops it to the ground next to the dead man. Then, Rig climbs over the balcony railing and jumps to the balcony below. He repeats the action to get to the ground floor.

Several minutes later, Rig opens the rear door of the panel van and tosses the rolled-up rug into the van. Then, he climbs into the back of the van and sits beside Pinero's body. Two minutes later, Rouston is driving the panel van toward the salt marsh that is located the other side of the valley's southern hills.

"Did ya get the tapes?"

"Yeah."

"Who's the dead guy?"

"A rookie," Rig answers calmly.

"Rookie?"

"Yeah, I smelled him coming."

"Did you leave a mess behind?"

Rig replies, "I don't think I left any mess. I think all the blood is trapped in the flokati rug."

"Are you sure?"

"No blood came through to the backside of the rug. His heart stopped pumping soon after I cut him."

"Okay, I won't chance sending in a cleanup crew, then."

After a few moments of silence, Rouston compliments, "You're a natural in this business. I see you as a mission planner and mission controller someday."

Twenty minutes later, Rouston parks the van at the end of a dirt road one-half mile from the main road. The odor of the salt water marsh fills their senses and the heavy damp air presses against their bodies.

Rouston keeps the motor running, turns off the headlights,

and turns on the interior light.

Rig searches the dead man's clothes for personal items. He finds a leather I.D. wallet. He hands the I.D. wallet to Rouston for examination. Then, Rig removes the dead man's shoes, clothes, and jewelry.

Rouston advises, "He is a private detective named Leoncio Pinero."

"Don't know the name," Rig lies.

"I do," Rouston informs. "He was investigating the death of those two hoods killed in the streets of Sedo Mare by a sniper—hired by Marcio Dario."

Rig carries the naked dead body of Leoncio Pinero, fireman style, along a dirt path with marshy water on both sides. A flashlight in his right hand illuminates the way.

Five minutes later, Rig opens the front passenger door of the panel van.

"I got blood all over my clothes. Hand me the bag with my change of clothes. I'll change out here."

Rouston turns off the interior light; he asks, "I heard a splash. How far down the path did you dump him?"

"At a turn in the path where I saw a large, four-legged, hairy animal that I could not identify."

Rouston states, "Good chance that the body will never be found."

Rig speculates, "Good chance that there will be no body by this time tomorrow."

At the compound on the Rota Naval Base where Rouston stores ONI vehicles, Rouston parks the van inside the Quonset hut garage. After exiting the vehicle, Rig and Rouston inspect each other under the overhead lights to ensure the other has no blood splatters. They are both clean.

Rouston advises, "I will have a cleanup crew scrub the

vehicle and burn the rug and burn your blood-stained clothes."

They each get into their own cars. Rouston drives back to his condo in Sedo Mare. Rig drives to the *Antares*. He plans to get some sleep before working hours start.

Chapter 44

Rig and Arleigh Rouston sit at Rig's kitchen table and sip coffee. Rouston has a mission for Rig. "I have something that I want you to investigate. You will need to go into the *Rota Gut*, specifically the *Texas Bar*. Are you familiar with it?"

"I haven't been to the *Rota Gut* in ten years, but I do remember some bars named after U.S. States."

Rouston explains, "Two nights ago, a sailor from the naval base, one Engineman Second Class Alvin Jones, was charged with one count of *Drunk and Disorderly* and three counts of *Assault and Battery*. According to witness statements, Jones had become drunk and loudmouthed while drinking at the *Texas Bar* and Hotel, located close to the Rota harbor waterfront. He had arrived at the bar around 6:30 PM. The bar patrons were mostly sailors on liberty from the USS *Coleman*, a destroyer. Jones attempted to pick a fight with every *Coleman* sailor that entered the bar. Eventually, several Coleman sailors became annoyed with Jones's insults and told Jones to *shut his fucking mouth*. Jones responded by throwing himself at the table while kicking and swinging his fists. A brutal fight ensued. The Spanish bartender called the Policía. The Naval Base Shore Patrol, augmented with USS *Coleman* Shore Patrol, was on the scene first and had Jones restrained and handcuffed by the time the Spanish Policía arrived.

"Because the *Texas Bar* owner would not press charges, the Spanish Policía did not arrest Jones. The Naval Base Shore Patrol locked EN2 Jones in the *drunk tank*.

"Normally, fights in bars between sailors on liberty are not of naval intelligence interest. However, photos of the fight scene came with the report from Naval Investigative Service."

Rouston hands three, five-by-eight color photographs to

203

Rig.

The second photograph causes Rig to flinch with surprise. Sitting on a tabletop are some empty cocktail glasses and three empty bottles of *Imperio Aqua* with red labels, which identify the water source as the underground river beneath the *Imperio Construir* warehouse in Sedo Mare Pueblo.

"Jones was sitting at that table drinking scotch and water for several hours before the fight."

Rig studies each photograph again, looking for more bottles of red labeled *Imperio Aqua* on other tables. He doesn't see any. Then, he asks, "Is NIS aware of the ONI investigation into the underground river at Sedo Mare?"

Rouston responds, "I was ordered not to reveal that investigation to anyone outside naval intelligence, and NIS has said nothing to me about it. I believe they are not aware."

Rig nods and expresses understanding. He asks, "Okay, what do you want me to do?"

"I want you to find out what's going on with that water at bars in *The Gut*, especially those bars frequented by U.S. Military personnel. You should start with the *Texas Bar.*"

"Looks like my nightlife is about to become interesting."

Near the Rota harbor waterfront, an economic zone exists that American sailors call *The Gut*. For most establishments in *The Gut*, a sleazy bar occupies the first floor, and a cheap whorehouse operates in the upper floors. Ageless, rundown stucco buildings of fading pastel colors line the narrow streets. The road surface is a patchwork of brick and cobblestone and zigzags at irregular angles around oddly shaped buildings. Alleyways dart into darkness and can end without notice. Windows caked in decades of grime and the smell of rotting garbage and sewer lend to the *unwashed* atmosphere.

The Gut exists in most foreign ports visited by the American

Navy. Business names like the *California Bar* and the *Texas Bar* attempt to defraud American sailors into a sense of belonging in a place far away from home. However, sailors are not attracted by the names of these enterprises. They are attracted by the honesty of those businesses' marketing techniques. Sex is for sale, and no business attempts a subtle *soft sell*. Sailors are willing buyers and do not haggle the price.

As twilight transitions, neon signs flicker to full illumination in random order throughout *The Gut*. Sailors stand outside the doors of their favorite bar. They came ashore with their friends in groups of three or four. More than half the sailors are smoking and when they inhale the night appears to be infested with fireflies. Many, who started drinking earlier, stagger along the sidewalk. The occasional inebriated sailor who wanders away from his friends and staggers alone becomes the target of thieves.

Rig parks the untraceable ONI car one block from the *Texas Bar*. He scans the area. U.S. Navy sailors crowd the narrow street. Although they are dressed in civilian clothes, U.S. Navy sailors are easily identifiable because of their short hair and American casual wear. Rig is dressed the same so that he blends in. However, for this mission, he colored his hair black and he applied fake sideburns and a mustache that are at the limit of navy grooming regulations.

Rig knows that most of the U.S. Sailors in *The Gut* tonight are assigned to the one submarine and three surface ships moored at the Rota Naval Base piers. Few sailors on shore duty in Rota party in *The Gut*. Rig observes about a dozen sailors wearing Italian Navy uniforms. Rig considers that he is at low risk of encountering anyone he knows.

The last time Rig came to *The Rota Gut* was ten years ago.

Back then, U.S. Navy sailors who were first class petty officers and below and assigned to ships on overseas deployment were required to wear their dress uniform in foreign liberty ports. Then, during 1970 when Admiral Zumwalt became Chief of Naval Operations, he changed the uniform requirements for ships on overseas deployment and allowed first class petty officers and below to wear civilian clothes on liberty.

Rig enters the *Texas Bar*. He stops inside the door and exhibits that he searches for an open table. Actually, he checks for rear exits and counts the number of American sailors and number of people of other nationalities. Rig determines that all the patrons are American sailors. He estimates thirty American sailors. None of the sailors wear their navy uniform.

Like most bars and brothels in sailor haunts around the world, the *Texas Bar* smells like a dirty ashtray mixed with the smell of body odor and sewer. Cigarette smoke hangs like a cloud. The floors are littered and dirty. Walls are caked with grime. Lights are dim to hide the crud. Loud voices with occasional bursts of laughter fill the room. Frequently, strings of foul language rise above the din. The staircase to the upstairs brothel is on his right, and sailors with their prostitute of choice flow up and down the stairs.

Rig counts ten *Texas Bar* employees. Two are male bartenders. Two are waitresses. Five are prostitutes—one is leading a sailor up the stairs to the brothel.

The tenth employee is a tall, wiry Spaniard with pitch-black hair and mustache and a deeply tanned and scared face—*the bouncer*. The bouncer sits in a straight-back, wooden chair at the foot of the stairs that lead up to the brothel.

No empty tables. So, Rig makes his way to an empty stool at the bar. Within seconds, the bartender, a lean Spaniard in his early twenties, asks in broken English, "What drink want you?"

Rig glances at the bottles on the back bar. Then, he requests,

"Chivas Regal and water—no ice."

"Chivas much money—one shot five American dollars."

"No problem," Rig responds, expressing a pleasing smile.

"No tap water," the bartender advises. "Bottle only—warm—no cold. One American dollar more. Six dollars all."

"No problem," Rig responds, maintaining his pleasing smile.

Rig watches the bartender. The bartender walks to the end of the bar where he reaches down under the bar and pulls a bottle of water from a cardboard box. The bartender returns to Rig's position and places the bottle of water and an empty glass on the bar top in front of Rig. Then, the bartender reaches to the back bar and grabs a bottle of Chivas Regal. An auto measure is attached to the bottle's opening. The bartender pours one shot—43 milliliters—into Rig's glass.

Rig slides a ten-dollar bill across the bar top and tells the bartender, "Keep the change."

The bartender expresses appreciation and says, "Thank you, sailor. All things you want you ask me." The bartender points at himself and says, "Me, Reinaldo."

"I will do that," Rig promises.

Reinaldo walks off to serve other customers.

Rig considers the overpriced shot of Chivas Regal. The same shot costs one-hundred-seventy pesetas—two dollars and fifty cents—at the beach bars in Sedo Mare Pueblo.

His attention turns to the eight-ounce bottle of water that came with his drink. He stares thoughtfully at the green label on the bottle. Then, he scans the room to locate other water bottles. He finds a total of four bottles among the twenty-some tables. All water bottles have the *Imperio Aqua* green label.

Normally, Rig drinks scotch *neat*—no water and no ice. He sips the scotch *neat*, followed with a gulp of water. He repeats sips and gulps until he consumes all the scotch and all the water from the bottle. Then, he motions to Reinaldo to deliver another drink.

Reinaldo acknowledges the order for another drink. He checks the water case and finds it empty. He walks out from behind the bar and turns right down a hallway.

Rig concludes that the stockroom is down that hall. He also notices signs for the toilet down that same hall. He assumes that a rear exit will be located in the stockroom.

Moments later, Reinaldo returns to the bar with a case of *Imperio Aqua*. Rig notes that a green-colored logo, identical to the green labels on bottles, is printed on the outside of the case.

Reinaldo places a clean glass and an eight-ounce bottle of *Imperio Aqua* in front of Rig. He pours a shot of Chivas in to Rig's glass.

Rig slides another ten-dollar bill across the bar top, and says, "Keep the change."

Reinaldo knows from experience that fleet sailors are not big tippers because they have little money. He senses that the big tipper is not an ordinary fleet sailor. He stares curiously at Rig as he asks, "You live Rota much time?"

"No."

"You work naval base, yes?"

"No."

Reinaldo expresses confusion. He decides not to inquire further because persistence might stop the generous tips. "Okay, sir. You want all things, you ask Reinaldo."

In an inquiring tone, Rig asks, "Toilet?"

Reinaldo points toward the hallway that leads to the rear of the building.

Rig slips off the barstool. His drink is only half consumed. He points at the stool and says. "Save."

"No problem. I watch."

Rig bypasses the door to the toilet and walks toward the storeroom door, which is halfway open. He slips through the door opening.

The store room is brightly illuminated. Within several seconds he finds the two side-by-side stacks of water cases. The five cases stacked on the right have the *Imperio Aqua* green label. The four cases stacked on left have the *Imperio Aqua* red label. Each of the red label cases has a large black **X** drawn on the box face over the red logo. Taped to the top red label case is a sheet of paper with tomorrow's date. Rig concludes that those cases with red labels will be picked up by the *Imperio Aqua* Company tomorrow.

The storeroom door opens wider and the other bartender enters. He catches Rig standing in front of the stack of red label water cases. "What you want?" the bartender asks in a suspicious tone.

Rig expresses confusion as he asks in an inquiring tone, "Toilet?"

The bartender points toward the doorway.

Rig walks out of the storeroom.

As Rig walks along the hallway, the bartender stares suspiciously at Rig's back. He had noticed Rig standing close to the stacks of water cases. The bartender knows that the red label water is not to be used; he does not know why. He also knows that the water supplier will pick up the stacks of red label water tomorrow.

After making a stop at the toilet, Rig returns to his barstool.

The other bartender returns to the bar. He whispers into Reinaldo's ear while staring at Rig. Then, he walks to where the bouncer sits and whispers into the bouncer's ear.

The bouncer stares suspiciously at Rig.

No one who works in the *Texas Bar* knows why they stopped serving the water with the red label. They just know that several nights ago they were ordered not to serve it and that the supplier would pick up the remaining bottles of water. The employees were also ordered by the owner to report to him anyone who showed interest in the water with the red labels.

Rig lays another five-dollar bill on the bar top. He slips off the barstool and motions for Reinaldo's attention.

When Reinaldo looks in Rig's direction, Rig points to the five-dollar bill on the bar top and says, "Thank you, again, Reinaldo."

Rig walks toward the door with his eyes straight ahead. He watches the bouncer out of the corner of his eye.

The bouncer stares at Rig until Rig disappears out the door.

After Rig exits the *Texas Bar*, he turns left and walks in the direction the *California Bar*.

During the next hour, Rig investigates the *California Bar* and the *Florida Bar*. He finds the same situation with red label water in the storeroom of both bars and with a sign not to use, as he did in the *Texas Bar*.

Now, Rig sits on a barstool in the *Florida Bar*. He concludes that someone fucked up at the Sedo Mare warehouse and shipped red label water to local distributers. He decides that he does not need to investigate another bar.

The bouncer from the *Texas Bar* and the bouncer from the *California Bar* enter the bar where Rig sits. Rig pretends to be nonchalantly sipping a drink, but he watches the two bouncers. The bouncers stare at Rig for a few moments. Then, they walk across the bar to the *Florida Bar* bouncer who sits on a barstool near the stairs leading up to the brothel. The three bouncers engage in conversation. Rig notes that the men wear cheap suits and that they are chain smokers.

A sense of trepidation flows through Rig's mind. He continues to sip his drink as he watches the three bouncers out of the corner of his eye.

Rig places his right hand on his left forearm and feels the

dagger in its sheath through the cloth of his jacket. The dagger is his only weapon. When he dressed earlier in his condo, the thought that he might need to fight his way out of *The Gut* never entered his mind. The only reason he had for strapping on the dagger is the field operative rule to never go on a mission without a weapon. Considering the look and manner of those three bouncers, Rig regrets not bringing a handgun. The small Beretta would have easily fit into his jacket pocket. Both Rig and Rouston underestimated the need for weapons and the need for a backup and emergency extraction plan.

Another Spanish man, equal in street-fighter appearance to the others, exits the bar office and joins the three bouncers. The four men exchange words. One glances in Rig's direction. Then, all four men exit the bar through the front door.

Rig has lost the opportunity to dash for the front door and get a leading run on these heavy smokers. Now, those tough street fighters lie in wait for Rig to exit the bar.

His ONI vehicle is three blocks away. During mission preparation, Rig had memorized a map of *The Gut*. He calculates four different routes to the ONI vehicle. Two of those routes include exiting the bar through the rear entrance. Rig puts a ten-dollar bill on the bar top, rises from the bar stool, and walks toward the storeroom.

Rig turns out the light in the storeroom and closes the door to the hallway. His eyes need to adjust to the dark before he dashes into the darkness of the alley.

Two minutes later, Rig is confident his eyes have adjusted.

As he approaches the rear door, he considers that thugs could be waiting just beyond the door in the dark of the alley. With his right hand, he reaches underneath the left cuff of his jacket and retrieves the dagger and holds it reverse style.

He keeps the blade close to his forearm, resulting with the knife being hidden from the sight of others. Rig conceals the knife because he needs to surprise any thug who gets close enough to harm him.

Rig opens the door; then dashes into the alley. He turns right and begins the three-block sprint to his vehicle. The familiar smell of *The Gut*, sewer and rotting garbage, fills his nostrils.

His memorized route specifies that he turn right at the first street.

Rig is thirty feet from the end of the alley when two of the bouncers walk from the street into the alley. Rig increases his speed and tightens his grip on the dagger.

The two bouncers, sensing that their target will not slow down, reach for their weapons. One bouncer is armed with a switchblade and the other bouncer is armed with an expandable steel baton.

Rig makes a leap toward the bouncer on the right.

The bouncer on the right has not yet cleared the expandable baton from his pocket when Rig swings out his right arm, holding the dagger in reverse position. The dagger blade cuts deep through the bouncer's neck—severing the jugular vein and slicing open the windpipe. The power behind the dagger knocks the bouncer down.

Rig lands on his feet and faces the other bouncer.

The bouncer stands between Rig and the street. They are seven feet apart and stand in the illumination of a street light.

The bouncer points his open switchblade at Rig and shouts a few words in Spanish.

Rig waves his left backhand toward the bouncer. Rig is motioning for the bouncer to run away.

The bouncer, who is an experienced knife fighter, glances at his compadre who lies dying in the filth of the alley. He fears for his own life knowing that the American will not hesitate to kill. Rig stands seven inches taller than the bouncer, outweighs the bouncer by thirty pounds, and has a longer reach. The bouncer looks into Rig's eyes; then, he glances at Rig's dagger. He understands that the American is telling him to run away.

Gasping gurgling sounds come from the thug who lies dying in the slime of the alley.

The switchblade wielding bouncer backs out of the alley, turns left, and runs away.

Rig runs out of the alley and turns right. During the run to his vehicle, Rig hugs the shadows of the streets and the darkness of alleys. In the streets he runs past dozens of American sailors. During the run, he glances over his shoulder several times. He sees no one chasing him.

During the thirty-minute ride to his condo building, Rig removes the mustache and sideburns and he slips on a pullover sweatshirt with a hood. He raises the hood over his head to conceal his black colored hair.

He parks the ONI vehicle in his condo parking lot.

The lights in the condo building lobby reveal dried blood splatters across his trousers and shoes. He enters the elevator and pushes the button for his floor. Two minutes later, he enters his apartment. He did not encounter anyone on his journey from the parking lot to his condo.

After taking a shower and washing the black coloring from his hair, he telephones Rouston and advises they need to meet immediately.

Three days later, Rouston and Rig sit at Rig's kitchen table. Rouston passes a copy of the local Spanish newspaper to Rig.

Rig reads the headline. His limited Spanish allows him to comprehend that the article is about the homicide of a Spanish man in an alley near the harbor. Accompanying the article is a police artist color sketch of the suspected killer's face.

Rouston comments, "The article claims the person in the

sketch is an American sailor and is a *person of interest* in the killing."

Rig responds, "The person in that sketch has black hair, sideburns, and a mustache. Don't think I have seen that sailor anywhere."

"He looks a little like you," Rouston claims.

"The eyes and chin are not the same."

Rouston expresses thoughtfulness.

"What are you thinking?" Rig asks.

"These Spanish criminals are rookies at international espionage. They do not understand the power of their enemy. That makes them dangerous and unpredictable."

Rig comments, "I just hope that life I took is worth the intel I gathered."

Rouston nods while expressing acknowledgement of Rig's comment. Then, he advises. "Your report has been sent to the ONI analysis section. The way I see it, someone in the *Imperio Aqua* Company fucked up by delivering that red label water to those bars. Had *Imperio Aqua* not retrieved that water, its effects would have become well known to American authorities within a few days. *Imperio Aqua* decided to protect that water with deadly force. Now they know Americans are investigating and know that our investigator is a trained operative who does not hesitate to kill when necessary.

Chapter 45

Rig was specific in his weapons request to Jack Tacker. Each sniper rifle must be custom made and untraceable to Americans. Each sniper rifle must come with a night-optic scope, day scope, and a suppressor and with custom ammunition. Jack called Rig last night and advised that he is ready to deliver the weapons. They agreed to meet aboard Rig's boat at Chipiona Marina.

Jack enters the cabin of Rig's boat.

Rig stands as Jack enters. He is slightly bowed at the waist to prevent hitting his head on the overhead beams.

The two men exchange handshakes and pleasantries.

Jack Tacker hands Rig two leather cases; he advises, "These two rifles are the same as the one that I gave you before."

"Did you have them made on my request?"

"No." Jack answers. "I have a dozen of these."

Jack removes his overcoat.

Rig hands Jack a snifter of French brandy.

The two men sit down at the galley table.

Jack hands Rig an envelope and informs, "This is the report on that navy lieutenant you requested."

"Thanks." Rig stuffs the envelope in his pocket; then says, "I will read the details later. Tell me the short version."

Jack reports, "Lieutenant Barry Gradinski pilots cargo planes. He has been based in Rota for nearly a year. He has been to captain's mast twice for beating up women—one was a woman he was dating when stationed in Norfolk and the other was a Barcelona prostitute. When he is in town, he frequents brothels on nights he is not with Christine Hawthorne. His flight crew thinks he is the biggest asshole they have ever served under. He was passed over for Lieutenant Commander last cycle. Interesting, though, my operative says he comes across as polite and charming when he is with your friend Christine Hawthorne. She spent some nights at his place, and he at hers. The nights you have spent with her are when he is out of town. More details about him in the written report."

"What about his physical appearance?" Rig asks.

"Five feet and nine inches, thin and wiry, brown hair, and in good shape. He spends two hours in the base gym on mornings when he is not flying. While stationed in Norfolk, he earned his blue-belt in Karate but has not continued his karate training since he left Norfolk a year ago."

"Thanks," Rig says in an appreciative manner. "My bill with *The Guardians* must be gigantic."

Jack smiles and chuckles. "Since you arrived in Spain, *The Guardians* have provided you with thirty-thousand-dollars-worth of weapons and equipment, and ten-thousand-dollars-worth of private investigations." Jack pauses for a moment; then, he comments, "During my years with *The Guardians*, I have never seen such willingness come from above to serve a field operative. My controller has not told me why *The Guardians* are so generous towards you. Obviously, you are an asset of value."

"*The Guardians* have been generous, and I know that I must provide services in return, which I do willingly. Anyway, I will return all the weapons before I transfer from Rota."

Jack states, "You have stirred up a blood-revenge crusade in the local crime family. They are all related. They will spare no expense in tracking you down."

"I will be careful."

"You need to be," Jack cautions. Then, he asks in a curious tone, "Where do I sleep?"

Rig points forward and says, "Bunks and head."

Chapter 46

Rig's sailboat drifts in a calm sea two-miles west of the Chipiona Marina. Both the mainsail and the jib are lowered and secured. Mid-afternoon sunlight is filtered by a partly-cloudy sky. A crisp and mild wind blows from the west.

One hour ago, Rig deployed two, man-sized, towed-target buoys. The buoys are now fifty yards astern and twenty feet apart.

Rig, Gordon Benedict, and Curtis Anderson stand in the stern well. During the past hour, Rig has instructed Gordon and Curtis on the safety features and operation of the custom-made sniper rifles that Rig obtained from Jack Tacker. As part of that instruction, they fired several rounds into the water.

Now, they fire at the human images on the towed targets, focusing their crosshairs on the center torso where the heart is. Curtis shoots at the target on the left, and Gordon shoots at the target on the right. The ripple of the water causes the targets to move slightly from side to side and bob slightly up and down.

After Gordon and Curtis fired a dozen rounds each, they retrieved the target buoys. A check of the targets revealed that every bullet fired hit the target and most hit mid-chest where the heart would be located.

Rig informs, "After dark, we will practice with the night scopes."

Gordon responds, "You said that you have prepared a plan."

"Yes. Let's go below and I will explain."

Several minutes later, they are sitting at the booth-style table in the sailboat's cabin. They are sipping ice-cold San Miguel beer from brown bottles.

Rig explains, "Those crooks who are after you are part of a mafia-style family that controls all criminal activity from Cadiz to the Portugal border, including the city of Seville. The head man is Marcio Dario. His brothers and their male children are his lieutenants. Every Thursday evening, they all gather at Marcio's villa on the Rota beach along *Avenida Punta Candor*. That is when we will hit them."

Curtis asks, "Is Herberto one of the family members who attends that meeting?"

"Yes," Rig confirms.

"Won't the place be guarded?" Curtis asks in an anxious tone.

"No. There is no reason to have guards. I mean, the place has the usual burglar systems, but no armed guards roving outside."

Curtis and Gordon exchange doubtful expressions. Curtis challenges, "How do you know these things?"

"I have trustworthy sources," Rig says confidently.

While shaking his head slightly and expressing doubt, Gordon questions, "But why would they not have guards. It makes no sense."

Rig advises, "Their crime organization has no competition. They totally own the criminal activities in this area. They annihilated what little competition existed decades ago. They own public officials and the Policía. They have nothing to fear; so, they have no reason to be concerned about being attacked."

"What about the assassinations of Cristóbal and Sandalio? That should have put them on guard."

"I don't think they are convinced that was an attack by other crime families. I mean they are still looking at Americans as suspects. Plus, during their last meeting at that Rota beach villa, more than a month after Cristóbal and Sandalio were killed, they had no guards posted. So, I do not anticipate any guards."

Curtis nods acceptance of Rig's assessment. He says, "Okay, Senior Chief, tell us your plan."

Rig spends the next twenty minutes explaining the plan. He uses drawings of the Marcio Dario's villa compound and approach streets. After he is done explaining, both Gordon and Curtis are ashen faced and express fear.

Rig says, "You two are thinking that when it comes time to pull the trigger and kill, you will not be able to do it, right?"

"That's what I am thinking," Gordon admits.

"Yeah, me too," Curtis confesses.

Rig counsels, "When it comes time to pull the trigger for the first time, you'll hesitate while considering the morality of killing and the mortality of your target. But you are not really considering your target's mortality. Subconsciously, you are considering your own mortality and how easily someone who does not know you can take your life. Get over those fears. Think about your families and their futures with these violent criminals pursuing them. Get it straight in your mind beforehand. If you hesitate, we lose and could be killed in the process."

Curtis promises in a sincere voice, "I'll be mentally ready when the time comes."

"Me too," Gordon asserts.

After a few moments of silence, Rig says, "Gordon, please go topside for some air. I need to talk to Curtis, privately."

After Gordon has departed the cabin, Rig asks Curtis, "During all those conversations you overheard in Spanish between those crooks, did they ever reveal that the Dario family owns the Sedo Mare Valley and *Imperio Construer*?"

Curtis appears thoughtful for a few moments; then, he answers, "No. Do they?"

Rig says, "You will be questioned by some American intelligence agents regarding what you know about the killing of those two officers in Sedo Mare and the connection to the Dario Crime family."

"Yes. I know. You told me. I'm ready for it."

"During your interview with those intelligence agents, I want you to tell them that you overhead conversations between members of the Dario family that revealed Marcio Dario owns the Sedo Mare Valley and *Imperio Construer.*"

"Okay, Rig. I can do that. Does he own it?"

"Yes."

"Wow! That answers some questions I was wondering about."

Chapter 47

Rig enters the lobby of the Chipiona Marina Yacht Club. He walks directly to the receptionist and asks, "Can I make a call to the United States from the club."

"Yes, sir, if you are a member."

"I am."

"Pick up any house phone and dial zero. The club operator will assist you."

"How do I pay for it?"

"Phone charges will be entered on your monthly statement."

Rig goes to the lounge and finds a house phone on an end table next to an overstuffed chair. He sits, picks up the phone handset, then dials zero.

"Si, digame."

"I would like to make a call to the United States."

"Your name and club member identification number and city and telephone number calling, please."

Rig provides the information.

"Thank you, sir. I will call you at this extension when your call is ready."

For the next twenty minutes, Rig anxiously waits for the call to be connected. He speculates as to what could be so important that would cause his father to send a telegram telling him to call.

The phone rings. Rig picks up.

"Mr. Page, your call to the United States is ready."

"Thank you, please patch me through."

"Hello, Dad."

"Rig! Son! Great to hear your voice! How are things in Spain?!"

"Routine, Dad. I am enjoying my tour. Doing a lot of

sailing."

"Great! Europe must be more fun now than when I was there during World War II."

"Dad, the telegram, what's up?"

"Strangest thing happened yesterday morning while your Uncle Dave and I were preparing the boat for a fishing trip to Catalina. The Long Beach Police and the FBI showed up on the dock and presented me with a search warrant. Uniformed cops searched the boat while some suits questioned me and Dave about Weston Pyth. You know. That reporter from the *Long Beach Times* that disappeared."

"What were the police searching for?"

"The warrant said personal belongings of Weston Pyth and other evidence of his presence onboard."

"Did they find anything?"

"Of course not. That asshole has never been aboard my boat."

Rig recalls finding Weston Pyth's wristwatch in the forward void of his father's boat during the weekend prior to Rig departing for Spain. Pyth had disappeared months before Rig found the wristwatch. Rig had concluded that his father killed Pyth and dumped Pyth's body into the sea. He also thinks that his Uncle Dave was a co-conspirator. Rig did not tell his father about the wristwatch. He did not want his father to know that he knows. Rig now fears that the police are closing in on his father.

"Son, are you still there."

"Uh, yes. What do you think it all means?"

"I guess they think I have something to do with that son-of-a-bitch's disappearance."

With a cautious tone, Rig ask, "Why would they think that?"

"Beats me."

Silence falls over their conversation.

A few moments later James Page states, "Something else was strange."

"What?"

"When the police started their search, they went directly to the forward void where we store the beer and scuba gear, as if they were looking for something specific and expecting to find it. They appeared befuddled when they found nothing in the void or anything anywhere on the boat for that matter."

"What about fingerprints?" Rig asks, hoping the police did not search for fingerprints.

"Yes, they spent hours going over the boat with fingerprint techs, but that bastard was never aboard my boat. Besides, I have marina services wash that boat down with soap and fresh water every three months. Last time was just a few weeks ago."

The confidence in his father's tone causes Rig to reconsider his father's involvement in Pyth's disappearance. For the first time since he found Pyth's wristwatch, he considers that his father did not kill Pyth and that his father might be the target of a frame.

Rig speculates, "Pyth could have boarded your boat and planted something to make it look like you held him aboard your boat. Remember that you threatened him outside the sheriff's office."

James Page inhales sharply; then he blurts, "That deceiving little shit. He is trying to frame me for something."

Rig exhales a sigh of relief as he concludes that his father did not kill Pyth. A heavy burden has been lifted off his shoulders. He comments, "Looks like Pyth failed at whatever he might be trying."

James Page responds, "I am thinking that Pyth and that fucking union are still trying to destroy our family."

Without much thought, Rig blurts, "It's what Marxists do! When protests and deceit fail, they turn to force!" Rig calms somewhat and then adds, "Pyth has gone underground for a reason."

"Don't worry son. I am taking precautions."

Rig offers, "I want to help with those precautions."

"How?"

"I will send someone. Please follow his instructions." Rig will ask *The Guardians* to send someone to help.

"Okay. I will."

The conversation pauses for a few moments, Rig says, "No use in paying for dead air. Thanks for letting me know."

"When will you be back in the States?"

"I don't know for certain."

"Keep in touch, son."

"I will."

For several minutes after hanging up, Rig considers the possibilities of why Weston Pyth went underground. Then, he picks up the phone handset and dials zero which connects him to the marina operator.

"Si, digame."

"This is Rigney Page, again. I need to call *La Línea da la Concepíon*."

"What is the number, Mr. Page?"

Rig provides the number. Less than one minute later, Jack Tacker answers.

"Hello, Jack, Rig here."

"Hi, Rig. I was about to call you. We need to meet."

Jack specifies the time and place.

Chapter 48

An overcast moonless night hides Rig as he crouches against the seaward wall of Marcio Dario's villa compound in Rota. The pounding surf and whistling twelve-knot wind cancel the sound of his movements. His black colored clothing and the black grease paint on his face and hands cast him as a shadow.

He wears his usual mission vest of many zippered pockets that contain the tools of his trade. His backpack contains the explosive devices that he will plant inside the villa. Tonight, the only weapon he carries is a short-barrel nine-millimeter Beretta in a holster on his belt. Although he does not anticipate that he will need to fight his way out of the villa, he must be prepared to do so. He checks his watch—2:28 AM. He knows from surveillance reports provided by Jack Tacker that the only person inside Dario's villa during this day of the week and at this time of night is a live-in, middle-age-woman housekeeper whose bedroom is located in the southwest corner of the villa.

Several minutes ago, he checked the gate on the seaward wall. The gate was locked, which did not surprise him. The gate is constructed of eight-inch-wide by four-inch-thick wood planks and is the same height as the wall—twelve feet.

He throws the grappling hook with rope attached to the top of the twelve-foot-high wall. The grappling hook takes hold. Rig climbs to the top of the wall. The top of the wall is flat and ten inches wide. He repositions the grappling hook grip on the top of the wall and tosses the rope to the inside of the wall.

He jumps to the ground; then, he sprints to the villa's backdoor.

After entering, he quickly discovers the layout of the villa. All the bedrooms are located in the villa's west side—closest to the ocean. Living room, library, dining room and kitchen are located on the east side.

He locates the housekeeper's room and quietly opens the bedroom door. The housekeeper snores deeply. He retrieves a sleeping-gas canister from his backpack and slides the canister across the floor into the bedroom; he flips up the vent snap. Sleeping gas flows from the pressurized canister. He closes the bedroom door.

During the next thirty minutes, he tapes firebombs to the back of standing wardrobes and standing cabinets that are too heavy for the housekeeper to move by herself. He also tapes a firebomb under the tabletop of the heavy and ornate dining room table and under a heavy couch. As he moves from room to room, he draws a detailed layout of the villa's floorplan. Before departing the villa, he retrieves the empty sleeping-gas canister from the housekeeper's bedroom.

Chapter 49

The time is early evening and Rouston and Rig sit in the living room of Rig's condo.

Rouston briefs Rig. "We have completed the investigation into the history of the water systems at Sedo Mare. We discovered that during the early days of construction in Sedo Mare, the water supply came from an underground source. As was common in this region back then, the water supply was not trusted as potable. The underground source was good enough for bathing, sinks, flushing, washing clothes but was not trusted as drinking water. Bottled drinking water was provided by competing water companies.

"During the early years, occasionally, reports of some Sedo Mare residents wandering the streets in a trance like state, sometimes naked, and sometimes copulating openly in public spaces gave Sedo Mare the reputation as a community where open sex and drug parties were often held. However, raids by Policía never found any drugs. When the residents finally came around, they denied taking drugs and did not remember their activities. People with solid reputations, including American and Spanish naval officers, were found to be in that drugged state by Policía.

"The cause of those occasional drug-induced states was not known. However, residents of Sedo Mare made a case against *Imperio Construer* that such incidents were occurring only in Sedo Mare; therefore, the owners of the land, the construction company, must be culpable. A dozen lawsuits were filed against *Imperio Construer.* Those lawsuits must have motivated the land owners to investigate the cause, which must have led them to discovery of the drug-like compound in the underground river water supply. *Imperio Construir* settled the lawsuits quickly and quietly and with settlement clauses that silenced the plaintiffs. *Imperio Construir* installed those water tanks along the east ridge of the valley, and those water tanks are supplied from public reservoirs to the east.

"After the water supply was switched to those distant public reservoirs, incidents of erotic behavior in the streets became so rare that the longtime residents were pointing to the old water supply as the cause. But the lawsuits had been settled and attention toward the old water supply diminished.

"Then, about two years ago, the frequent occurrences of naked dancing in the streets and public sex started up again. Sedo Mare Pueblo regained its reputation as a *free love* community.

"Anyway, societal morals change. The Policía no longer come to the scene of such incidents. There has never been a serious injury. Public intoxication and public nudity are not crimes. And copulation in public is not prosecuted unless someone swears out a complaint.

"Now, here is an interesting coincidence uncovered by our ONI analysts. During the last two years, there have been nine reported incidents of residents appearing in drug-induced states and roaming naked in the streets, and a few incidents of naked people copulating in public areas. During each of those incidents, the *Imperio Construir* Superintendent had foreign guests visiting his home in Sedo Mare. Our analysts are proposing that the underground water was purposely delivered in bottles to selected Sedo Mare residents during those foreigner visits to demonstrate to those foreigners the effects of drinking the water. ONI operatives tracked two of those foreign visitors to Syria where they work in the local offices of *Saint Claire Shipping*—owned by a Turkish billionaire named *Mustufa Aydin*."

"Muslim?" Rigney asks.

"Analysts don't think so, because he has been seen spending time in Christian churches and his behavior and eating habits are not Muslim."

Rig stares down at the floor as he attempts to grasp the meaning of it all. He cannot determine a connection between all the bits of information. He stares into Rouston's face and asks, "So what do our analysts conclude?"

Rouston asks, "Have you kept up on the Egypt, Israel peace talks that are being negotiated by President Carter?"

"Yes. I've read about it in the papers."

"The treaty is scheduled to be signed next week. Most of the Middle Eastern countries are against the treaty. Military forces of those opposing countries are staging for attack against Egypt and Israel. Intel reports say those countries will attack if the peace treaty is signed.

"Pockets of U.S. military advisors and U.N. peacekeeping troops are all over the Middle East. And, then, there are U.S. Embassies and consulates in every Middle Eastern Country. The U.S. Sixth Fleet has positioned troop ships, an aircraft carrier, and heavily armed cruisers and destroyers in the Eastern Mediterranean.

"Countries invading Egypt and Israel must neutralize U.S. military advisors and U.N. peacekeepers already on the ground there. Those countries can't do anything about the U.S. warships, but they can neutralize U.S. and U.N. elements already on the ground."

"They wouldn't dare," Rig states confidently. "America would not stand for it. Even President Carter would retaliate militarily against an assault on American military advisors and embassies."

Rouston responds, "Those countries do not need to physically assault U.S. and U.N. elements. All they need to do is neutralize them for twenty-four hours."

Rig furrows his brow and expresses thoughtfulness as he considers all the information. Then, his eyes go wide as it all comes together. He casts a confident grin at Rouston and says, "*Imperio Aqua*! Everywhere you go on U.S. managed compounds there are stacked cases of free bottled water. Dehydration in that heat is a major concern. Bottled drinking water is provided free to anyone who wants it. Logistic departments in those compounds have contracts with local bottled-water companies, and those companies maintain a plentiful and constant supply of bottled water in offices, dining rooms, and lobbies of living quarters. I have been there. Bottled water is stacked everywhere."

Rouston adds, "And analysts at ONI, DIA, and CIA conclude that the normal supply of water to those compounds will be substituted with *Imperio Aqua* from Sedo Mare during the twelve hours leading up to invasions of Egypt and Israel. American military advisors and U.N. peacekeeping forces will be drugged out for a day or more before someone finally discovers a problem with the water."

Rig shakes his head and remarks, "Diabolical!" Then after a short pause he states, "There will be little or no sensible intel coming from American, U.N., or Western media assets inland. American commanders at sea will not know where to effectively deploy and use their forces."

"That's right," Rouston confirms. "The recommended action from intelligence agencies is to confiscate the Sedo Mare water upon delivery to those compounds and confine the delivery people. And that is what intelligence operatives from three agencies will do. The object of American actions is to make it clear to those invading countries that we uncovered their plot, which should deter them from attacking Egypt and Israel."

Rig takes a few moments to consider all that he heard in this briefing. Then, he asks, "Do I have a mission?"

"Yes—to be executed at the same time that American operatives are confiscating Sedo Mare water in those Mid-Eastern compounds and arresting delivery personnel. Your mission is to destroy that bottling plant operation in Sedo Mare."

Rig reports, "Security is tighter around that construction compound than during my last intrusion. The building superintendent has installed security cameras around his house, and I must assume some are aimed at the compound."

"No problem," Rouston declares. "An ONI geology team has found another way in. I have already submitted my plan, and I am waiting for approval from Washington."

Chapter 50

Rig climbs the seaward wall of Marcio Dario's Rota villa. The lights for the villa's rear patio are not on. His black clothing and a black ski mask allow him to easily hide in the shadows. A two-way radio is clipped to his utility belt and the radio headset and microphone are sewn into his ski mask.

He conceals himself by kneeling behind a stack of firewood. He checks his watch—9:15 PM. Marcio's weekly meeting with the lieutenants of his crime organization began fifteen minutes ago.

All weapons and equipment for this assault on the Dario family were provided by *The Guardians* via Jack Tacker. ONI knows nothing about this operation, and Rig must take extreme care tonight to ensure his identity is not compromised.

According to the plan timeline, Gordon and Curtis should now be positioned at the open windows of a hotel room one-half block away. The room is on the top floor of a nine-story hotel.

At 9:20 PM, in accordance with the plan timeline, Rig flips the power switch of his two-way radio. The frequency is clear. The transmit function is voice activated. Softly and clearly in a low volume tone, he speaks into the radio, "Bravo Bravo."

"*Charlie Charlie,*" Gordon responds over the radio.

The code word exchange signals that everyone is in place and ready to continue with their plan. The exchange in code words confirms that Rig is hidden in the rear patio of the villa and that Gordon and Curtis are positioned at open windows in their darkened hotel room. The exchange of code words also confirms that Gordon and Curtis have a clear line of fire into Marcio Dario's courtyard.

Rig unclips another hand-held radio from this belt. This

transmit-only radio has twelve channels. Each channel will key a detonation of individual firebombs planted in Marcio's villa and firebombs taped to the gasoline tanks of cars belonging to Marcio's crime lieutenants. The firebombs hidden inside the villa contain low yield explosives and a flammable liquid. The firebombs in the villa are positioned so that when ignited will drive the criminals from inside the villa out the front door and into the courtyard.

The low-yield charges taped to gasoline tanks under vehicles will spray burning gasoline over anyone within twenty feet.

Although the explosives are low yield, a person could be killed if standing within six feet of the charge when it explodes, especially those charges planted behind glass-door cabinets containing dishes and glass and ceramic figurines.

Rig is about to activate the detonators of the first six firebombs when the woodpile topples over him. A heavy log of wood hits him in the back of the head. He becomes dizzy; then, he falls to the ground. The last thing he sees before unconsciousness is two men in suits standing over him with guns in their hands.

One-half block away in the top-floor hotel room, Gordon and Curtis exchange worried expressions. The timeline called for Rig to detonate the charges in the villa ten minutes ago, which would result in driving those gangsters into the villa courtyard.

They glance at their watches again.

Gordon casts a concerned stare at Curtis and declares the obvious. "Something's wrong."

Rig hears voices coming from the dark. He cannot understand what they are saying. After a few more moments, he sees light, followed shortly with images taking shape.

Within seconds, the situation becomes clear to Rig. He sits, unrestrained, in a wooden chair in front of a large, carved-wood desk. Two men guard him, each standing on opposite sides of the desk and holding large automatic pistols. Rig notes the gun safeties are off; he calculates each automatic holds ten rounds and he assumes each automatic has a round chambered.

Marcio Dario sits behind a desk. He points to Rig's two hand-held radios, now sitting on Marcio's desktop. Dario speaks in Spanish.

Rig does not understand most of what Dario says and remains silent. Then, he expresses concern and looks around the room.

Rig's actions are interpreted by the three Spaniards as a man who has just regained consciousness and attempts to understand his surroundings.

In actuality, Rig is searching for a clock. He dares not glance at his wristwatch for fear he may reveal that the time is important to him. He finds a clock sitting on a shelf behind and above Marcio's head. Rig's eyes do not rest on the clock, but he does note the time. He continues his study of the room. He peers around the back of the high-back wooden chair in which he sits. He sees a large painting, behind which he planted a firebomb just two nights before. Rig also notes that the throne-like, ornate wood chair in which he sits unrestrained has a high back that extends six inches above his head.

He takes a moment to sense the presence of his weapons. After a moment he knows he has been stripped of his weapons, and he did not see his weapons when he scanned the room. He still wears his thin leather gloves. His ski mask lies on Marcio's desktop.

The time on the clock tells him that Gordon should

have initiated the backup plan ten minutes ago. He is wondering if Gordon and Curtis have been caught in that hotel room. He refuses to believe that they fled in fear after becoming aware that Rig must have been caught. They know the safety of their families depends on their actions tonight. Rig anticipates that Gordon and Curtis are discussing the situation and they will initiate the backup plan soon.

Marcio speaks tersely in Spanish.

Rig turns his head and eyes toward the crime boss.

The guard standing on the left side of the desk speaks a few words of Spanish to Marcio.

Marcio casts an appraising stare toward Rig. Then, Marcio questions in English, "You are British or American, perhaps?"

Rig appraises the manner of the two guards. They are not alert to Rig's every move. Their bodies are relaxed. Their pistols are not continuously aimed at Rig's torso. They do not fear him. They do not see him as a threat.

"Who are you?!" Marcio demands in a loud and threating voice.

Rig now has a better understanding of his situation. He cannot suppress a grin. *These men do not understand that a skilled and ruthless killer sits before them.* Rig formulates his plan of action for when the backup plan is eventually initiated, which should be shortly, if he accurately judged Gordon's and Curtis's dedication to the task.

Curtis views Marcio's courtyard through the night-scope of his suppressor-equipped sniper rifle. The courtyard is empty of people. Three black, late model Mercedes sedans are parked near the front door of the villa.

Gordon no longer stands at an open window. He sits at a small table and stares at the spare radio detonator that Rig provided. The radio has the same number of channel switch positions.

Gordon shifts his attention toward Curtis who stands at an open window. He speaks with a fearful tone. "We do not know Rig's location. I could kill him, if I use this."

Curtis argues, "Come on, Gordon. Rig said this might happen. That's why he gave us a backup radio detonator. He said for us not to worry about him and detonate the explosives. Shit, for all we know, he is in a bad situation and wants us to blow up that house."

Gordon responds, "The explosives are low yield mixed with flammable material—won't blow up the house—just start fires in a pattern that will drive those assholes through the front door and into the courtyard."

Curtis rolls his eyes and challenges in a loud frustrated tone, "Then what the fuck are you waiting for?!"

Gordon takes the radio detonator and his sniper rifle to the other open window. He turns the knob of the radio detonator until it clicks into place at position one. Hesitancy appears in his manner. The radio detonator shakes in his hand.

Curtis pleads, "Do it Gordon! The lives of our families count on it!"

Rig concludes that when the explosive detonates behind him, the three-inch-thick wood chair-back will protect him. He is confident that he is probably in the safest location in the villa. Nevertheless, as the minutes tick by, the chance of these thugs moving him to another room increases.

Marcio is now standing and converses in Spanish with the two guards. Rig knows they are discussing where to move him.

Rig considers action to keep him sitting in that chair as long as possible.

The two guards move toward Rig.

"I am an agent with the United States Federal Bureau of Investigation." Rig see no harm in lying to these three men who will be dead soon.

Marcio returns to his chair behind the desk. The two guards return to their posts on either side of the desk. The three men appear confused at the mention of the FBI.

"I am an American federal policeman. The American government knows that I am here. So, I suggest you let me walk out of here or you face the punishment of the U.S. Government."

Marcio exhibits understanding. He translates for the guards.

"Why are you here?" Marcio asks.

"I am observing your movements and actions and reporting back—"

Two explosions, separated by three seconds, shake the villa.

Marcio jumps to his feet.

Two seconds later, the blast that comes from behind Rig knocks Marcio and the two guards backward and off their feet. Their heads hit the corners of the wood bookcase.

The blast slides Rig's chair forward less than twelve inches.

Marcio and the two guards are dazed and crumpled

on the floor but not unconscious. Both guards have dropped their guns.

The desktop is on fire. Rig's radios are on fire and melting.

Rig leaps out of the chair toward the guard on the left. He slams a karate punch to the man's larynx.

Rig picks up the guard's gun; then, he stands and quickly aims at the other guard. He fires two shots into the guard's torso. The guard utters a yelp of pain. Rig takes careful aim and fires a bullet into the guard's brain.

Then, Rig takes aim at the dazed Marcio Dario. A shard of ceramic protrudes from Marcio's right cheek, and his suit is on fire. Marcio moans in pain. Rig takes time for a head shot and pulls the trigger. Blood oozes from Marcio's head.

Rig turns toward the guard whom he had karate chopped. The guard is choking. Rig takes time to aim and fires a bullet into the man's brain.

Killing those three men took Rig thirteen seconds. During that time, another five explosions rocked the villa.

On his way to the door, Rig picks up the other guard's gun. He does not have time to search for his own weapons. He knows that Marcio's men elsewhere in the villa heard the shots and are currently arming themselves.

At the door, he turns and scans the room—the fire is spreading. Marcio's body is being consumed by fire. The smell of burning flesh is nauseating.

He steps into a debris-cluttered hallway. He has a gun in each hand. The west end of the hallway is on fire, which should drive people attempting to escape toward the front door and out to the courtyard. Smoke fills the air, but the air is still breathable. He can see twenty feet ahead.

Two men who wear dark suits exit a room near the fire. One carries a pistol and the other carries a shotgun. They turn and run in Rig's direction. The smoke is too thick for them to recognize Rig as not one of them. Rig raises the pistol in his right hand and fires two bullets rapidly into the man on the right, then, two bullets into the man on the left. The magazine empties. The two men fall to the floor.

Rig tosses the empty gun to the floor; then, he shifts the pistol in his left hand to his right hand and moves closer to the two men that he just shot. He needs to shoot them in the head to ensure the kill, but his need to shoot them in the head ends when flames jump to the men's clothes and begin to burn. Neither man moves.

In the darkened hotel room, Curtis stands at one open window, and Gordon stands at the other open window. They both aim their suppressor equipped sniper rifles at the villa's front door. Thirty seconds have passed since Gordon detonated the explosives.

They both worry about having the nerve to kill and if they do kill will they be able to live with it.

A man in a dark suit dashes into the courtyard and runs toward one of the parked Mercedes sedans. Seconds later, another man in dark clothing runs into the courtyard.

According to their plan, the first target belongs to Curtis. The Second target Gordon's. After that, the plan calls for firing at will.

Curtis and Gordon have the crosshairs of their night-scopes on their individual targets. Both Curtis and

Gordon are remembering Rig's instructions: *"Do not pull the trigger while the target is moving because you will miss and probably warn the target. They'll want to escape in their cars. So wait until they stop to open the doors of their cars."*

Their targets run to separate cars. When their targets stop to open the car door, Curtis and Gordon pull their triggers. Their targets collapse to the ground.

Gordon pulls his head back from the scope. Now, he has a wider view on the courtyard. The movement of one of the Mercedes inside the courtyard causes Gordon to pick up the radio detonator. Positions eleven through thirteen on the radio will detonate explosives attached to the gasoline tanks of each vehicle. He quickly cycles the switch through the positions. The moving Mercedes is the second vehicle to explode in flames. The Mercedes drifts across the courtyard and comes to rest against the gate. Flames from all three vehicles light up the night. Burning pieces of metal blown away from all three vehicles lie around the courtyard.

Curtis pulls his eye away from the scope but keeps his eyes on the courtyard. He asks, "How did Rig plant those explosives in those cars?"

Gordon answers without taking his eye from his scope, "He didn't say, exactly. He said he knows someone who would take care of it."

The few people walking the streets nearby stop and gaze at flames rising above the high courtyard wall of the villa on the beach. They exchange comments about hearing three separate explosions. Pedestrians who walk closest to the villa will later report that they heard gunshots coming from within the villa walls several minutes before the vehicles exploded.

Flames provide the only illumination inside the villa. The electricity failed several minutes ago.

Rig moves on hands and knees along the hallway. He can see about eighteen inches ahead as he moves through the hallway. The smoke is thinner near the floor, but the smoke-filled air is close to unbreathable. Tears continually flow from Rig's eyes. His cough is nearly continuous. He sweats profusely from the effort of his movements and from the heat of the fires. The marble tile floor plays hell on his knees.

A survival idea comes to him. He halts; then rises and rests on his knees. He places the pistol on the floor. As he removes his shirt, he shifts his weight to adjust his balance. While shifting his weight, his foot kicks the pistol away into the smoky distance. He ties the shirt around his nose and mouth as a smoke filter. Knowing that searching for the pistol by feel would be an unwise use of time. He continues his trek towards the front door but—now on his hands and toes.

He feels his way around a corner in the hallway. His knowledge of the floorplan tells him that the front door is approximately thirty feet ahead. As he moves toward the front door, the smoke becomes thinner.

At the doorway he stands up, then, pauses to scan the courtyard. Through the smoke, he sees three vehicles burning and two bodies lying on the ground. Rig assumes the bodies are the work of Curtis and Gordon. That makes at least seven thugs taken down. He does not know there is a dead thug in the burning car next to the gate. Rig considers there are two criminals unaccounted for. Usually, nine members of the crime family are present at the weekly meeting. The housekeeper is an unknown factor.

Rig hesitates walking through the doorway and entering the courtyard because a couple of amateurs, one-half block away, are aiming high powered sniper rifles at the patch of ground that he must cross.

At the open windows in their hotel room, Curtis and Gordon have their night-scope sniper rifles aimed at the villa's front doorway. Each has his trigger finger resting against his rifle's trigger. The car fires are dying but still illuminate the courtyard. Occasionally, wind gusts blow the smoke and temporarily block their view of the front door. They worry that their targets may get away through the smoke. Every time the wind gusts and clears smoke away from the doorway, they increase the pressure on their triggers. They had expected more than three targets to come through that front door during the elapsed time since detonating those explosives inside the villa.

While Curtis still aims through the night-scope, he questions aloud, "Do you think the rest went out the back?"

"How should I know?" Gordon answers in a frustrating tone. Those explosives were planted to block the rear exit. Something has gone wrong."

"Maybe we should get out of here?" Curtis proposes.

"No!" Gordon orders. "We must give it more time."

Rig stands just inside the doorway and is about to walk slowly through the doorway and into the courtyard with his hands raised when he is slammed in the back and knocked forcefully ten feet into the courtyard where he trips over Mercedes debris and falls to the ground.

Both Curtis and Gordon are aiming through their rifle's night-scopes when they observe a darkly clad figure with soot covering his clothes, face, and hands stumble into the courtyard and fall to the ground. Then, almost immediately, a second person not so covered in soot runs from the villa into the courtyard.

"I'll take the first one," Gordon states.

Curtis shifts his aim to the second person and immediately recognizes Herberto.

Both targets are stationary.

Curtis and Gordon increase the pressure on their individual triggers.

The wind shifts. Smoke now hides their targets.

Rig is flat on his face when he hears a nearby male voice speaking Spanish in a loud, frantic tone.

Herberto stands ten feet from Rig. He was one of the two Dario family criminals who captured Rig by the woodpile. He has not yet recognized Rig, and he moves toward Rig to help him stand.

Rig assumes the thug is armed, and he fears for his life. Then, a solution flashes through his mind. He knows it is risky, but he must chance it. He pushes himself up from the ground and positions himself facing the hotel and staring up at the windows of the darkened room where Curtis and Gordon should be aiming their rifles. Rig snaps to attention and renders a military salute. Then, he quickly drops to the ground and lies flat and face down. Only four seconds elapsed from the time he pushed himself up to the time he was again lying face down.

Herberto recognizes Rig as the man caught at the woodpile. He quickly pulls his pistol.

The wind gusts and clears the field of fire for Curtis and Gordon. They search for their individual targets through their night-scopes. Then, Gordon sees his target facing him and saluting.

"Damn, Rig's in the courtyard!" Gordon says excitingly. "Be careful with your aim."

Gordon shifts his aim to Curtis's target.

Herberto, the last living lieutenant of the Dario criminal hierarchy, walks into the view of both night-scopes. Gordon and Curtis become alarmed when they see Herberto pulling a gun from his shoulder holster.

Emergency vehicle sirens sound in the distance.

Rig stills lies face down on the ground. He hears footsteps approaching. He turns his head in the direction of the footsteps.

The thug moves toward Rig and is in the act of taking close aim on Rig's head.

Suddenly, the thug falls to the ground. Two seconds later, the thug's head explodes.

Rig rises slowly to his feet. He looks toward the direction of the hotel windows where he knows Curtis and Gordon stand. He raises his right hand and makes an *okay* sign. Then, he runs from the courtyard along the side of the villa and to the beachside of the wall. He climbs the wall; then, he jogs along the beach in the direction of his parked vehicle.

Moments later, a fire truck pulls up to the locked front gate of the villa. Firemen exit the truck and begin conversations on how to get their truck inside the villa's wall.

Chapter 51

Several hours later, Curtis Anderson is driving his car north toward Sedo Mare Pueblo. Rig sits in the passenger seat.

A rabbit runs across the road within the illumination of the headlights. Curtis steps lightly on the brake pedal to avoid running over and killing the rabbit. The rabbit makes it across the road safely.

"Compassionate act," Rig says softly with a slight tone of amusement in his tone.

Curtis understands Rig's amused tone is to lighten the burden of guilt that Curtis feels after killing two human beings tonight. He is also burdened with worry that killing the Darios might not keep his family safe."

After moments of silence, Rig asks Curtis, "What is bothering you?"

"That what we did tonight will keep my family safe."

"We killed every Dario that wanted to do you harm, and probably a few who didn't even know who you are."

Curtis considers Rig's words, then, asks, "What about the men watching my condo?"

"They stopped watching your condo after their boss went missing."

"Boss?"

"The Pinero Detective Agency. Pinero went missing. Those men sitting in your parking lot waiting for you were hired by Pinero. They did not know why they were waiting for you. They were hired to observe and report, nothing else. Pinero disappeared. So, those men no longer have a job."

Curtis shakes his head and shoots a curious glance at

Rig, then puts his eyes back on the road. With some challenge in his voice, he asks, "How do you know these things?"

In a confident tone, Rig explains, "I know people who know people who know these things."

Curtis bypasses the turn into Rig's condo building and drives to his own condo building.

Ten minutes later, they stand at the front door of the condo belonging to the now deceased Herberto.

Rig pulls out his lock pick set and goes to work.

Curtis paces and nervously glances at the other condo doors on the floor. He does not expect to see anyone at this time of night, but the possibility gives him the shakes.

Rig opens the door to the condo. They enter, and Rig closes the door behind them.

They discover that the walk-in closet has been converted to a small office and black-market goods storeroom. The filing cabinet has a key lock that is easy to pick.

After opening the top draw of the filing cabinet, Rig tells Curtis, "Find your stuff. I will check the desk."

After some minutes pass, Curtis advises, I found all my files and address books they stole."

Rig states, "And I found Herberto's ledger. It contains the names of all he traded with both buyers and sellers."

"What are you going to do with it?" Curtis asks—his manner and tone apprehensive.

"Don't worry," Rig says in a comforting voice. "We are not interested in prosecuting sailors for selling rationed products. We are after those who bought classified information from Herberto."

"Who do you mean by *we*?" Curtis asks.

"The people I know who know people who know things. Do not be concerned. You gave us full disclosure in your statements and your audiotapes. Unless you lied to me about not passing classified information, you are safe and free to continue your navy career."

Curtis expresses relief.

Several minutes later, Curtis steps off the elevator at the floor of his condo. He turns and holds the elevator door for a moment and faces Rig who stands inside the elevator. In an appreciative and admiring tone, he tells Rig, "You are one special friend, Rigney Page. If you ever need help with anything, you let me know."

Rig casts a friendly smile and responds, "I might do that someday."

The elevator door closes.

Ten minutes later, Rig enters his condo and finds Christine sleeping on his couch.

Christine awakens when he closes the door.

He shakes his head and expresses bewilderment. "I thought that you and Lieutenant what's his name were on a vacation cruise to the Eastern MED."

"He is a drunk and a woman beater. I got off the cruise ship in Malta. I am afraid he will come after me and beat me. I need a place to stay where I feel safe." She starts sobbing. "I was so wrong about him."

Rig places his gear bag on the floor. He goes to the couch, sits, and places his arms around her. She rests her head against his chest and cries more.

Several moments later she pulls back and stares into

Rig's face.

Rig gets a good look at her black eye and her cut and swollen lower lip. Silent rage wells within him—brought on by his lifetime hatred of bullies. He does not expose his rage to Christine.

Christine is no longer crying. She reaches for the half glass of wine on the end table.

Rig's arm hugs her shoulder. He comforts her with his strong and confident tone. "You can stay here as long as you want. I will protect you."

"He said he would kill me if I walked out on him."

"Did he say that in front of witnesses, and do you think he meant it?"

"Yes, in front of witnesses and I think he meant it. He is a monster. I just never saw it in him before."

"I will protect you. And you should report everything he did to his superiors."

"I can't do that," she states in a fearful tone.

"Why not?"

"Reporting it would do me more harm than good."

"How's that?"

"Rig, you would need to be a woman in the navy to understand."

Rig sighs deeply, then commits again. "I will protect you no matter what."

"Thank you."

"He still doesn't know about me, right?"

"No, I never—" Christine's eyes go wide and she expresses fear. "What are you going to do?!"

"Keep you safe."

Christine takes a few minutes to consider Rig's words. Finally, she concludes that Rig did not mean what she first thought he meant. She calms; then she glances up at the clock on the wall. She asks, "What has kept you out until early morning?"

"I was destroying the Evil King and his kingdom."

Christine slides away from Rig so that she can comfortably stare into his face. She expresses bewildered amusement. Possibilities of what Rig is talking about rush through her mind. Then, she believes she knows. "Earlier, AFRTS Rota reported a large villa on fire near the beach. Later reports said bodies were found and the Policía are investigating multiple homicides. The last report said the villa belonged to a criminal godfather."

Rig declares in a firm, mild tone, "Looks like another evil king got his just due."

Chapter 52

Three days have passed since Rig, Gordon, and Curtis eliminated the Dario crime family. Rig has been called to a naval intelligence safe house for a briefing. He wears his European jet-setter disguise.

The murders of Dario family members are the lead subject of the briefing by Mr. Arleigh Rouston.

"Local newspapers are reporting a revived war between the Darios and criminal families to the north and to the east. More than twenty-five years ago, Marcio Dario was an ambitious petty criminal attempting to take turf away from the ruling Raya crime family of the time. One night twenty-five years ago, all leading members of the Raya crime family were killed aboard Raya's yacht when the yacht exploded in Cadiz harbor. All onboard were killed.

"Dario and his criminal family quickly established their dominance throughout Cadiz Province. During the first two years after the Dario family took control, criminal gangs from adjacent provinces attempted to eliminate the Dario family. But Marcio Dario led a vicious and brutal battle against those gangs and those gangs never again attempted to tread on Dario's turf.

"The Darios became so comfortable and arrogant in their dominance that they gradually let their guard down, believing that no one dare challenge them, which probably led to their demise three nights ago. Local Policía are anticipating that within the next few weeks a new gang will rear its ugly head and that new gang will claim Cadiz province as their own.

"Our focus is on how elimination of the Dario family

affects control of the *Imperio Construir* water-bottling operation in Sedo Mare. We have recently learned that the Dario family has owned Sedo Mare Valley, *Imperio Construir*, and *Imperio Agua* for more than twenty years. As you know, a distant cousin of Marcio Dario is Superintendent of *Imperio Construer* in Sedo Mare. They could have been using that water to drug and compromise naval personnel; then, extort classified information from those naval personnel who had been compromised. The Darios could have been doing that for the past twenty years. We are hoping our raid will uncover more details on the Dario family's espionage activities.

"Headquarters has approved our operation plan. We go in two nights from now.

Chapter 53

At 1:34 AM, Lieutenant Barry Gradinski opens the door to his bottom floor condo along the *Calle Principe de Astunas*. He enters, flips on the hallway light, closes the door, and drops his navy-blue canvas suitcase onto the ceramic tile floor.

He landed his cargo plane at the Rota Navy Air Terminal just one hour ago after completing an eighteen-hour round trip flight to Athens and three other stops along the way. He still wears his flight suit and is now ready for a shower and eight hours of sleep.

Barry is pulling down the zipper of his flight suit as he enters the bedroom. He flips the light switch, which turns on a low wattage lamp on the nightstand. Barry immediately sees a stranger standing against the wall near the nightstand. The stranger aims a large, suppressor-equipped automatic pistol at Barry's chest.

"No sudden moves!" Rig demands. "Sit on the Bed!"

Barry quickly realizes that his karate training will not help him in this situation. The intruder is more than ten feet away. *No way that I can cross that distance without being shot.*

The stranger warns menacingly, "I know about your karate training. Take one step toward me and you will be dead before you hit the floor."

Rig wears his business man disguise, which consists of a curly long black-hair wig, a thick dark mustache, contact lenses, Italian tailored suit, expensive gold watch, and expensive gold with diamond stud cufflinks. He applied tan colored makeup to his face and wears light-weight leather gloves to hide his ruddy complexion. In the dimly lit room, Barry cannot tell that the stranger wears a disguise.

As Barry sits on the bed, Rig moves along the wall toward the bedroom doorway, keeping at least ten feet between him and Barry.

"Wha' Whadda ya want?" Barry stutters out in a fearful tone.

Rig stops in the doorway. He stretches out his gun hand and aims directly at Barry's head.

Barry shakes with fear, expressing astonishment that his life is about to end suddenly and violently.

"Stop stalking Christine."

Barry flinches and expresses surprise that this is about Christine. His level of fear diminishes, now knowing that he has an out. The stranger has a deep, vibrant voice that he knows he can recognize later.

"If you come within two blocks of Christine, I will give you the beating of your life with weapons that you cannot overcome with your karate skills."

Again, Barry is surprised how much this intruder knows about him. With his thought processes no longer blocked with fear, he assesses that the stranger is capable of inflicting such a beating.

"If you lay a hand on Christine, you will go through life with only one functioning limb. You will not be given the choice of which limb. If you attempt to find out who I am, you will go through life with only one functioning limb. Do you understand?"

Barry, now no longer fearful of being shot unless he makes a sudden move, nods his head.

Rig places his left hand on the doorknob and says, "I will lock you in here. I will be gone by the time you get the door open. If you move too quickly to get out of here, I will shoot you. Do you understand?"

Barry nods.

Rig closes and locks the bedroom door. He slips the key in his coat pocket and tucks his weapon into his belt.

Forty seconds later, Rig arrives at the side of the road of *Calle Principe de Astunas*.

Ten seconds later, Jack Tacker brings a car to a stop where Rig stands. Rig gets in and sits in the front passenger seat. One minute later, they are blocks away.

Chapter 54

Because of the dark moonless night, Rig wears night vision goggles to see his way along the recently-cut dirt path from the road to the clearing at the river's edge— a distance of one-half mile. When he is one-hundred feet from the clearing, he sees the glow of the perimeter lights that have been erected by his mission support team.

When Rig steps into the small rock-lined clearing at the river's edge, the mission support team is waiting for him. The low-wattage, battery-powered, directional lamps around the perimeter of the clearing are sufficient for mission preparation actions. The clearing is in a valley that is miles from the nearest building and protected from view by rocky hills.

Rig removes his night goggles and hands them to one of the team members. While one team member readies the canoe, two other members help Rig with readying his weapons.

Rig wears black-colored clothing that includes a black long-sleeve cotton sweater over a black t-shirt. He has applied black grease paint to his face, neck, and to the back of his hands. Instead of combat boots, he wears steel-toed, steel-heeled construction boots. A combat knife in its sheath is strapped to his utility belt. He wears a steel combat helmet modified with a battery powered lamp; a leather chinstrap holds the helmet firmly on Rig's head. His radio headset is wired into the helmet, and the wire to his voice-activated microphone curves around his right cheek. The two-way radio is strapped to his utility belt. Rig will use the two-way radio to inform *control* and the backup team of his location and progress and to receive instructions from *control*.

The support team has stocked Rig's mission vest with weapons that he requisitioned during a mission meeting two days ago. They help him slip on the black-colored, canvas combat vest. Rig connects the metal clasps that serve as buttons. The vest now feels snug against his body.

During the pre-mission simulations, Rig rejected the use of a bullet resistant vest because it constrained his movements and added width to his form. Width that he estimated would make it difficult to pass through those narrow passages that he knows he must go.

A support-team member hands Rig a nine-millimeter machine pistol. The machine pistol has a long leather sling and is equipped with a twelve-inch-long noise suppressor.

Rig inspects the machine pistol. The suppressor is screwed tightly to the barrel of the pistol. The thirty-two-round magazine is correctly inserted. He slips the sling over his head and positions the sling bandolier-style across his torso.

The support team leader advises, "Double-check to ensure all your weapons and equipment are easily reached."

Using his right hand, Rig tugs on all the pouches that contain spare magazines, spare batteries for his miner's lamp, and several styles and lengths of screwdrivers.

Then, he lightly tugs on each of the four, custom-made hand grenades to ensure the safety pins are secured to the leather loops that run off-center down the length of his vest. By design, a hard tug on a hand grenade will pull the safety pin clear.

Lastly, he tests his ability to reach all pockets. Using his right hand, he reaches for all pockets at the bottom of the vest that hold explosive devices and tests the zipper of those pockets. Then, he tests his reach to those pockets with his left hand.

"Okay. I'm ready," Rig confirms with a nod to the team leader.

"The canoe is ready," advises another team member at the water's edge.

Rig steps into the end of the canoe where a rudder and tiller have been installed. He turns on the two battery operated lamps and the two battery operated spotlights that will illuminate the inside of the cave. The support team pushes him into deeper water. The river's current takes him to the rocks that hide the mouth of the cave. He maneuvers around the rocks and enters the cave.

He kneels on foam padding inside the eight-foot-long aluminum canoe. His right hand is on the tiller. The river current pushes the canoe through the waterway. The battery-operated spotlights and lamps illuminate the inside of the cave.

Mushrooms that give the water its hallucinogenic quality grow inside the cave near the entrance. Millions of mushrooms grow on the walls, floor and ceiling of the cave. An uncountable number of mushroom pieces float on the water. During one three-day period, members of the geology team estimate thousands of mushrooms fell from the walls and ceiling into the moving water. Also, during a heavy rain, the water level rose and became more forceful causing more mushrooms than normal to break free and enter the underground river.

As part of his briefing for this mission, Rig had read the geologists' report. Although the report was saturated with scientific terms that Rig did not understand, he was able to understand the geographic formation of this underground river. Five-hundred-thousand years ago, seismic activity caused a change in direction of the *Rio Guadalquivir*. The seismic activity also created numerous tributary waterways. One of those tributaries flow for nine-hundred meters above ground and then enters a cave that was created by the same seismic activity that changed the direction of the *Rio Guadalquivir*.

Entrance to the cave is hidden by large rocks, but the entrance was easy to find because the geologists knew where to look. For a casual uneducated observer, the tributary ends in a pool surrounded on three sides by rocky hills.

The water flows inside the cave for three miles. Then, the water flow breaks away from the cave and enters a lava tunnel that was formed millions of years ago. The geologists conclude that the same seismic activity that redirected the *Rio Guadalquivir* and created the cave also caused a crack in the lava tunnel wall, connecting the lava tunnel to the cave.

Rig guides the canoe as it moves swiftly along the underground river. The cave widens and narrows along the route. No area has been wider than thirty feet or narrower than fifteen feet.

Rig assumes that the fast running water was the natural force that smoothed the cave walls. He is not concerned that he will encounter any dangerous obstacles during his journey to the river location below Sedo Mare because, recently, the cave was traveled by a geologist team in the employ of the U.S. Defense

Intelligence Agency, and Rig read their report.

DIA organized and funded the geologist team after ONI analysts speculated a connection between red-label *Imperio Agua* and the upcoming signing of the Egypt-Israel Peace Treaty. When that connection was published in classified intelligence documents, Defense Department funding and resources were poured into this operation. Rouston had told Rig that he never before had an operation budget this large, which includes establishment of two Spanish translator billets approved and funded.

The water flow falls one meter between the cave and the lava tunnel. Rig easily maneuvers the fall but does not avoid a drenching splash of water soaking him from head to toe.

The water flows faster in the lava tunnel than in the cave because the lava tunnel has a steeper angle of decline on its way to the ocean.

Because of the faster flow, changes in rudder angle result in more significant direction changes than the same rudder angle did in the cave. After several bounces off the tunnel wall, he decreases rudder angles and now moves swiftly down the center of the underground river. For a moment, Rig remembers learning the interaction of rudder angle versus speed when he was qualifying as helmsman on the fast attack nuclear submarine USS *Barb*.

Several minutes later, the spotlight finds the equipment and footbridge that lie directly underneath the *Imperio Construir* equipment warehouse at Sedo Mare Pueblo. As previously planned, Rig takes holds of the grappling hook and thick-gauge elastic bungee cord. The grappling hook is connected to one end of the thirty-foot-long bungee cord and the other end of the cord connects to the stern of the canoe.

When the canoe is ten feet distant from the footbridge, Rig tosses the grappling hook over the footbridge's handrail.

The canoe passes under the bridge.

Rig pulls on the bungee cord. The grappling hook grabs the bridge's handrail. The canoe travels another twenty feet before the tension on the bungee cord slows the canoe to a stop.

Using hand-over-hand pulling motions, Rig brings the canoe back to the bridge. Using hemp line, he moors the canoe to a handrail post on the footbridge.

He takes a moment to stare toward the west where the underground river continues into darkness. Access to his primary objective hides in that darkness.

The damp draft of the tunnel chills his already wet clothes. He shivers; then, blocks the discomfort of cold wet clothes from his mind.

He turns on his helmet lamp; then, he turns off the lamps and spotlights mounted in the center of the canoe. After climbing up onto the bridge's walkway, he quickly steps toward the ladder that accesses the shaft. The shaft leads to ground level. His helmet lamp illuminates the way.

Chapter 55

Rig climbs out of the shaft; then, stands on the floor of the bottling room. The bottling machinery appears in the illuminated beam of his helmet lamp.

The warmth from the bottling room heating system begins to dry his clothes.

Now is the time specified in the mission plan for Rig to make radio contact with the two operatives of the backup team who are watching the construction yard and the superintendent's house. They watch from their vehicles on elevated positions several blocks away. Their task is to warn Rig of anyone who approaches the warehouse.

Rig speaks into the microphone, "*November*, this is *Romeo*, over."

No response.

Rig calls the other operative. "*Sierra* this is *Romeo*, over."

No response.

Thinking that he might not be speaking loud enough to key the radio transmitter, Rig attempts the radio checks again with a louder voice. Still no response with either operative.

Rig considers that the metal walls enclosing the bottling room could be blocking signals. He exits the bottling room and walks into the warehouse area. Construction equipment and vehicles clutter the warehouse.

He climbs to the top of a bulldozer with the intent of improving radio transmitting distance and better reception. He pulls the two-way radio from its holster on his belt. The radio is soaking wet. He eyes the transmit indicator as he speaks into the microphone. The transmit indicator does not illuminate.

Arleigh Rouston observes the construction compound from Rig's balcony. He becomes worried because Rig is late in making radio contact. He decides to check with *November* and *Sierra*.

"*November, Sierra* this is *Control*—no contact with *Romeo*. Do you have contact?"

"*This is November—no contact with Romeo.*"

"*This is Sierra—no contact with Romeo.*"

"*November, Sierra* this is *Control*—implement backup plan."

"*This is November—WILCO, out.*"

"*This is Sierra—WILCO, out.*"

Without radio contact, Rig cannot be warned of approaching danger nor be issued revised orders from *Control*. This possibility was discussed at the mission briefing. Rig was ordered to continue with the mission, regardless of radio contact. The primary mission plan called for events to be initiated based on radio confirmations from *Control*. The backup plan calls for events to occur by a time schedule.

Rig glances at as his watch—0245. He knows that *Control*, Rouston, must have ordered the backup plan implemented by now. His next task must be completed during the next twenty minutes. Then, he must move on to his primary objective.

The *Imperio Construir* security manager woke Superintendent Jacinto Orrantia several minutes ago with a telephone report that someone is moving around inside the warehouse.

Jacinto now sits next to the surveillance room technician and views the surveillance video screens. The security manager stands behind Jacinto.

To deter intruders, security cameras are usually installed in plain view and are high and unreachable. However, this is not the strategy employed by Jacinto Orrantia. The recent assassination of his cousins at the Dario seaside villa and the killing of a distant family member in the streets of Sedo Mare several months ago compelled Jacinto to install hidden security cameras around his home and around the construction compound. He decided to hide the cameras instead of displaying them openly because he does not want to deter intruders; he wants them to enter and be captured, interrogated, and then terminated. These are Jacinto's thoughts as he views the surveillance system video screens.

"There!" announces the surveillance room technician as he points to a warehouse window. Light flashes through the window from the inside; then, the light fades.

Jacinto turns in his chair and looks up into the face of the security manager and asks, "How many guards on duty?"

"Five, including myself."

"They all have radios?"

"Yes."

"Call them in and arm them with automatic rifles; then, meet me at the gate to the compound. Tell them to be quiet. Tell them to plug in their radio headsets. I do not want blurting radio speakers to alert our intruder."

The security manager nods, turns, and steps quickly from the room.

Jacinto turns his attention to the surveillance room security guard and asks, "Where did he climb the fence and where did he enter the warehouse?"

The guard shrugs his shoulders and expresses ignorance. "I did not see him. I saw the flashes of light in the windows and I called the supervisor."

Jacinto shakes head and expresses disgust at the technician's incompetence. He orders tersely, "Keep watching the monitors. Call me on the radio when you see anything unusual. You are not to take your eyes off the monitors for any reason." He pauses for effect and then demands in a loud authoritarian tone, "Do you understand?!"

"Yes, Señor. I will be alert."

Several minutes ago, Rig planted an explosive device in the center of the bottling machine.

Now, he searches for stanchions that when destroyed should bring down the roof. Then, he comes upon *a target of opportunity*—a two-ton cargo truck. He crawls under the truck and wedges an explosive device between fittings where truck fuel lines connect to the fuel tank. He flips the safety switch to the *armed* position; then, he extends the device's radio antenna.

He has one more explosive device to plant. He moves toward the east wall looking for another target. Suddenly, he hears what he believes to be the sound of a sliding door in motion. He glances in the direction of where he knows the sliding door to be and he sees the door opening. He runs to a ten-foot-high stack of cement bags, which hides him from the view of anyone standing in the open doorway.

Jacinto moans frustration at the noise made by the motion of the sliding door. As the door opens, he glimpses a figure with a miner's helmet dashing toward a pile of cement bags. *The intruder knows we are here!*

Rig peers around the stack of cement bags. He sees five men backlighted from security lights shining through the open doorway. They wear the khaki colored *Imperio Construir* security guard uniform that is seen so frequently about Sedo Mare Pueblo. They are fifty feet away and stepping cautiously in his direction. Their rifles are at high ready position.

Rig's training and experience spark a quick assessment of his situation. A hand grenade is the best weapon for this scenario. The stack of cement bags will protect him, and that one-thousand-gallon fuel tank is behind him. Smaller gas tanks on other vehicles are a risk, but a risk he must take. He yanks one of the hand grenades from his vest and lobs it over the stack of cement bags.

The hand grenade explodes three feet off the floor, ten feet in front of the approaching guards. A wave of shrapnel takes out the first row of guards. The explosion blows out windows and shakes the foundation of the warehouse. The shock wave and shrapnel slams into the concrete floor—producing a crack nine feet long.

Rig glances around the side of the cement bag stack. He sees three men lying motionless on the floor, oozing blood from their wounds. Five rifles lie on the floor. A fourth and fifth man are rising to their feet. Rig raises his machine pistol and aims in the direction of the two men. They are not armed. Rig hesitates. Then, he glances at the five rifles on the floor. The two men limp off toward the door. Rig reasons: *They are just security guards doing their job and are no longer armed. They are no longer a threat.* Rig decides not to kill the remaining two guards. He lowers his weapon. Just before the two men step out of sight beyond the lighted doorway Rig recognizes one of the men as the *Imperio Construir* Superintendent.

Rig considers chasing after Orrantia and the guard. He glances at his watch and calculates that he is running out of time to plant the third explosive device. He must dedicate the next few minutes to planting the explosive. He hopes he does not come to regret his decision not to kill Superintendent Orrantia.

He walks toward the bottling room, looking for another spot to plant a charge. A metal stanchion that supports the roof near the center of the warehouse with a stash of five-gallon cans of paint thinner near the base provides an excellent target for the third explosive device. He straps a charge to the stanchion five feet up from the floor, arms it, and extends the antenna.

In one of the pockets of Rig's ammo vest is a transmit-only radio detonator. When the transmit button is pressed, all explosive devices that have been armed and are in range of the transmit frequency will explode.

Ten minutes later, Rig is in the canoe and drifts rapidly westward to his primary objective.

Chapter 56

Jacinto Orrantia and the security manager enter the well-lit kitchen of Jacinto's house. They have recovered from dizziness caused by the blast of the hand grenade that slammed them to the concrete floor of the warehouse.

They dampen towels and wipe away blood from their bodies. Their wounds are not serious. They have shallow shrapnel wounds on their legs and arms. They were lucky. The three guards in front of them absorbed most of the deadly flying shrapnel.

After applying bacteria killers and bandages to the deeper cuts, they go to the weapons closet and arm themselves with two automatic pistols each. All the rifles were left behind in the warehouse.

As Jacinto closes the door to the weapons closet, he says, "We will go to my office."

"We should call the Policía," the security manager asserts.

"No Policía!"

"But the intruder will escape. We should go back to the warehouse."

"No." Orrantia objects in a strong authoritarian voice. "The intruder is heavily armed. We risk our lives by going back to the warehouse where he can ambush us from any location. You must call for more guards."

Rig sits in the back of the canoe and uses the rudder to guide the canoe along the underground river toward his primary objective. Then, the tunnel widens, and banks appear on each side of the river. A large crack in the lava tunnel's side and overhead appears in the illumination of the spotlights. Rig maneuvers the canoe to the north bank of the river. The speed of the canoe drives the canoe onto the bank. The canoe's metal hull scraping across solidified lava makes a shrieking, finger-nails-across-a-chalkboard sound.

He moves to the center of the canoe and positions one of the spotlights toward the tunnel's overhead. Large cracks become visible. The spotlight beam finds the nautical-style ladder, called a Jacob's ladder in navy terminology. The Jacob's ladder hangs from a ten-foot-wide opening in the tunnel overhead. Rig runs the spotlight beam down the ladder. The bottom of the ladder touches the bank only a few inches from the flowing river.

On their way to Jacinto's office, Jacinto and the security manager stop at the door to the surveillance room. Jacinto opens the door and asks the technician, "Has anyone exited the warehouse?"

"Only you and Señor Mendez. What happened? I heard an explosion."

Jacinto asks the technician, "You did not notify the authorities after hearing the explosion?"

"No, Señor. The procedure manual says not to notify them without your permission."

"I will be in my office. Call me immediately when that intruder exits the warehouse and take note of which direction he goes."

Rig pulls the canoe to the bottom of the Jacob's ladder. Then, he positions the beam of both spotlights to illuminate the opening in the tunnel overhead. He repositions the beams of light several times so he can view as far up the opening as possible. The light illuminates about thirty feet into the opening.

During the geologists' pre-mission briefing, the team leader had explained, "We were drawn to that location because it was the only spot in the underground river with banks. On the banks, we discovered old Viking tools about one-thousand years old. Then, we discovered ancient artifacts of Scandinavian origin under piles of lava dust on the bank and buried in the river bed. The river is only four feet deep there. The deeper we dug into the riverbed, the older the artifacts we found. Some of those riverbed artifacts dated back more than three thousand years; we suspect the oldest artifacts to be of Scandinavian origin. Mixed in with some of the two-thousand-year-old Scandinavian artifacts were Roman soldier spears and swords dating back to the time of Roman occupation in this area. Broken clay jars were abundant on the bottom of the river. We found animal bones at all levels from five-hundred to three-thousand years ago but no human bones. We believe that their culture required burying the dead at sea. Wondering why that part of the river was so rich in artifacts and animal bones, we searched for an entrance close by that might lead to ground level.

"We concluded that the cracks in the tunnel overhead must provide the path to the surface. We built scaffolding thirty feet high, which placed the scaffold platform only three feet from that gapping whole in the tunnel overhead. Some in our team are skillful rock climbers. They used their skills and equipment to ascend that opening in the overhead. After climbing about twenty-five feet the lava rock ends and a man-made well begins. The circular walls of the well are lined with multiple-type rocks and ancient mortar mix made of sand, cement and lime. The man-made well runs a total of eighty feet up to surface level. When we explored the interior of the well, we found patch repairs in the walls. During ancient times, that well was kept in good repair. The well has not been used for the last five-hundred years. Our team had to shore up some of the well wall to keep it from collapsing.

"In the lava tunnel we found the remnants of leather ropes and wood tied together that must have formed what, today, we call a nautical Jacob's ladder, which gave us the idea to install our own modern-day Jacob's ladder from the top of the well all the way down to the lava tunnel river bank.

"From other artifacts we found on the river bank and along the walls, we believe that people lived on that river bank for periods of time. The remains of ancient camp fires were found. The smoke from those camp fires would have easily rose up through the well.

"Uh, getting back to the task at hand. When we vacated the tunnel, we removed the scaffolding. We left the Jacob's ladder because we plan on going back in there to conduct a thorough scientific dig. You can use that ladder to climb to the top of the well."

"What will I find at the top of the well?"

"Oh, sorry!" the lead geologist had responded. "I thought you knew." He had cast a questioning glance at Rouston.

Rouston then advised, "We haven't briefed Rig on that, yet."

The lead geologist had nodded his understanding; then, he explained, "You will find yourself inside a dirt-floor room in a shed on the grounds of the Sedo Mare construction superintendent."

In Jacinto's office, Jacinto and the security manager

sit in overstuffed chairs separated by a coffee table. Jacinto pushes a phone toward Mendez and tells him, "Bring in five more off duty guards. I want them here immediately. Tell them to bring any personal weapons they own."

"But Señor Orrantia, the intruder will be gone by the time my other guards arrive."

"Do as a say!" Jacinto demands in a loud and irritable tone.

Mendez pulls a notebook from his breast pocket, opens it, and begins dialing.

While Mendez calls off duty guards, Jacinto pours two glasses of cognac.

Rig pushes up on the wooden, disk-shaped well cover. He carefully and silently sets the cover aside, then, climbs out of the well. The lamp on his helmet provides the only illumination.

He looks down the well. The canoe spotlights resemble distant candles in the night.

Mendez hangs up the phone and advises. "I called six guards who live closest. I estimate thirty minutes for them to arrive, be armed, and be briefed."

Jacinto places a glass of cognac in front of the security manager.

Mendez advises in a concerned tone, "A great possibility exists that residents called the Policía after hearing the explosion in the warehouse."

"Possibly," Jacinto concedes. "But construction explosions are common in the Sedo Mare, and the nearest house, except for mine, is one-hundred meters away. I want to capture him. I do not want him arrested by Policía. We learn nothing if the police hold him."

"Señor Orrantia, please excuse me for asserting my opinion, but you hired me to advise you on security for Sedo Mare. There are three dead men in the warehouse. Eventually, we must notify the Policía."

Jacinto asserts, "I will worry about the Policía later. What is your assessment of this situation?"

Mendez expresses contemplation for a few moments, then he answers, "Perplexing. Why is a thief in the night armed with hand grenades? If he is a thief, what is there of value in the warehouse that he can carry away? There is nothing, right? If he is not a thief and is the assassin that you have been expecting, why trespass into the warehouse when obviously you are in your home. He must have another purpose."

Jacinto shakes his head and expresses he has no answer. He is not a knowledgeable participant in the plot unfolding in the Middle East. He was ordered to ship the *Imperio Agua* from Sedo Mare to the Rota docks. That is the limit of his knowledge.

Then, the security manager's eyes go wide as he expresses revelation. "A commercial saboteur! He is an operative for a competing construction company commissioned to destroy inventory and equipment—blow up buildings to scare away customers from buying or renting homes in Sedo Mare."

Jacinto recalls the incident in those waterfront bars where someone, allegedly an American sailor, showed interest in the red label water and later killed a guard in an alley. But no one had proof that the red label water was the man's interest. Hundreds of products are in those storerooms. There was no evidence the man was an American other than a bartender's judgement. The

272

Policía logged the incident as a thief who got caught and had to fight his way out, and the Darios accepted that conclusion. Now, Jacinto considers that the man at the waterfront could have been an operative for a competing company or rival criminal organization.

Jacinto nods acceptance of the possibility of a commercial saboteur stalking his warehouse. He comments, "Insurance will cover destroyed buildings, and we can rebuild and restock the warehouse. Those who hired this intruder know that. I do not see destruction of the warehouse scaring away home owners. Potential buyers might be scared off for a while. However, owning a residence in Sedo Mare is a good long-term investment. Too good of an investment to scare off buyers forever. There is more going on here than a competitor attempting to put *Imperio Construir* out of business in Sedo Mare."

Mendez advises, "The intruder will use explosives. There are many flammable materials in the warehouse. We should get as far away as possible."

Jacinto jumps to his feet and announces, "No! We will be safe here because the intruder knows he must destroy the warehouse soon, before we can assemble another assault team. He will not be far away when he blows it. This house is solidly built. We must go to the surveillance room and wait for him to exit the warehouse. Then, we will follow him."

Rig circles the well and inspects the square shaped room. The walls are concrete block and the floor is dirt. There are no windows. He finds the light switch and flips it to the *UP* position. The room illuminates.

In one corner he finds a carved marble statue in the

shape of a person. The statue is five feet high. The outstretched arms are broken off at the elbows. The features have been worn away by two thousand years of erosion.

As briefed, the thick wooden door has no lock. There are no sounds of people moving about on the other side of the door.

Jacinto, Mendez, and the surveillance room technician sit before the six security monitors. All six surveillance cameras cover the entire compound. The two monitors that normally monitor inside the courtyard walls of Jacinto's house are now aimed at the construction compound. The three men continually shift their focus from monitor to monitor.

Jacinto challenges the technician "You are sure that no one has exited the warehouse?"

"Not since you and Señor Mendez. I am sure."

Jacinto glances at the clock on the wall. Forty minutes have passed since Jacinto and Mendez exited the warehouse.

Jacinto shakes his head and expresses befuddlement. "This is not making sense," he announces.

Before opening the door of the well room, Rig turns out the light. He opens the door a crack and peeks into the next room. Artificial light enters the next room through two small windows.

He removes his helmet and turns off the helmet lamp; then, drops the helmet down the well.

The next room has a dirt floor, also. Gardening tools, bags of soil, and bags of fertilizer lie randomly about. He is in a large, concrete-block garden shed. He moves to one of the windows. A manicured garden lies between the shed and house. Two high-wattage security lights cast illumination on the garden and the gardening shed. No one is walking about.

The security camera on the house's roof is disguised as an exhaust vent and currently points away from the garden and toward the warehouse compound, as anticipated. He knows from the maps of the area that the warehouse is on his left about fifty yards away.

The door that leads to the garden has no lock. Rig is not surprised by a garden shed door without locks because a ten-foot-high, concrete-block security wall surrounds the grounds of the house—making locks on the gardening shed door unnecessary.

He exits the gardening shed and locates a shadowed area between the shed and the security wall.

Had the house surveillance cameras been aimed to scan the house's grounds in their normal pattern instead of aimed toward the warehouse, Rig's movement in the garden would have been noticed by the men in the surveillance room.

Rig steps up onto a three-foot-high tree stump next to the security wall. He retrieves the radio detonator from a pouch on his weapons vest, extends the antenna, and holds it over his head, which places the detonator antenna above the top of the security wall.

When the red button is pushed, the radio detonator will transmit a radio frequency one-quarter of a mile. The radio frequency will be received by those armed explosives that he planted in the warehouse. However, explosives within range that are not armed, like the ones stored in his vest, will not receive the radio frequency.

Jacinto, Mendez, and the surveillance technician watch the six surveillance monitors. Their eyes continually jump from monitor to monitor. The intruder has not yet exited the warehouse.

A buzzer sounds in the surveillance room, signaling that someone has activated the intercom on the outside of the front gate.

The surveillance technician presses the talk button on the intercom and directs, "State your business."

"This is Munoz and three other guards. Señor Mendez called us in."

Jacinto leans toward the intercom, presses the talk button, and orders, "Go to the guard room. Señor Mendez will equip you and brief you."

The surveillance technician presses the button that activates the motor to open the gate.

The guards enter, cross the courtyard, and enter the house's service entrance.

The explosion shock wave shakes the house. The explosion disables the four surveillance cameras in the warehouse compound. Those monitors in the surveillance room that are fed from warehouse cameras go blank. The two surveillance cameras mounted on the roof of the house are still working and record the damage to the warehouse.

When Jacinto refocuses on the two working monitors, he sees half of the warehouse collapsed and the entire warehouse on fire. Debris from the explosion falls to the ground.

"The Policía will surely come now," Mendez comments.

"And the fire department," the surveillance technician adds.

Mendez turns and starts for the door.

Jacinto turns away from the monitors and grabs Mendez's arm and orders, "Make sure our guards are in uniform. I don't want the authorities mistaking our men as perpetrators."

Mendez nods acceptance of the order; then starts for the door.

On the balcony of Rig's condo, Rouston observes the explosion. He raises binoculars to his eyes and spends a few moments analyzing the damage. Then, he glances at his watch. The explosion happened ten minutes later that the scheduled time in the backup plan. However, the destruction of the warehouse tells Rouston that Rig is now inside the security wall of the superintendent's grounds.

Rouston picks up the radio microphone and orders, "*Sierra, November* this is Control relocate to position *Oscar.*

"*This is November, WILCO out.*"

"*This is Sierra, WILCO out.*"

November and *Sierra* drive their vehicles toward their designated locations for extracting Rig.

"Are you sure that you did not see him?!" Jacinto questions in a demanding tone toward the surveillance technician.

"I am positive, Señor," the technician answers in a defensive tone. "He did not exit the building before it exploded. We can play the videotapes."

"There is no time for that!" Jacinto's manner turns irritable as frustration overcomes him. He advises, "I am going to the guard room. Then, I will take the guards to surround the warehouse."

Rig stands near the backdoor of the superintendent's house. He considers where he will plant explosives in the house. According to Rouston, obtaining the floor plan of the superintendent's house was the most expensive, single item purchased for this mission.

Rig hears the sound of multiple heavy-booted footsteps on the other side of the door. He quickly searches for a hiding place and finds a granite bench in a shadowed alcove some twenty feet from the backdoor. He ducks behind the bench and observes the backdoor from the shadows.

Several moments later, five men wearing khaki colored *Imperio Construir* security guard uniforms exit the door, followed by the construction superintendent— Jacinto Orrantia.

Orrantia's men are armed with automatic pistols. Rig mentally prepares for a shootout should he be discovered. He clicks off the safety of his machine pistol.

The guards and Orrantia pass by Rig's hiding place and walk along the side of the house toward the front gate.

One minute later, Rig dashes from behind the granite bench and enters the backdoor of the house. He steps quickly along the well-lit hallways toward Orrantia's office. The lights make him more susceptible to being detected, but turning off lights risks drawing attention. Rig calculates there is one guard in the house—the one in the surveillance room.

The door to Orrantia's office is open and the light is on. He enters and immediately locates the four-drawer metal file cabinet. The top three drawers are labeled *Imperio Construir*. The bottom drawer is labeled *Imperio Agua*.

Rig pulls a folded, cloth, draw-string duffle bag from one of his vest pouches and unfolds it. Then, he stuffs all the files and ledgers from the file cabinet into the duffle bag. He draws the string tight and knots it so the bag will not open.

After planting an armed explosive device on Orrantia's desktop, Rig steps quickly out of the office and moves rapidly along the hallway. He holds the duffle bag in his right hand.

On his way toward the surveillance room, he stops and plants an armed explosive device in the guard room, which contains the transceivers and auxiliary communications equipment for *Imperio Construir* security communications.

Rig stops outside the closed door of the Surveillance Room. He drops the duffle bag to the floor and pulls out the last explosive device from his weapons vest. Then, he extends the antenna and arms the explosive.

With the explosive device in his left hand and his machine pistol in his right hand, he pushes the Surveillance Room door open with his foot.

The surveillance technician turns his head toward the door. At the sight of the tall, menacing figure before him, his heart starts to pound and sweat pours from his body. He expresses fear for his life.

"Estar! Manos levantadas!" Rig orders; he jerks the barrel of the machine pistol once to emphasize his meaning.

As he stands and raises his hands, the technician stares fearfully at the machine pistol pointed at his chest. He detects an accent in the intruder's voice and as he notices the intruder's imperfect Spanish.

Rig notes that the man wears casual clothes instead of a security guard uniform. The man is not armed, indicating the man is not a trained guard. He raises the explosive device a few inches and asks, "¿Sabes lo que es esto?"

Now, the technician knows Spanish is not the intruder's first language. He raises his eyes and stares into the intruder's blackened face as he attempts to determine the intruder's intent. For the first time, he notices the intruder wears damp and wrinkled clothes. The technician perceives the intruder's intent is not to kill him. He gambles and replies in English, "It is a radio bomb, Señor."

Not surprised his language has been discovered, Rig warns in a menacing tone, "You have one minute to go far away from this casa before many bombs explode."

With his hands raised, the technician takes one step toward the door; then stops. He looks into Rig's face for permission to continue.

Rig nods permission and orders harshly, "Go through the front door!"

The technician runs from the room. Then turns toward the front door of the house and increases his speed.

Rig places the explosive device on the top of one of the surveillance monitors. Then, he runs from the room.

In the street, the surveillance technician runs as fast as he can. As he passes by two guards and Jacinto Orrantia, he warns them that the house is about to explode and they should run to safety.

Orrantia expresses a combination of fear and surprise. Then, the situation becomes clear to him. The warehouse was a distraction. The real target was his home—his office. He turns and runs with the others off into the distance.

Rig exits through the back door; then, sprints to that shadowed nook between the garden shed and the west wall where he previously stood on a tree stump. He jumps up onto the tree stump; then, tosses the duffle bag over the wall. He jumps from the tree stump to the wall, grabs the top of the wall, pulls himself over the top, and drops to the other side.

He runs two blocks and stops at *Sierra's* vehicle. He tosses the bag of files into the back of the vehicle.

Before getting into *Sierra's* vehicle, Rig turns and faces Orrantia's house. He presses the transmit button on the radio detonator. A fireball blasts into the sky and casts illumination over the remains of the once large and elegant home. The blast shakes the ground beneath his feet. The courtyard walls focus the shockwave upward instead of outward and level with the ground.

Sierra drives south toward Rig's condo building. They pass Policía and fire trucks going in the opposite direction. During the drive, Rig removes all his gear and weapons and he wipes off the black grease paint from his face.

Chapter 57

Jack Tacker and Rig sit on Rig's balcony and watch the sunset over the ocean. They sip expensive French bandy that Jack brought with him.

Jack informs Rig, "Lieutenant Gradinski hired a private detective to follow Christine. He's trying to identify and locate you."

Rig expresses irritation as he comments, "I warned him not to do that."

"What did you say to him?"

"I told him that if he tried to discover who I am, I would cripple him."

"Are you going to carry out that threat?"

"I don't want to, but I am worried about Christine."

"Do you want my operative to continue following Lieutenant Gradinski's hired detective?"

"Yes, I need to know if he is getting close to discovering me."

Jack warns, "You must stay away from Christine until this situation is settled."

"I know. I will tell her that Gradinski has a private detective following her and that she and I cannot be seen together off the ship. She would be pissed if she finds out that I threatened Gradinski, even though I did it in disguise."

They are silent for a few minutes while the sun completely descends below the horizon. They pour more brandy.

Rig asks, "I have been asking a lot of *The Guardians*— I am truly in their debt."

"Someday you will pay the bill."

Rig responds, "Yeah, I know. I agreed to that when I signed up. I am just curious about where *The Guardians* get their funding. Aren't you?"

"I wonder about it sometimes, but I'm not so curious as to inquire about it."

Jack pauses; then he comments, "You would be good at what I do—being a covert representative of *The Guardians*."

"Is the pay good?" Rig asks in a curious tone.

"I do not do it for the money. It's enough to allow me a comfortable life. *The Guardians* would not employ someone who does it for the money. I was offered more money by defense contractors when I retired from the Air Force, but I wanted to do something significant. I believe in *The Guardians'* cause."

Rig comments, "Appears to me they do more than protect the constitutional rights of Americans. Like the help I got with fighting those criminals.

"Yes, and highly unusual."

"I guess I am keeping you busier than usual."

Jack raises his brandy glass in a toasting-like manner and says in a slightly amusing tone, "That you are, Rig. That you are."

Chapter 58

Rig sits at the conference table in Commodore Weller's stateroom. The commodore sits across the table from Rig. Both are dressed in their Working Khaki uniform.

A mess cook pours coffee for both Rig and the commodore; then, the mess cook departs the stateroom.

"Senior Chief, my squadron transfers to Kings Bay next month, along with all the submarines under my command. The *Antares* will change home port to Charleston and become the flagship for COMSUBRON EIGHTEEN.

"Several days ago, I called the bureau of personnel to discuss transferring you from *Antares* to my staff. I was informed that you were already slotted to fill a billet at Commander Submarine Group Eight in Naples, transferring you next month. I attempted to change that. Instead, I was given an AUTOSEVOCOM telephone number to call.

"I called that number on my secure-voice phone and talked with a navy commander at BUPERS Special Assignment Branch. He told me your orders to COMSUBGROUP EIGHT were final and could not be changed. Did you know about those orders?"

"No sir," Rig lies.

"Do you know about the Special Assignments Branch?"

Rig responds, "I think they are the branch that assigns people to NATO billets."

"Yes, that is true. They're also the BUPERS interface with the Office of Naval Intelligence for undercover assignments. A fact that I know because of my rank, command, and previous assignments."

Rig expresses thoughtfulness for a few moments. Then, he comments, "If I am remembering correctly, Commander Submarine Group Eight wears the NATO hat for Commander Submarines Mediterranean."

"Yes, Senior Chief. That's true."

Rig stares at the commodore, anticipating there is more.

"Senior Chief, have you been serving as an undercover agent for naval intelligence while serving under my command?"

"Yes, sir."

The commodore flinches and blinks his eyes several times. "You revealed that easily, Senior Chief."

"ONI policy, sir. Not being honest with my seniors once they discover who I am can lead to a lack of cooperation."

Commodore Weller casts a curious smile at Senior Chief Page. Then, he asks, "Is there anything about my command that you should tell me?"

"Commodore, I assure you that no one in your command was the subject of my naval intelligence work."

"Good to hear that," The commodore comments in a cheerful tone. Then, he asks, "You have resided in Sedo Mare during your time here, correct?"

"Yes, sir, that is correct."

"There has been a lot of unusual activity in Sedo Mare during your stay. And a lot of message traffic recently about the murders of Lieutenant Coleridge and Lieutenant Willmont being solved. Both officers were in my command."

"Sir, I am not permitted to confirm or deny my involvement

in that investigation."

The commodore casts a knowing smile. Then, he opens a file and signs a form. "With my signature, I have recommended you for continued overseas duty, which is a navy procedural requirement prior to transferring naval personnel to another overseas command."

The commodore stands and offers his hand to Rig— signaling that the meeting is over.

Rig stands and shakes the commodore's hand.

The commodore advises, "I wish you success in your next assignment."

Chapter 59

Rig stands in Main Comm and shifts through the morning message stack. A message from Naval Recruiting District Louisville Kentucky with the subject of *RM2 Robert Baylor* catches Rig's attention.

NRD Louisville reports that RM2 Baylor is applying for reenlistment. NRD is requesting a copy of Baylor's transfer evaluation from the *Antares*. NRD Louisville advises that time is of the essence because if Baylor reenlists no later than ninety days from his discharge date, he will not lose any time in service credit or time in rank credit and his service will be officially continuous with no break in service. NRD Louisville specifies a facsimile telephone number. The message is action to the Admin Department with information copies to CO, XO, Personnel Officer, and Command Career Counselor.

Rig knows that the message will receive quick action. If Baylor reenlists within ninety days of discharge, credit for the reenlistment goes to the re-enlistee's last command, USS *Antares*.

This reenlistment action takes Rig by surprise. The day that Baylor left the ship Rig had walked Baylor to the Quarterdeck. During the walk to the Quarterdeck, Rig had told Baylor about the ninety-day grace period. Baylor had showed no interest and politely asked Rig to *back off*. Baylor's bitterness toward the navy and toward USS *Antares* was clear and adamant. Rig remembers that while he watched Baylor walk to the head of the pier, he was convinced that the navy lost this one.

Rig rereads the NRD Louisville message one more

time. He notes that the message states Baylor now has two dependents—a wife and newborn child. He wonders what happened to cause Baylor to change his mind. He speculates that Baylor did not find selling cars in Kentucky to be as interesting as a career in the navy. Rig also speculates that Baylor's wife applied a lot of pressure as the cost of healthcare in the civilian world became a reality to the Baylors.

He folds and pockets the Baylor message. He is sure that throughout the day a number of chiefs and officers will approach him with salutations of *"I told you so."*

A message from Naval Hospital Rota reports that Lieutenant Christine Hawthorne was admitted at 1045 last night. The message informs that the lieutenant had been physically assaulted but did not give details of her injuries.

Rig places the unread message copies back into his slot box.

At the technical control desk, Rig calls the base hospital. After being transferred several times, the floor nurse tells Rig that she cannot release Lieutenant Hawthorne's condition. The nurse advises him that Lieutenant Hawthorne is allowed visitors after 1:00 PM.

He is worried about Christine and decides to go to the hospital immediately to evaluate her condition firsthand. He exits Main Comm and moves swiftly down ladders to the main deck and then toward the brow. He is five feet from the brow when he suddenly stops. He engages in thought for a few moments. Then, he departs the ship with the purpose of going to the base telephone exchange and calling Jack Tacker.

Chapter 60

Jack Tacker picks up after the third Ring. "Si, digame."

"Jack, Rig. What's the latest information you have about the private detective following Christine?"

"I got a report this morning. That detective hired by Lieutenant Gradinski did not follow Christine yesterday, which was odd because he usually follows her when she drives off the base. Yesterday the detective stayed home."

Rig informs, "Last night, Christine was beaten up and now she is in the hospital."

Jack warns, "Don't go to the hospital, Rig. It's a trap."

"Yeah, I came to the same conclusion. The detective was not producing any results on my identity. So, Gradinski is attempting to draw me out."

"Rig, Gradinski's actions reveal that he is not afraid of you. He will be armed when you approach him. What are your intentions?"

"Can you have your operative follow Gradinski? I want to know his routine."

"Sure, Rig, but only for a couple of days. I have some other priorities arising, and I need that operative for other things."

"That's okay, I understand."

Chapter 61

Forty hours later, Rig calls Christine's hospital room.

Christine reaches to pick up the phone on the stand next to her hospital bed. Although she is on an intravenous pain-killer drip, her broken right arm and three cracked ribs cause her pain as she reaches. Her swollen lips, jaw, and tongue cause her to answer in a weak, mumble tone. "Hewo."

"Hello, Christine. Please do not talk. I know it must be uncomfortable. I must explain to you why I haven't come to see you." Rig pauses and takes a deep breath before continuing. "Some weeks back, I disguised myself and threatened Gradinski with a gun. I told him to stay away from you. I told him that if he came close to you or attempted to discover my identity, I would cripple him. Obviously, I did not scare him because he hired a detective to follow you, thinking that you would lead the detective to me. When the detective was unsuccessful, he beat you up badly enough to put you in the hospital. Gradinski watches the hospital to see who comes to visit you. I have confirmed that he hangs out in the waiting area on the floor of the hospital you are on. I'm sorry about all this."

Christine is silent for a few moments as she considers Rig's words. She knows he must be planning something. Her whole face hurts as she mumbles the words. "Yo wa disguise. How culd he 'dentify yo?"

"By my size, shape, and manner; and, then, there is my unique voice. Once he sees me, especially in uniform, he will become immediately suspicious that I am the one."

"Wha ya gonna do?"

Rig responds with commitment in his tone, "Cripple him so that he can never harm you again."

Christine starts to weep. She cannot stop Rig. She feels guilty for being involved in a brutal act to ruin the life of another human being, even one as evil as Barry Gradinski.

Rig says, "I will call you in a few days." Then he hangs up.

Christine's head rests against her pillow. She shakes her head to express denial of the situation in which she finds herself. For a moment she indulges in self-pity for being deceived by Barry Gradinski.

A sudden feeling of fear for Rig overcomes her as she remembers that Barry is a karate fighter. She hopes Rig knows that and is careful.

Chapter 62

Barry Gradinski walks down the stairs from the second-floor brothel of his favorite bar in *The Gut—El Blanco Toro*. He walks across the barroom to the bar and orders a beer.

El Blanco Toro is also a favorite bar and brothel of fleet sailors from U.S. Navy ships anchored in Rota harbor. The Rota Harbor is crowded with two U.S. Navy cruisers, three U.S. Navy destroyers, and two U.S. Navy submarines. On this Saturday night, sailors from fleet ships pack into the bar and there is a constant stream of sailors going up and down the stairs leading to the second-floor whorehouse.

All the U.S. sailors wear civilian clothes. You can tell who they are because of the type of clothes they wear, their short haircuts, and boisterous manner.

Barry is not bothered by all the sailors occupying the bar because his presence is hidden in the crowd. No one would suspect him of being an eight-year navy pilot of lieutenant rank.

Barry is not the only sailor obscured in the crowd. Standing at the bar next to Barry is one Operations Specialist First Class Curtis Anderson. He is disguised with a wig and fake beard and glasses. Curtis is there at the request of Rigney Page. Curtis owes Rig big time and will always help Rig when asked.

Curtis does not attempt to engage Barry in conversation. Curtis pretends to be interested in the six young barmaids who scurry about the place taking orders and delivering drinks. He awaits his opportunity for Barry to be distracted.

Several minutes later, some sailors start shouting alcohol

slurred insults at each other. Barry turns his head toward the ruckus as one sailor shoves another sailor to the floor.

While Barry's head is turned away, Curtis slips two large white colored pills into Barry's beer.

When the ruckus settles, Barry turns his head back toward his beer. He takes a large gulp.

Curtis slips away and exits the bar. He crosses the street and enters the rear door of a gray-colored panel van that has U.S. NAVY markings on the door.

Inside the van, Rig sits in the passenger seat. He wears the summer white uniform of a navy lieutenant, junior grade and wears a Shore Patrol band on his left arm. He is also in disguise with a blond wig, thick sideburns, and mustache.

Curtis's father-in-law, U.S. Navy Chief Petty Officer Gordon Benedict, sits in the driver's seat and wears his own summer white uniform with a Shore Patrol band on his left sleeve. He wears a wig and fake beard.

Their disguises portray them with longer hair, sideburns, mustaches, and beards; all within uniform regulations so as not to draw undue attention.

Curtis begins his shift from civilian clothes to white summer uniform. He removes the beard but keeps the longer hair and a mustache.

"How did it go?" Rig asks.

"Like clockwork," Curtis responds. "He should collapse in about two minutes."

Sixty seconds later, Curtis is dressed in his summer white uniform with a Shore Patrol band covering his chevron. He discards the fake glasses. "Ready," He advises.

The three disguised sailors exit the van, cross the street, and come to a stop five feet from the front door of *El Blanco Toro*.

Inside *El Blanco Toro*, Barry Gradinski collapses to the floor. Several sailors come to his side and stoop down beside him. One of the stooping sailors requests loudly, "Any corpsmen here?"

A young sailor comes to Barry's side and stoops; he directs, "I am a corpsman. Please stand back while I check his vitals."

All sailors step back and clear space for the corpsman to work.

One minute later, the corpsman announces, "This man needs to go to a hospital."

A sailor in the crowd says loudly, "I saw the Shore Patrol outside! I'll get them!"

Rig is the first to appear at Barry's side. Curtis and Gordon stand behind Rig. "What's wrong with him?" Rig asks the sailor taking Barry's pulse.

The corpsman looks up at the officer who wears a Shore Patrol armband and states, "Weak pulse, sir. Shallow breathing. He's unconscious. He needs to go to a hospital."

"Are you a medic or a corpsman?" Rig asks.

"Corpsman, sir."

Rig inquires, "Any broken bones? Any reason why he can't be moved, now?"

"No broken bones that I can see. You can move him."

"We'll take him to the navy hospital," Rig announces to the crowd. Rig points to four sailors and orders, "Carry him to the Shore Patrol vehicle across the street."

Outside at the van, the four sailors load Gradinski into the cargo area; then, they step aside. The corpsman is about to climb into the van when Rig raises his hand in a halt gesture and says, "We got it from here, sailor. Go back to having a good time."

The corpsman expresses surprised confusion at the officer's order. His training tells him that the proper, by-the-book action is for him, a medical professional, to accompany the incapacitated sailor until that sailor is delivered into the hands of hospital staff.

The Shore Patrol officer explains, "The navy hospital is only ten minutes away. We are all trained in first aid. We can handle this."

The corpsman is not convinced. He knows standard procedure is for him to go with the patient, but he does not protest. He turns and walks toward the door of *El Blanco Toro*.

Rig enters the van and sits in the passenger seat. Gordon steps on the gas and the van spurts forward. Curtis sits in the cargo area with the unconscious Gradinski.

After driving several blocks, Gordon says, "I was nervous as hell in that bar, worried that I would be identified. Wouldn't it have been easier and less risky to have taken him in the street outside the bar or near his condo?"

"No," Rig asserts. "He knows someone is after him. He would be on his guard when alone in the street. Inside that bar he felt safe with all those people around. Besides, they were all fleet sailors in that bar and the fleet departs Monday morning."

Gordon states the obvious: "We didn't anticipate the presence of a corpsman. He could have blown the whole thing."

"No operation plan is perfect," Rig asserts.

Gordon responds in an amused tone, "Yeah. So, I am learning—the hard way."

In the back of the van, Curtis places a hood over Gradinski's head; then, he injects Gradinski with strong sedatives and pain killers.

Three blocks north of the *El Blanco Toro*, Gordon turns into a dark alley that they had previously surveyed.

Gordon and Curtis remove their Shore Patrol armbands and hand the armbands to Rig.

Gordon and Curtis exit the van.

Gordon peels off the PROPERTY OF U.S. NAVY decal from the driver's door.

Curtis peels off an identical decal from the passenger's door.

Rig moves into the driver's seat. He takes off the officer's hat and removes the officer-rank epaulets from the shoulders of his white uniform shirt. He dons a blue, cloth cap that is often worn by Spanish laborers.

Gordon and Curtis toss the decals into the back of the van.

Now, anyone observing Rig will only see a man in a white shirt and cap driving a gray panel van.

Gordon talks to Rig through the open window on the driver's side. "Rig, are you sure you do not need us to help finish this job? No problem with helping you."

Rig expresses an appreciative smile while he responds, "Thanks, Gordon, but no. I need to finish this by myself."

Rig drives off in the van.

Gordon and Curtis begin the two-block walk to where they know they can find available taxis. Gordon and Curtis will spend the rest of the weekend in Gordon's condo. Come Monday morning, the fleet will be gone, and so will the risk that they will be identified as the fake Shore Patrol inside *El Blanco Toro* on Saturday night.

Rig drives the van to the predetermined location, a clearing on a remote dirt road in the agricultural district five miles from the Rota Naval Base. In the back of the van, Rig takes Gradinski's wallet, all the contents of Gradinski's pockets, and Gradinski's watch.

Rig drags the hooded, unconscious Gradinski from the back of the van and brings him around to the front of the van. He lays Gradinski on the ground in the beam of the van's headlights.

Rig retrieves a four-foot-long crowbar from the back of the van. Then, he returns to the front of the van and stands over Gradinski. He raises the crowbar over his head; then slams the crowbar down onto Gradinski's left kneecap.

Although heavily sedated and doped with pain killers, Gradinski utters a sharp, high pitched scream.

In total, Rig slams the crowbar eight times onto Gradinski's left leg and left arm. Each time, the crunch of bone is audible over the hum of the van's idling engine, followed by Gradinski's sharp, high pitched scream.

Rig gets into the van, tosses the crowbar into the back, and drives off. Gradinski still lies in the dirt.

One block inside the Rota town limit, Rig parks the van next to a public pay telephone booth. Inside the telephone booth, Rig places a miniature battery-operated tape player on the metal shelf where the telephone book lies. He dials the local telephone emergency number for the Naval Base Shore Patrol office. When the phone is answered, Rig lowers the phone handset to within one inch of the tape player and presses the play button. A woman's voice with a Spanish accent explains in English where a navy officer lies injured. The message plays only once. No repeats are necessary because the Shore Patrol records all calls to their emergency number.

Ten minutes later, Rig parks the van in a garage rented by Jack Tacker. Inside the garage, Rig changes into civilian clothes. He exits the garage, leaving behind all of Gradinski's belongings and all items used in the deceptive abduction. Jack Tacker will ensure the van and its contents disappear forever.

Rig walks the one-half block through the residential area to his parked car.

Forty minutes later, Rig enters his condo in Sedo Mare Pueblo.

Chapter 63

Special Agent, Theodore (Ted) Wallace, of the U.S. Navy Investigative Service Rota Office, enters Christine Hawthorne's hospital room. He quickly notes that Lieutenant Hawthorne has fewer bandages and less bruising and swelling on her face than during his last visit two days ago.

Christine turns her head toward the door to see who entered. She is disappointed at the presence of the NIS agent. The tall, lean, and athletic NIS Agent in a summer-weight gray suit casts a friendly smile at her. She was hoping that Rig would change his mind and come to the hospital to see her. Rig does call each day, which is a comfort to Christine.

Special Agent Wallace tells Christine, "There is an interesting turn of events regarding the person you accuse of assaulting you."

Christine fakes an expression of sincere interest because she believes that she already knows what the agent is about to tell her.

"Lieutenant Gradinski is now a patient in this hospital. He is in intensive care on the first floor."

Christine feigns concern.

"Don't worry. Lieutenant Barry Gradinski is heavily sedated and is incapable of walking. You have nothing to fear from him."

"What happened to him?"

"Someone beat him with a club. His left arm is broken in four places and his left leg is broken in four places. He also had some crushed veins in his legs. He was in emergency surgery for three hours last night."

"Who beat him?" Christine asks while faking an astonished tone.

"We don't know. Lieutenant Gradinski has been unconscious since he was found out in the woods late last night. You were involved with him. I was hoping that you might have some ideas who his enemies are."

"I don't understand. He wasn't mugged?" Christine still portrays astonishment.

"He was found with a hood over his head. His wallet and watch were missing, but muggers would not take the time to methodically beat him. No head injuries, which normally accompanies a mugging. Appears that he was heavily sedated and drugged with pain killers before he was beaten. No doubt about it. He was deliberately and methodically beaten with coldblooded premeditation."

"I have no idea," Christine says. "He never told me about anyone who wanted to hurt him."

Agent Wallace pulls out a pocket notebook and flips some pages. After reading his notes, he casts a suspicious expression at Christine as he asked, "Were you dating someone else while you were also dating Lieutenant Gradinski?"

Christine responds with an immediate and confident, "No."

"You previously stated that Lieutenant Gradinski beat you the first time when you and he were on a Mediterranean Cruise Ship. You said you left the ship in Malta and arrived back here the next day—April 4th. That is your statement, correct?

"Your land lady, who looked after your condo and collected your mail, said that you did not return to your condo until April 9th. Where were you during those five days?"

Christine thinks quickly and responds, "I have a stateroom on the *Antares*. I stayed there—where I thought I would be safer."

Agent Wallace looks down at his notes. With a suspicious tone in his voice, he asks, "Yet, ship's records show that you did not check off leave until April 10th. I confirmed that you were on a flight that landed at Jerez Airport on April 4ᵗʰ. What do you have to say about that?"

Christine attempts to come up with an answer that is believable, but she cannot. Her face flushes. She exhibits nervousness. She has been caught in a lie, and both she and Agent Wallace know it.

Agent Wallace smiles, "Okay, Lieutenant, now that we both know that you avoided the truth, it's time to be truthful. Why did you not report to your superiors or to his when Lieutenant Gradinski assaulted you the first time?"

"His word against mine, and I wasn't injured badly that time. I was able to walk off that cruise ship and travel back to Rota on my own."

Wallace advises, "Same this time—your word against his."

"You're an official investigator for the navy. I only told you because you asked. NIS is the one filing the charges. I would have never filed charges against him."

"Why not?"

"Mr. Wallace, if you were a woman officer in the navy, you would already know the answer to that question."

Wallace expresses thoughtfulness for several moments; then, he asks, "Where were you and what were you doing during those five days from the time you returned from the cruise ship until you checked off leave?"

"I was healing. I wanted the swelling and black and blue marks on my face to fade before I went back to work."

"Where did you do that?"

"I stayed with a friend."

"Who?"

"No. I will not reveal my friend's name."

"Male or female?"

"No. I will not reveal any information about my friend."

"Is that because your friend is the one who beat Lieutenant

300

Gradinski with a club?"

Christine's manner becomes angry, "Mr. Wallace, are you forgetting that I am the victim here!"

Agent Wallace nods and says, "Yes, you are a victim, and, now, Lieutenant Gradinski is a victim."

"Oh, I see!" Christine retorts back. "Barry is a navy pilot and much more valuable to the navy than a female communicator!"

"NIS is investigating both incidents with equal effort. You have identified your attacker. Your landlady confirms Gradinski was at your condo the night you were beaten and she states that she heard him shouting at you and you screaming and a lot of smashing noises. The local JAG office has already prepared the charge sheet.

"Now, I must also investigate the assault and battery on Lieutenant Gradinski, and I must consider the possibility it was a revenge beating by someone you know. Will you tell me who you know that is capable of inflicting that beating?"

Christine avoids looking at Wallace as she answers. "I don't know anyone that brutal."

"Alright, Lieutenant, we will talk again."

Christine watches Agent Wallace exit the room. She is confident that her relationship with Rig is still a secret. They never met on base, and also spent their time together far away from Rota. The several times that she did show up at Rig's condo, she is certain she was not recognized during the walk from the parking lot to his condo building. She was always in civilian clothes and wore a scarf and sunglasses. Inside Rig's condo building, she never encountered anyone in the lobby or elevator who knows her. Christine is determined not to reveal her relationship with Rig.

Four days later, Agent Wallace returns to Christine's hospital room.

Christine has recovered enough that her doctor has set her release date as two days from now, assuming no unseen problems arise.

Wallace tells Christine, "I have more information regarding the beating of Lieutenant Gradinski. According to Gradinski, he was drinking in *El Blanco Toro* near the Rota waterfront, and the next thing he remembers is waking up in the hospital twenty-four hours later. He says the beating he took was like a painful nightmare. He has some memories of it, but nothing is clear.

"Anyway, we have interviewed *El Blanco Toro* employees who remember Gradinski collapsing and the Shore Patrol taking him away. However, Shore Patrol Headquarters have no record of the incident. The evidence shows that Gradinski's abduction at the *El Blanco Toro* was the result of a well thought out plan. *El Blanco Toro* employees have described the fake Shore Patrol sailors. I have some artist sketches.

Agent Wallace pulls three sheets of large sketch-artist paper from a leather satchel and hands the sketches to Christine.

Christine knows she must spend equal time on each sketch. She cannot spend more time on one sketch over the other two because more attention to one sketch will alert Agent Wallace.

She looks at each sketch, spending about fifteen-seconds on each. The second sketch, the one with the officer rank, was the only one that might be Rig; but she does not clearly recognize Rig in the sketch.

"I do not recognize any of them."

Agent Wallace exhibits amusement as he responds, "I didn't think you would, but procedure requires that I ask."

Christine hands the sketches back to Wallace.

As Agent Wallace inserts the sketches into the leather satchel, he advises, "Lieutenant Gradinski was medivac'd to

Bethesda yesterday. His doctors say that Gradinski will never pilot again. He is disabled for life and will receive a disability discharge."

Tears come to Christine's eyes in an act of self-pity as she accepts her culpability in destroying a person's life.

Agent Wallace misreads Christine's tears as sadness over the destroyed life of a former lover—a woman-beating lover, but a lover, nonetheless.

Chapter 64

Lieutenant Christine Hawthorne sits at her desk in the USS *Antares* communications office. This is her first day back to work after being released from the hospital yesterday. She wears her Working Khaki uniform that includes short sleeve blouse and long trousers. Only a faint evidence of her beaten face remains. Her right arm is still in a sling.

Senior Chief Rigney Page sits on the other side of the Lieutenant's desk. He also wears Working Khaki uniform. His garrison cap is tucked into his belt.

The door is closed and locked.

In the outer office, Christine's yeoman shakes his head and expresses acceptance toward the COMMO's continuous violation of the rules against male and female sailors behind locked doors aboard ship. He has never mentioned to anyone that Lieutenant Hawthorne and Senior Chief Page frequently close and lock the office door. He is resigned to the fact that they will eventually be caught, but not because of him. He considers it none of his business what those two do behind closed doors.

Christine tells Rig, "When the *Antares* departs for the States, I will transfer back to NAVCOMMSTA Rota. I will be relieving the departing Communications Department Head. You are going to Naples, right?"

"Yes, COMSUBGROUP EIGHT. I've always liked Southern Italy. I am looking forward to my tour there."

"What will be your duties there?"

"Leading radioman. My sponsor did not provide any more detail than that."

Christine expresses anticipation as she comments, "There are direct flights between Madrid and Naples ... only half-a-day's travel."

Rig expresses willingness as he responds, "I am looking forward to utilizing such convenient travel schedules."

"Me, too," Christine says in a satisfied tone.

A thought about Christine's earlier comment causes Rig to ask a question. "If you are assuming the NAVCOMMSTA COMMO slot, you must have agreed to extend your obligation to the navy. I thought you were planning to resign."

"I think life would be boring as a civilian. At best, I would become a teacher. I think of Doctor Sally Macfurson. She was successful and revered in academia, but she gave that up and chose the navy over academia."

Rig nods and expresses his approval of Christine's decision. Then, he questions, "Have your feelings about the navy changed? I am thinking about the situation with Lieutenant Gradinski."

Christine answers, "Barry Gradinski was medivac'd to Bethesda last week. There has been no resolution as to the charges against him for beating me. Agent Wallace said the investigation into Barry beating me and into who beat up Barry will continue. Agent Wallace told me that he thinks the two beatings are connected. Agent Wallace thinks that Barry was beaten in revenge for beating me, but he has not yet accused me of being involved in Barry's beating.

"According to Agent Wallace, Barry said he was drugged at a bar in *The Gut*. Bar employees gave descriptions of the three Shore Patrol sailors who took Barry out of that bar. The Shore Patrol sailors were fakes. Agent Wallace has artist's drawings of those three fake Shore Patrol sailors. I looked at the drawings. I did not recognize them.

"I am not confident that Barry will ever be court martialed for beating me, but he will pay for it the rest of his life."

Rig exhibits satisfaction that justice has been served.

Christine shakes her head slightly and expresses her guilt. "Did you have to be so brutal?"

Rig stares curiously at Christine. He wonders if it is possible that she is so naïve. He explains, "Barry Gradinski is an evil person. Beating up women is in his blood. He learned it from his father. Should Barry ever have sons, he will pass that evil on to them. Should he ever have daughters, they'll become accustomed to taking beatings from men. The only way to deal with such evil is to disable its ability to perform evil acts. Now, because Barry is disabled, women will be able to escape his grasp. Had he not become disabled, you would need to spend the rest of your live looking over your shoulder. You know that, don't you?"

Christine disagrees with Rig's logic. She counters, "You don't know Barry. He will be a threat to me as long as he lives. Being disabled will not stop him from revenge."

"Would you rather that I killed him, instead of just disabling him?"

"No, of course not!"

"It's a hell of a dilemma, Christine. Even if I had never entered the picture, Barry Gradinski would have stalked you over the years. When you left him after that first beating aboard that cruise ship, you rejected him. Women beaters do not take rejection well, especially from women. They see it as a rejection of their manhood, and they worship their manhood above all else. They learn from their fathers at an early age that women are subordinate beings. When women reject them, they will spare no effort to punish such women. Disabling him instead of killing him was the lesser of the two evils."

"I still need to fear him, then?"

"Yeah, but not so much."

"How do you know?"

"I just know."

Chapter 65

Barry Gradinski lies in a bed at Bethesda Naval Hospital. There are two beds in his room, but he is the only occupant. Anger stirs every thought. He was just advised by his doctors that the cast on his arm and the cast on his leg must remain intact for another month. Then, the casts will be removed and he will be immediately fitted for an arm's length brace and a leg's length brace.

His doctors predict that even with the left arm brace, he will only have twenty percent arm movement. He will be able to take a light grasp of objects with his hand, but his fingers will have practically no dexterity. The arm brace must be worn at all times except when bathing. During initial physical therapy, he will be taught how to remove and attach the brace using his right hand.

Although he will be able to stand with the leg brace, he will need the aid of a crutch to keep his body weight off his left leg when walking. He is right-handed; so, he will also require a lot of therapy to properly manipulate a crutch on his left side.

Loneliness overcomes him as he stares out the window. Then, he thinks about events over the past month. His hate for Christine Hawthorne and her unknown defender burns inside his evil soul. The pain and tranquilizer medications administered to him thirty minutes ago do not suppress his hate. His anger rises as he thinks about her again. *That bitch whore was fucking someone else while she was fucking me! That entire pretense about being a sophisticated Brown University graduate. She's just another privileged and educated slut who cannot get enough cock!*

Knowing that Christine and her lover will continue with a normal life while he goes through life crippled raises his rage so high that tears come to his eyes. Knowing he was not enough man to satisfy Christine torments his ego. His manhood has been insulted. Although he will be mobile on his own, he sees himself as a pathetic invalid living on military disability retirement. *What woman will want me?!*

He spends most of his hours planning how he will make Christine and her *champion* lover pay for what they have done. He considers all the deadly weapons that can be operated with only one hand.

An orderly enters the room and puts Barry's mail on the table next to the bed.

Barry scans the three envelopes. One is from the Military Medical Board, one is from Barry's mother, and the third does not have a return address. He selects the envelope that has no return address and examines it. His address at the Bethesda Naval Hospital is typed in capital letters. He is annoyed that his rank is not specified with his name in the address. He notes the Spanish stamps and a Cadiz, Spain postmark.

Barry has learned to open his mail by holding the envelope between his knees while sliding the letter opener under the sealed flap. The cast on his left leg makes it easy. He pulls out the single sheet of folded paper. He flicks the sheet of paper outward and the paper unfolds. His eyes go immediately to the single typed line centered on the page.

"NEXT TIME I WILL KILL YOU"

Chapter 66

Rig and Christine lie naked in Christine's bed. They are resting after their first sexual routine of the evening, which is always prolonged foreplay followed with each performing oral sex on the other. They anticipate that one or more traditional and pleasurable acts of sexual intercourse will follow.

Rig lies on his back. Christine lies on her side, cuddled up to Rig. She runs her hand through his chest hair.

Moonlight and a warm, summer-night breeze flows through the open balcony doorway. The moonlight flickers sensually over their bodies. The sheer curtains across the balcony doorway flutter delicately in the breeze.

"I will miss you dearly," Christine says softly, sadness edges her tone.

Rig responds in a tender tone, "You sound like this separation is permanent."

"You gave me flowers and an expensive parting gift."

"I've done that before."

"Flowers and thoughtful gifts, yes—but nothing says goodbye more than an eight-hundred-dollar bracelet. I saw it in the jewelry counter at the Navy Exchange last week."

"The gift expresses my love for you."

"You don't love me, Rig."

"Sure I do. Not marriage-like love, but love nonetheless."

Christine moves away from Rig and raises herself up on one elbow; so that she can look into his face.

Rig turns his face towards her and looks into her eyes.

"I think your true love is Sally Macfurson. You were with her when you were stationed in Washington last year, right?"

Rig responds sincerely in a caring tone, "Sally and I have no commitment toward each other. And, yes, I was with her when

I was in Washington. You are the only woman I have been with during my time in Rota. And I did not see other women during our time together in Thurso."

"I know, Rig, and I love you in the same way; although, if you were to propose, I would accept."

An appreciative smile appears on Rig's face. "I am flattered and honored, and I will remember that. But no marriage while I lead a dangerous life."

"Rig, my heart is yours anytime you want it."

Rig reminds her, "There are daily navy logistic flights between Rota and Naples. No reason why we cannot spend some time together."

"Okay, we will do that, when you are not with your new Italian girlfriend, whoever that will be."

Rig casts a smile and shakes his head.

"What time is your flight tomorrow?"

"Oh-nine-hundred."

Christine slides closer. She wraps her hand around his flaccid penis.

"I am not ready yet." He states the obvious.

She slides down his body and takes his penis into her mouth.

Fifteen seconds later, Rig is ready.

Christine rolls over on her back and spreads her legs.

"Make love to me, Rig."

"You have an insatiable sexual appetite, Christine."

"Only with you, Rig. I can never get enough of you."

He rolls on top of her. He kisses her. She kisses back. Their arms are wrapped around each other.

Rig enters her. He caresses her neck while pumping his hips in slow, gentile, rhythmic motion in the sequence she likes.

Christine groans with pleasure. She whispers, "Please never forget me, Rig."

"I won't," he whispers back sincerely.

Chapter 67

Rig looks out the window of the Lockheed C-130 cargo transport airplane. He recognizes the island of Mallorca twenty-thousand feet below. He recalls the events leading up to him killing three American sailors in Palma who attacked him. That was during his first mission with naval intelligence eleven years ago. A secret military court ruled that Rig's killing of those three sailors was an act of self-defense and was a necessity to continuing his mission. The whole incident remains classified.

He sighs deeply as he attempts to get comfortable in the metal seat. The fourteen-hour trip from Rota to Naples includes two stops. The next stop is Olbia airport in Sardinia; then, Naples.

He reflects back on his time in Rota. His job as the USS *Antares* Communications Department Leading Chief and as the COMSUBRON THIRTEEN Communications Chief was productive and successful as his transfer evaluation so specifies. *Easy job*, Rig considers. Having five chiefs subordinate to him allowed him the spare time he needed to accomplish his naval intelligence missions.

His naval intelligence controller, Mr. Arleigh Rouston, wrote a glowing report on Rig's successful missions in the Rota area. Specifically, Rouston credited Rig for observing suspicious activity at the *Imperio Construer* warehouse that led to discovery of the water source that was the key element in a plot by terrorist organizations to sabotage the Egypt-Israel Peace Treaty. A plot that was thwarted by U.S. intelligence agencies before it began. The signing of the treaty occurred on schedule and without significant incidents.

Rouston rated Rig's raid on the *Imperio Construer* warehouse and the superintendent's home office as standard for a field operative.

In the Spanish press, the destruction of *Imperio Construer* property in Sedo Mare was attributed to war between rival crime organizations.

The most recent TOP SECRET intelligence report on U.S. and European government actions against *Imperio Construer* and *Imperio Agua* stated that all assets and accounts of those companies had been confiscated by European governments. The report informs that the Turkish owner of *Saint Claire, Limited* and key corporate officers had been abducted and placed in secret prisons and are being interrogated. The disappearance of those corporate officers was leaked to the public press as persons missing—implying that those corporate officers went into hiding after a fraud scandal within the company had been exposed.

Sedo Mare now has a Spanish government official managing those operations once managed by Sedo Mare Building Superintendent, Jacinto Orrantia. American and Spanish authorities judged Orrantia too low in the *Imperio Construer* corporate structure and too distant a relative (second cousin) of Marcio Dario to be considered a culpable co-conspirator in the plot to sabotage the Egypt-Israel Peace Treaty. Orrantia now lives in Cadiz and is currently unemployed.

The latest Spanish news advised no one had been arrested for the sniper killings of those two hoods in Sedo Mare and for the killings of the Dario family in Rota. Rival crime families are still the prime suspects.

Surprise transfer orders arrived last month for Curtis Anderson and Gordon Benedict. NAVPERS gave no reason other than *Needs of the Service* for the transfers.

Two days ago, Rig met with Jack Tacker and Rig retuned all weapons, gear, and reports provided to him while in Rota. Jack reminded Rig that *The Guardians* are always ready to help.

Jack provided Rig with the telephone number of *The Guardians* contact in Rome.

Rig spent last night with Christine. Their love making lasted beyond midnight. His penis is sore from excessive use, and he is physically exhausted. When she got out of bed this morning, Christine complained about being too sore to walk normally.

Christine drove him to the U.S. Navy Air Terminal. Before parting, they committed to arranging visits with each other.

Last week, he received a letter from the COMSUBGROUP EIGHT Chief of Staff who advised that Rig would be assigned as Communications Operations Chief. His job will be to supervise communications operations and investigate all communications problems reported by submarines on patrol in the Mediterranean. He will be the Leading Chief in the Communications Center and will supervise two chiefs and sixteen other enlisted. One of his duties will be riding all submarines during their first week in the MED. During his one-week ride, he will verify that the submarine is equipped and trained to communicate with both U.S. and NATO military forces as specified in the Mediterranean Communications Plan.

Rig glances out the window and observes the sea twenty-thousand feet below crowded with ships. He imagines submerged submarines under the operational control of COMSUBGROUP EIGHT attempting to avoid detection by those surface ships. He already has an excellent understanding of how his duties as COMSUBGROUP EIGHT Leading Radioman affect the operations of those submarines. What he does not know is his naval intelligence role in Naples; he will be informed of that tomorrow when he checks in with his ONI Controller.

BELLA

From Dunoon to Naples and NATO installations in between, an alluring communist-operative weaves a web of extortion and espionage against the U.S. Navy.

Bella has American sailors wrapped around her little finger. Then, she encounters Senior Chief Rigney Page and her world begins to crumble.

*For Mature Readers

Michael R. Ellis

BELLA

A Rigney Page Adventure

#7

GLOSSARY OF NAVY TERMS

1MC - Ship's announcing system; ship-wide reports and announcements made over this sound system; announcing general quarters, chow time, ship's time by bells, flight quarters, reveille, taps, commence ship's work, liberty call.

2-Kilo - A 3-M form used for reporting technical problems and repair actions for all navy equipment by serial number. Also used as a work order. The information on the form is entered into central computer databases. An accurate, up-to-date, and centralized 2-Kilo database is crucial to rapid equipment improvements, legitimate manpower authorization levels, parts and maintenance support, and assignment of trained technicians.

3-M (Maintenance, Material, Management) - The U.S. Navy system for managing maintenance and maintenance support in a manner that will ensure maximum equipment operational readiness. The 3-M system standardizes preventive maintenance requirements, procedures, and reports on a fleet-wide basis.

4.0; four-oh - 4.0 was the highest numerical value a sailor could be assigned in a performance evaluation.

96 - The number of hours between watch strings. For most navy watch standing [shift work] organizations, watches are organized as two day watches, two mid watches, and two eve watches; then 96 hours off until the next watch string.

ACP 127 - Allied Communications Publication 127 – Tape Relay Procedures

Adonis Crypto Machine / device - An electromechanical typewriter style machine used for offline encryption and decryption of military messages of all classifications and accesses. Codes changed daily.

Admiral Zumwalt - Chief of Naval Operations from 1 July 1970 to 1 July 1974. Zumwalt's policies led to reduction of so called "chicken-shit regulations" meant to improve morale. Many accused Zumwalt of undermining good order and discipline and encouraged junior enlisted to jump the chain-of-command, thereby weakening the chain-of-command.

AFRTS - Armed Forces Radio and Television Service

ARI / GCT - Scores resulting from navy enlistment tests for math, knowledge, and reasoning skills.

ASC - AUTODIN Switching Center; Communications complexes located throughout the world that provide interface with tributary stations to AUTODIN and perform computerized relay of messages from one ASC to the other and to distant tributaries.

ASROC - Antisubmarine Rocket; launched from ship, parachuted into sea, motor and guidance systems activate, seeks to destroy submarine

ASW - Anti Submarine Warfare; systems and processes used to combat enemy submarines

BAQ - Basic Allowance for Quarters; Expense paid by navy when sailor authorized to live off base.

Baudot code - A character set predating EBCDIC and ASCII and the root predecessor to International Telegraph Alphabet No 2 (ITA2), the teletype code in use until the advent of ASCII. Each character in the alphabet is represented by a series of five intelligence bits; sent over a communication channel such as a telegraph wire or a radio signal. Example: Baudot code for the alphabet character "A" = 11000; for "E" = 10000

BCP - Ballast Control Panel; located in submarine's control home contains controls for adjusting submarine's ballast / weight. Underway, BCP manned by the Chief of the Watch.

Blue Jacket - navy slang for a U.S. Navy sailor; a junior enlisted sailor

Boatswain's mate of the Watch (BMOW) – Bridge watch position; responsible for rendering bridge related ceremonies and traditions; armed when needed for additional bridge security; makes announcements and sounds bells over the ship's announcing system

Boomer – Navy colloquialism for a ballistic missile submarine

BOQ - Bachelor Officer Quarters.

Brown shoe navy - Navy jargon for those who work in naval aviation; based on a uniform that was unique to naval aviators that required wearing of brown shoes.

BUPERS - Bureau of Naval Personal; assigns personnel to

ships and shore stations; establishes manpower requirements; maintains central personnel records

burn bag - A paper bag used for storing discarded classified paper.

burn run - Communicator jargon for the action of destroying classified material – normally paper bags full of classified paper.

butterfly wrapped - A method of wrapping teletype tape around fingers of the hand to produce compact product on long paper tape messages.

Captain's Mast - Navy terminology for Uniform Code of Military Justice (UCMJ) Article 15 punishment. Process by which commanding officers punish sailors for minor infractions.

CASREP; casualty report - Report of un repairable equipment onboard; tells the senior chain-of-command that ship's personnel unable to fix equipment. Report will request outside technical help and / or parts.

CCU - Correctional Custody Unit

CDO - Command Duty Officer – 24 hour duty. Represents Commanding Officer after normal working hours

CIC - Shipboard Combat Information Center; central location on warships that funnel all battle and combat information.

CINCEUR - Commander in Chief of all U.S. military forces in Europe

CINCUSNAVEUR - Commander in Chief U.S. Navy forces in Europe

CINCLANT - Commander in Chief U.S. military forces Atlantic area

CINCLANTFLEET - Commander in Chief of U.S. Navy forces Atlantic area

CINCPAC - Commander in Chief of all U.S. military forces Pacific area

CINCPACFLT - Commander in Chief of U.S. Navy forces Pacific area

cleaning bill - Specifies what is to be cleaned, when it is to be cleaned, and who is assigned to clean it.

CMS - COMSEC (cryptographic) Materials Systems – manages distribution and accountability of crypto devices, codes, key-lists, and ciphers for both online and offline communications security systems.

CO - Commanding Officer

commercial re-file - A telecommunications activity that serves as interface between military and civilian communications channels.

COMDESRON - Commander Destroyer Squadron

COMMO - Communications Officer; Communications

Department Head

COMNAVCOM - Commander Naval Communications; predecessor to COMNAVTELCOM

CWO2; CWO3; CWO4; Chief Warrant Officer - Officer ranks between chief petty officer and ensign. Officers in these ranks are selected from the senior enlisted ranks, and selected because of their technical expertise and demonstrated leadership.

Communications Watch Officer; CWO - The person who supervises all command-wide communications operations during the shift. Originally, junior officers were assigned. As navy manpower lessened, the position was assigned to chiefs and, then, to first class petty officers.

Communications Watch Supervisor; CWS - The senior enlisted technical advisor to the Communications Watch Officer. Originally, chiefs were assigned. As navy manpower lessened, the position was assigned to first class petty officers and below.

COMNAVACTS UK - Commander U.S. Navy Activities United Kingdom; located in London.

COMNAVTELCOM - Commander Naval Telecommunications Command Washington DC; normally a rear admiral; operational and Administrative commander for shore based naval communications stations throughout the world; develops, writes, and distributes navy communications doctrine, policies and procedures. Previously named COMNAVCOM

COMRATS - Commuter Rations; expense paid by navy for food when sailor authorized to live off base.

COMSEVENTHFLT - Commander Seventh Fleet; operational commander of U.S. Navy in Western Pacific

COMSIXTHFLEET - Commander Sixth Fleet; operational commander of U.S. Navy ships in the Mediterranean

COMSUBGROUP EIGHT - COMSUBGRU EIGHT; Commander Submarine Group Eight

COMSUBPAC - Commander Submarines Pacific

COMSUBRON - Commander Submarine Squadron

CONUS - Continental United States

CR Division - Communications Radio division; Shipboard division with all the radiomen

crow - navy slang for rating chevron.

Cutler, Maine - Location of the U.S. Navy's most powerful submarine broadcast transmitter; transmits in the VLF range.

CW - continuous wave; a mode of radio communications using Morse code.

Chief Warrant Officer; CWO2; CWO3; CWO4 - Officer rank between chief petty officer and ensign. Sailors in this rank are selected from the senior enlisted ranks.

DCA - Defense Communications Agency

Deck and Conn - Deck: At sea, in charge of ship navigation and safety; Conn: control of ship's engines and rudder.

dink list; Delinquent in Qualifications list - A list published weekly aboard submarines reporting who in the crew is behind schedule in submarine qualifications a program.

DIA - Defense Intelligence Agency

DNI - Director, Naval Intelligence

Dolphins (Dolphins Insignia) - Submarine Warfare Insignia. Earned by those who completed a submarine qualifications program.

dungarees - U.S. Navy working uniform; denim fabric shirt and trousers; phased out during the1990s

ECM - Electronic Counter Measures; electronic equipment used to detect and combat radiated signals from the enemy.

ELINT; Electronic Intelligence - ELINT is the collection of electronic intelligence, typically the collection of the target's electronic countermeasures capabilities, including areas such as jamming capability, electronic deception capability and other electronic emanations. Specifically, intelligence is derived from non-communications electromagnetic radiations from foreign sources (other than radioactive sources). ELINT covers operations including RADINT (Radar Intelligence), COMINT (Communications Intelligence), and TELINT (Telemetry

Intelligence, i.e. interception of space vehicle telemetry during launch, in orbit, or during terminal stages) since these areas are also concerned primarily with electronic emissions. ELINT can be gathered by means of airborne platforms, ships on or below the sea, and in rising numbers via satellites.

EMI - Extra Military Instruction; a process used by midlevel leadership to punish sailors for minor infractions. Called "instruction" to get around the legalities that only a commanding officer can award punishment. Usually a dirty job loosely related to the infraction.

EMO - Electronics Material Officer; officer responsible for maintenance, repair, allocation of electronic equipment

ET - Rating designator for navy electronics technician

ETOW - Electronics Technician of the Watch; submarine control room watch position

eve watch - Navy communicator jargon for the swing shift

Exclusion Area - a Security Area defined by physical barriers and subject to access control; where mere presence in the area would result in access to classified material.

field day - Organized and scheduled activity to clean decks and spaces

FITREP - Annual report of officer performance

First Lieutenant – The officer who is responsible, in general, for the upkeep and cleanliness of the ship's exterior (except machinery and ordnance gear), for boats, ground tackle, and deck seamanship.

five by five; fivers - A radio communications term meaning loud and clear, high quality radio signals.

fleet broadcast - Shore based teletype, one-way transmit system that ships at sea are required to copy.

frock; frocked - The process by which a sailor who has been selected for advancement is allowed to wear the uniform and rank of the next pay grade before the official advancement date.

galley - chow hall; dining facility;

Galley Master at Arms - A navy petty officer who enforces regulations and provides crowd control in the navy dining facility.

GCT / ARI - Scores resulting from navy enlistment tests for math, knowledge, and reasoning skills

GMG / GMM - Rating designator for navy gunners mate; GMG – guns; GMM - missiles.

GMT - Greenwich Mean Time; Zulu time zone.

Green E –Command efficiency award for Communications Command and Control for navy ships

Green C - Communications Department Excellence award for navy ships

gut; the gut - The area of a port city with a heavy concentration of bars and brothels catering mostly to visiting sailors.

Head - bathroom

Helmsman - Mans the steering control on the bridge of ships

HF; High Frequency - Radio frequency range 3 – 30 Megahertz

HM - Rating designator for navy hospital corpsman

HUMINT - Human Intelligence; method of gathering intelligence using people watch, listen, and interact with other people.

IFF - Radio system that receives interrogation signals from air, surface and land IFF-equipped units and automatically replies with a coded response signal that provides own ship identification.

JANAP 128 - Joint Army Navy Publication 128 – AUTODIN

JASON Crypto – An electronic inline crypto device used for encrypting and decrypting teletype signals. Primarily used for fleet broadcasts.

JOOD - Junior Officer of the Deck; assists the OOD (Officer of the deck)

KGB - The security agency of the Soviet Union government, which was involved in nearly all aspects of life in the Soviet Union since March 1954. Yet its roots stretch back to the

Bolshevik Revolution of 1917 when the newly-formed Communist government organized Cheka, a Russian acronym for "All-Russian Extraordinary Commission for Combating Counter-Revolution and Sabotage. Headquartered at dom dva (House Number Two) on Dzerzhinsky Street in Moscow, the KGB had numerous tasks and goals, from suppressing religion to infiltrating the highest levels of government in the United States. They had five main directorates into which their operations were divided:

- Intelligence in other nations
- Counterintelligence and the secret police
- The KGB military corps and the Border Guards
- Suppression of internal resistance
- Electronic espionage

LAMPS (helicopter) - Light Airborne Multi-Purpose System (LAMPS) helicopter; evolved in the late 1960s from an urgent requirement to develop a manned helicopter that would support a non-aviation ship and serve as its tactical Anti-Submarine Warfare arm. Known as LAMPS Mark I, the advanced sensors, processors, and display capabilities aboard the helicopter enabled ships to extend their situational awareness beyond the line-of-sight limitations that hamper shipboard radars and the short distances for acoustic detection and prosecution of underwater threats associated with hull-mounted sonars.

LDO - Limited Duty Officer; previous first class petty officers and chief petty officers advanced to officer rank; duties normally involve managing departments related to previous enlisted specialty

Lee Helmsman - on the ship's bridge, mans the engine order telegraph (orders ship's speed) and RPM indicator

LF; Low Frequency - Radio frequency range 30 – 300 kilohertz

LORAN – A terrestrial radio navigation system which enables ships and aircraft to determine their position and speed from low frequency radio signals transmitted by fixed land based radio beacons.

MC - circuits 1MC through 59MC; transmit orders and information between stations within the ship by amplified voice communication by either a central amplifier system or an intercommunication system.

MED – Mediterranean

Message minimize - A period of time when non-essential messages are prohibited from entering the military communications networks; usually initiated during periods of high-level defense alerts.

MI6 - British Military intelligence

mid watch - Navy communicator jargon for the graveyard shift

MS - Rating designator for navy Mess Management Specialists; cook

mustang - A sailor who was advanced to officer rank from senior enlisted rank.

MWR - Morale, Welfare, and Recreation (department); a non-appropriated fund activity on military bases used to provide recreational services that is directed to improve the morale and welfare of personnel; usually includes baseball fields, basketball courts, swimming pools, sports equipment check-out, gymnasiums, bowling alleys, enlisted clubs.

NATO - North Atlantic Treaty Organization; multinational coalition of mostly European countries.

NATO Message Re-file Center - A message center operated by U.S. Military communications facilities that receives messages from NATO in NATO message format and converts to U.S. message format and for converting U.S. formatted messages destined for NATO into NATO message format.

NAVCAMSMED - Naval Communications Area Master Station; located in Naples Italy.

NAVCAMSWESTPAC - Naval Communications Area Master Station Western Pacific; located on Guam Mariana Islands.

NAVCOMMSTA - Naval Communications Station

NAVCOMOPNET – A navy tape relay network that processed top secret message between operational units ashore and afloat.

NAVPERS - Chief of Naval Personnel, Washington DC

NEC - Navy Enlisted Code; Code assigned to navy enlisted personnel that defines technical specialties and skills

NESTOR – Mythological designator for KY-8 encrypted voice devices

NOFORN - No foreign dissemination

NPA - New People's Army; Philippine communist rebels

NTP - U.S. Navy Telecommunications Publication

ONI - Office of Naval Intelligence; Located near Washington DC

OOD (underway) - Officer of the Deck; captain's on watch representative; in charge of ship's maneuvering and operations during watch (shift); The OOD underway is designated in writing by the commanding officer and is primarily responsible, under the commanding officer, for the safe and proper operation of the ship. The OOD under way will: 1. Keep continually informed concerning the tactical situation and geographic factors that may affect the safe navigation of the ship, and take appropriate action to avoid the danger of grounding or collision according to tactical doctrine, the Rules of the Road, and the orders of the commanding officer or other proper authority.

OOD (in port) – Officer in charge of quarterdeck; controls access to ship in port

orderwire - A channel within a multichannel radio teletype configuration used to facilitate radio circuit management. Usually channel 1 of the multichannel configuration; normally operated from the technical control facility at the shore station and technical control room on the ship.

Orestes crypto - An electronic inline crypto device for encrypting and decrypting teletype signals. Usually used for ship-to-shore two way communications circuits.

peak loader - Additional operators assigned during busiest message volume periods.

PMs - Preventive Maintenance actions; part of the 3-M system

Pontus - Greek god of the deep sea; ONI Code name for one of its field operatives

port-and-starboard watches - A situation when those who work shifts are required to stand watches for 12 hours on and 12 hours off.

PPO - Division Police Petty Officer; supervises cleaning and maintenance of divisional spaces.

PRI-TAC – encrypted voice radio circuit used to issue tactical orders and responses

Quartermaster of the Watch (QMOW) – Bridge watch position; primarily assists with ship's navigation while on watch; enters deck log entries

quarters - An event when divisions gather prior to start of working hours for muster, reading of the plan-of-the-day, and to hear other announcements.

Restricted Area - Access controlled to specifically authorized personnel only.

RM - Rating designator for navy radioman.

RMSN - Navy rate *radioman seaman*; E-3 Radioman

Romulus crypto - An electronic inline crypto device (KW-26) for encrypting and decrypting teletype signals.

Routing Indicator - A four to seven alphabet character sequence; every military unit is assigned a routing indicator; similar in function to an email address.

SACEUR - Supreme Allied Commander European NATO forces

SCP - Ship's Control Panel; located in submarine control room; a panel containing controls and displays for steering and driving the submarine.

Sea and Anchor Detail – Sailors assigned to specific positions to perform actions and to be held responsible for getting ship underway and for entering / departing port.

Seabee - A person in the navy construction ratings

SEA; Senior Enlisted Advisor - Advises commanding officer on enlisted matters. Usually, the senior enlisted man in the command, and usually a collateral duty. SEA was the predecessor to the Command Master Chief position / program.

ship over - navy jargon for reenlisting

ship to shore circuit - A radio teletype or radio Morse Code circuit in the high frequency range between a U.S. Navy ship and U.S. Naval Communications Station. Used to transmit and receive messages to and from the ship.

short time - Philippine jargon for a quickie with a Filipina bargirl.

slot-buoy - A four-foot-long by six-inch-wide cylindrical transmit-only radio device used by submerged submarines. Submarine radiomen program a coded voice message into the buoy and launch the buoy from a slot-buoy ejector. When the buoy reaches the surface, the antenna extends and the buoy transmits the voice message in the Ultra High Frequency range.

SOP - Standing Operating Procedure

Sound-Powered Phone – Intercommunications device aboard ships; normally used during battle stations; powered by the sound of human voice. Consists of earphones and microphone that rests on a chest plate.

squared away - Navy terminology for situations or people that significantly exceed minimum performance and uniform requirements.

SSN - Submersible Ship Nuclear; fast attack nuclear powered submarine

SSBN - Submersible Ship Ballistic Nuclear; nuclear powered submarine carrying intercontinental ballistic missiles; boomer.

suspended bust - A reduction in rank, but suspend for the specified period of time. Any misconduct during the specified time will result in actual reduction in rank.

synching - Military telecommunications slang for cryptographic synchronization between transmit and receive electronic cryptographic machines

TAD - Temporary Assigned Duty

Tape Relay - A teletype message relay system in which the paper tape punched by a re-perforator is torn off after each message is received and manually transferred by an operator, who examines the tape for the destination address and feeds it to a transmitter-distributor connected to a teletype line leading to that destination.

Technical Control - Facility within Naval Communications Stations responsible for radio circuit management and quality control

Tempest - Electronic specifications for minimizing classified information riding on electromagnetic waves.

Tender / Submarine Tender / Destroyer Tender - U.S. Navy ships specializing in providing maintenance and repair facilities

The East - Cold War term referring to the communist countries; primarily, Eastern Europe and the Soviet Union

The West - Cold War term referring to the democracies and republics of Europe and North America

tracer(s) messages(s) - Official messages that request

information regarding processing, handling, and disposition of other official messages. Usually initiated after or non-delivery or delayed delivery of important official messages.

traffic channels - Channels within a multichannel radio teletype configuration that are used to transmit and receive specifically formatted military message.

UCMJ - Uniform Code of Military Justice; The foundation of military law in the United States; established by U.S. Congress in accordance with U.S. Constitution, Art I, Section 8.

U.S. Base at Forss - Scottish local name for U.S. NAVRADSTA Thurso

Upward Seminars - Conducted during the early 1970s; race relations seminars designed as confrontation sessions between white sailors and black sailors to air foundation and essence of prejudice and racism; discontinued after several years because of negative and antagonistic results.

VLF; Very Low Frequency - Radio frequency range 3 – 30 kilohertz

Watch - Shifts to cover 24 / 7 work schedule

watch bill - Document, usually updated monthly, that lists who is in which watch section, specific watch positions by name, and the dates and times watches are stood.

WESTPAC - Western Pacific

WILCO - Radio telephone abbreviation for "will comply"

WWVH - The call-sign of the U.S. National Institute of Standards and Technology's shortwave radio time signal station in Kekaha, on the island of Kauai in the state of Hawaii.

XO - Executive Officer (second in command)

Yard bird - Navy jargon; refers to civilians who work in shipyards.

ZBO - Communications signal; list of messages by precedence

ZULU - Military communications operates on the same time worldwide. All communications clocks are set to ZULU (GMT) time zone.

NAVY RANK

Pay Grade	Rank	Abb.
E-1	Seaman Recruit	SR
E-2	Seaman Apprentice	SA
E-3	Seaman	SN
E-4	Petty Officer Third Class	PO3
E-5	Petty Officer Second Class	PO2
E-6	Petty Officer First Class	PO1
E-7	Chief Petty Officer	CPO
E-8	Senior Chief Petty Officer	SCPO
E-9	Master Chief Petty Officer	MCPO
W-1	Warrant Officer	WO1
W-2	Chief Warrant Officer	CWO2
W-3	Chief Warrant Officer	CWO3
W-4	Chief Warrant Officer	CWO4
O-1	Ensign	ENS
O-2	Lieutenant Junior Grade	LTJG
O-3	Lieutenant	LT
O-4	Lieutenant Commander	LCDR
O-5	Commander	CDR
O-6	Captain	CAPT
O-7	Rear Admiral (one star)	RDML
O-8	Rear Admiral (two stars)	RADM
O-9	Vice Admiral (three stars)	VADM
O-10	Admiral (four stars)	ADM

Made in the USA
Middletown, DE
18 June 2020